D1078589

*The Weight of Water*

a&b

# *The Weight of Water*

PENELOPE EVANS

Allison & Busby Limited
13 Charlotte Mews
London W1T 4EJ
*www.allisonandbusby.com*

Hardcover published in Great Britain in 2009.
This paperback edition published in 2010.



A CIP catalogue record for this book is available from the British Library.

10 9 8 7 6 5 4 3 2 1

ISBN 978-0-7490-0798-0

Typeset in 10.5/15 pt Sabon by
Allison & Busby Ltd.

The paper used for this Allison & Busby publication has been produced from trees that have been legally sourced from well-managed and credibly certified forests.

Printed and bound in the UK by
CPI Bookmarque, Croydon, CR0 4TD

Penelope Evans was born in Wales and grew up in Scotland. She read Classics at the University of St Andrews before becoming a criminal lawyer in London. Her previous novels, *The Last Girl, Freezing, First Fruits, A Fatal Reunion, My Perfect Silence* and *Saving Grace*, were published to critical acclaim. She currently lives in Buckinghamshire where she combines writing fiction with journalism.

Available from
ALLISON & BUSBY

*First Fruits*
*A Fatal Reunion*
*My Perfect Silence*
*Saving Grace*

*For Anthony, Katharine and Alice,*
*with love.*

# Chapter One

I had the dream again. And there she was again. The little girl.

She was standing, as she always stands, on the bank of the river. Grass green beneath her feet. Little red shoes, little white dress. Dark hair caught in a red ribbon at her neck. She never changes. She just stands, while beyond her the river is brown and rushing, waits for nobody. Except maybe for just one person.

I have never seen her face.

Then it comes – the fear. The absolute certainty that any moment she is going to take a step. Her small red shoes will carry her into the river, and the waters will close over her head. The bank will be empty and it will seem as if she had never been...

At which point Tom rolls over in his sleep, flings his arm across my shoulders and instantly I'm awake. There is no child, no riverbank, no little red shoes. All gone – until the next time. And there will be a next time. I've dreamt this dream since I was four years old, about the same age she is. I've grown older, but she stays the same; poised on the riverbank, about to take that one step away from me. Away from everything.

The dream is an old one. It will come again. And again. And I will always be afraid.

I move Tom's arm from off my shoulders, gently, without waking him. Every night he sleeps with his arms flung round me like a drowning man clinging to a spar. Then I wait, listening to the traffic reaching all the way from Archway in the glowing dark that is London. A steady throb of engines from far off, like the engine of the world itself, the thing that keeps us all going, keeps us alive.

I've always liked it, the sound of the city. I would sleep with the windows wide open, lulled by the sound of distant lorries echoing in the spaces below the bridges. Not like Tom.

In London, the bridges span not rivers but roads. That's not to say there are no rivers but they run secretly, through underground channels or else disguised as canals. Straight sides carved by men. When they emerge, it's shyly, trickling out of tunnels into the Thames, only visible at low tide. Away from the Thames, you don't have to think about rivers at all if you don't want to.

Tom's arm creeps back across my shoulders. Maybe that's it: maybe he really does dream he's drowning, even if he doesn't remember the next day. It's heavier than ever now, but I don't have the heart to move it again.

That dream. I haven't always been frightened. When I was little I just wanted to see her face. So long as she looked at me before she stepped into the river, it wouldn't have occurred to me to worry about what came after.

It's only at night I think of Tom as drowning. In the daytime he's a swimmer. A survivor.

'We're both survivors,' he said the first night we got together. 'Both the same. Right down to the wreckage.'

And I could see how he was right. Firemen lifted me out of a car that had been squashed down to the height of a carrycot. Lucky I was in a carrycot, then. Those child seats everyone has now, reinforced and braced, they would have done nothing for me. They had to cut the roof open with every kind of tool devised by man, just so they could get to the baby inside, as difficult to extract as a soft nut from a shell. It took them all night, but I just lay there asleep – apparently. Maybe that's why I don't mind the sound of engines now, the *krrrum* of working steel. To me it can only be the sound of safety. Of arrival.

You could see it as a second birth. Metal-working midwives to bring me back into the world. When the firemen go on strike, I'm always on their side. Give them all the money there is, I say. I owe my life to them, never so soft as I was then. So in need of others to help me survive.

Tom's the same. Although he was older when it happened to him, and swears he remembers. 'What if?' he said that first night (the night we got together). 'What if I was in the other car, and no one ever told us? What if your parents' bad driving killed my parents?'

And that made me laugh. I laughed so much I cried. Then cried and cried. It's the only time I have cried for my parents. Ever. Safe for the first time, wrapped up in the arms of someone else. Safe and sad with someone who was just like me.

Does it seem strange? When you're an orphan, and you don't remember being anything but an orphan, it's embarrassing how much sadder everyone else is about it than you. I don't remember my parents. I was four months old.

I remember nothing. Thinking it odd when my great-aunt – my chilly Marietta – occasionally would crumple if she came across a letter from my mother lying in a drawer. Or an old dress. Even the photograph on her desk could catch her off guard. Poor Marietta – if she had ever thought to put her arms round me, I would have known to put my arms round her. But that was never Marietta's way. And she did her best. After my extraction, she took a whole month off from the museum. It makes me smile now, imagining a woman who had studied babies in the Amazon Basin, confounded by this baby who had turned up in Highgate. In the end she gave in and hired a nurse. I suspect it was a relief for us both.

Meeting Tom – that night we got together – it was a relief too. More than that. It was a liberation. I wrapped my arms around him and discovered I could be sad. Sad and happy at the same time.

He wasn't in the other car, of course. In our case I don't think there even was another car. He was somewhere up in the north of England. Newcastle way. Different road, different time of year. Different way of surviving. He joined a scrum of male cousins and grew up with them. He found it more difficult than I ever did. Marietta never tried to be a mother. I got by on a dry, clear-eyed kind of love. If people could meet her now, they wouldn't believe how anyone could have thrived in such arid soil. But I did thrive. Perhaps it was all those years playing amongst the glass cases in a museum dedicated to mankind; you learn there are different ways of bringing up a child. Of being a child. If you look at photographs of me then, you'd see a little girl with a close, almost guarded stare. Mouth set just so. Marietta standing beside me, ramrod straight, studying the camera with exactly the same look. Two generations between us and I was growing up in her image. We might have looked as if we were frowning, but that's just because we were thinking.

Tom grew up in a proper family. But his trouble was it had already been complete for years. No one was thinking about having another child, let alone someone else's child. They were just doing the decent thing when they took him on. So he grew up on the inside, when really he was on the outside. He saw his aunt with her own children, noted the difference – and knew exactly what he was missing. It would have been better if he had been lifted away altogether, held up for the auction they call adoption. Love would have been the highest bidder and he would have grown up – who knows – a different man. A different kind of Tom.

That first night – the night we got together – he drifted off long before I did. Already he was sound asleep, clinging to me like Arrian to his dolphin, a boy-man naked on the ocean swell. I found his arm heavy even then. But I didn't mind. I felt light. Buoyant, still smiling in the dark, I liked the way he smelt, the scent that lay in the whorls of hair at the nape of his neck. I breathed him in, believing I could have carried him for ever.

We'd only just met but already I knew. Some people are impossible to make happy. But with Tom it was simple. All he needed was love – a lot of it. And to my utter amazement, suddenly I had love to give; love that seemed to have come from nowhere, protective and tender. Unsuspected, not existing before this moment. Like mother love, I suppose. Born at the same time as the child, because of the child.

Mother love – first the child, then the love.

Ten years ago. He was nearly thirty then. I was twenty-five. It's late to find what you've been missing since the day you became orphans. It makes you careful with what you have. You don't tamper with an engine that's been running like clockwork.

We have no children. Something understood between us: a promise, a pledge to be all the family we could ever need.

When Tom wakes up, his arms fall away almost instantly. Perhaps deep down he does know, after all, about the way he sleeps.

This morning he's up before me. Standing by the window looking out over the roofs of Highgate, his back to the bed. He is tall and slender, despite the muscles smoothed along the lengths of his calves and thighs. If you saw him from behind you would take him for a boy just broken out of adolescence. He likes himself like this and takes care to stay this way. If it were the weekend, he would be getting dressed to go running. Sometimes I'll go with him, winding down to Waterlow Park, legs scissoring on the pavements tilting past Kenwood House. Slowing as we make the climb back up the hill. He doesn't stop for me when I fall behind, but at the end of it he'll have something waiting for me. A drink, an ice cream. Something.

But today is Monday and he's dressing for work. Slowly. His heart is not in the search for socks that match, or a tie with the right pattern. Since I am supposed to be asleep he's making a pretence of not waking me, but his heart isn't in that either. When he can't find what he is looking for he swears out loud.

So I open my eyes, smile at him. And he smiles back. I'm awake; he's got what he wants.

'I woke you. Sorry.'

'No, it's good. I'd have overslept otherwise. I was awake in the night. I had that dream again.'

But he doesn't really know about the dream of the little girl. Tom ploughs through the day as if there's nothing beneath him, no unseen depths. The challenge is all on the surface, he's a swimmer, not a deep-sea diver. I could dream the same dream every night and tell him about it and it would mean nothing. And why should it?

'Have you seen the tie with the clocks on it?'

I get out of bed and help him look.

By the time he's done, I am washed, dressed, breakfasted and ready. Readier than he is. Out on the pavement, he looks down at the sun reflected in his shoe, and says, 'Who'd want to be stuck on the Tube on a day like today?'

'Catch the bus, then.'

'I'd have to have left half an hour ago.'

I take his arm and walk him to the Underground. 'So what sort of day are you expecting?'

'Guess for yourself. Joaquin's over from Portugal for the week.'

Tom edits a financial magazine. He can do it because he's a man who knows about lots of things – money markets, formatting a newspaper, commissioning writers. He knows about art and design and fashion. He knows exactly what shoes to wear and would tell me too if only I would listen. It's all reflected in the pages of what he produces: a journal that looks like the magazines waiting for you in the first-class seats of an aeroplane. It has adverts for expensive watches and executive luggage, and carries articles you might want to read even if you weren't an investment manager or pension fund holder.

Tom has come a long way from where he started. But he doesn't give himself credit. He gets uncomfortable when old traces of Geordie catch his tongue unawares, goes quiet at smart dinner parties when people start talking about their old schools. He can't see a reason to be proud of his progress, and that lack of pride, it makes him vulnerable, needing protection.

His problem today is Joaquin, the owner, who is over from Portugal and doesn't seem to know how much Tom knows. He'll take up space between the white walls of the offices and poke a long Portuguese finger into the business (which, after all, belongs to him). Tom will feel hemmed in and threatened. He will come home depressed and I will have to cheer him up. And tonight he will open a second bottle of wine, and say: 'I don't know how much longer I can stand this.'

And I will take hold of his hand, and say, 'There's no reason for you to stand anything. Find another job, or try not working at all. We could afford it.'

We could too, for reasons we don't discuss. Reasons that have to do with Marietta and museums and a hundred years of family money.

And he will say, 'Oh but it's not just the job, Sara. It's everything. London, the pace of life. The people, the traffic. There has to be a better way. Somewhere else we could be. Nobody who can leave is staying anymore. Everyone's getting out.'

He's talking about the achievers, the high-flyers who pick up his magazine. The people who can actually afford the products in its pages. Who lately have been turning their backs on what made them rich to concentrate on the vineyard, the herds of alpaca, the small organic farm in the country. Confident that, in contrast, the world will never turn its back on them. Feature writers will come after them, to interview them over organic lunches at well-scrubbed tables, listen to them talk about life the way it should be. Yin and yang. Give and take. Balance and flow.

Lately Tom's been talking a lot about flow. I hold his hand, but say nothing.

Outside the tube station, we stop and kiss. Properly, holding on just that extra second. Anyone passing would think we were a pair of lovers not spouses. It's because we know what we have; take nothing for granted.

All the same, it's like coming awake again, a second start to the day. Tom takes his leave and I carry on walking with a kick in my heels. Almost guilty. Unlike Tom, I'm looking forward to my day. I like my work, what there is of it.

He couldn't believe it at first, the job I did.

'So, you work in a museum...?'

'The Ravenscroft Museum of Man.'

'Ravenscroft...' He mulled over the name. I knew he'd have heard of it, the way people mostly have heard of it – attached to some collection or work of art. Or, as in this case, an entire museum.

But it turned out he knew more than even most people.

'The Ravenscrofts – American robber barons, right?

Made all their money flogging Chinamen to their deaths on the railroads, cleaned up selling arms to absolutely everyone in the First World War, made a packet while others topped themselves during the Depression...'

'They weren't all like that.'

'No? I suppose they had their eccentrics. All those families did. The ones who travelled, trolling round the world collecting things, pretending not to know where their fortune came from. Isn't that how most museums get started?' He looked at me.

'And you do...what at this museum? Are you a curator?'

'No.'

'Research? Cataloguing? Archivist?'

I shook my head each time. Then nodded, because all of those things I did – a little.

'Ravenscroft Museum of Man. Anthropology, that's what they're about there. Right?'

I nodded. It was like a game of twenty questions. That was the night we met, and this was just the first five minutes.

'So...you go off in the rainy season and live with tribes in the Amazon? Run around with men with artificially elongated penises?'

'No. Mostly I'm just an attendant, one of the people in the corner watching you. I get to sit on a stool if I'm lucky.'

'Making sure I don't try nicking a three-hundred-year-old loincloth.'

'Exactly.' I paused. 'Marietta, my great-aunt, did all those things – the jobs you mentioned. It's her museum. She inherited it. It was a family thing. She even used to go off and live with the men with very long penises. Actually it was ears. They weighed down their ears where she went, so the lobes were elongated. She had to give that up to look after me.'

'Your aunt? Why was that?'

'My parents died when I was a baby.'

He smiled slowly. 'You know what? So did mine.'

And suddenly we were staring at each other with a new kind of interest. Studying each other like the last two remaining members of a tribe, astounded to find they are not alone.

If things had been different, if only one of us had been the orphan, the child without parents, we might have smiled our sympathy – then talked about something else. Moved on to somebody else. I wasn't Tom's type in those days, not really, being tall and thin, with hair too mousy to be brown. Serious. Slow to smile, like Marietta. Growing more like Marietta every day.

He asked me my name.

'Sara,' I told him. 'Sara Ravenscroft.'

Today I head off for the museum as I have nearly every day since I was old enough to keep Marietta company. Not for much longer, though. It's the end of an era. Marietta died two years ago and now the hundred-year lease has run out. The museum – her museum – is closing. Its contents transferred to the British Museum, to be sorted and stashed for ever amongst countless other collections of enthusiasts, wealthy amateurs with the tendencies of magpies.

So we're packing. African fly switches tribal thrones, shrunken heads and shaman's purses – everything to go.

Except for me. Proper museums, the sort that aren't inherited, don't need members of the family firm – knowledgeable about most things, but expert in none.

I doubt if there will be a Ravenscroft Room, there in the British Museum. They already have everything we have, and more.

I don't want to think about it too much, though, what comes after. Today I will be in a sea of bubble wrap and artefacts. But before that I will half skip down Highgate Hill in the sunshine, avoiding the ambulances careening into the Whittington, buy a newspaper from the man on the Holloway Road – and only then, when I'm running out of time, catch a bus. I'll find a seat on the top deck with the teenagers and look out of the window. Watch the children walking to school, small hands clutching the hands of their mothers.

Tom meanwhile will be on the Tube, avoiding the eyes of the nutters, trying to ignore the farting and the jostling. Probably he'll delve into his briefcase and bring out a book, the one he keeps quoting to me. It's by Thoreau, and is all about real life being the life lived away from the town, away from people. The happy man depends on no one, he says.

Marietta – if she were alive – would have said he is wrong. Civilisation is all about men and women learning to depend on each other. She had a whole museum to prove it.

He doesn't have to go on the Tube if he doesn't like it. Tom and I, we use the city in different ways.

Mid morning I stop packing and peel off the surgical gloves we have to wear when we handle things. Phone Tom.

'Yes?'

One word. He doesn't even know it's me he's talking to. But I can hear the edge in his voice. He's not having a good day.

'I forgot. We're going out to dinner tonight. Did you remember?'

'Charlie and Jen's? Of course I remembered.'

I open my mouth to ask about work, then close it again. He'll tell me later, blow-by-blow. The funny thing is, I've met Joaquin a few times, and I like him. For all the reasons Tom doesn't.

Perhaps *like* isn't the word I'm looking for.

Tom rings off and I put my gloves back on. I'm sitting in a puddle of all things Chinese, and the next object to hand is a pair of tiny scarlet slippers, concertinaed as if they have been in a collision. Made out of wood and bright silk, the colour has hardly faded since the day they were fashioned for the shrunken feet of a court lady two hundred years ago. Little red shoes, small as the shoes of a child.

And suddenly I'm back in my dream, watching her stand on the riverbank. Little red shoes poised to take her over the edge.

Have to blink it away. Fold the shoes up in bubble wrap and put them out of sight.

Jen meets us at the door, baby on her hip.

'Come in. Charlie's upstairs with Pig and I'm just about to put this one down. Go and do what you usually do.'

So we do what we usually do and make our way into their kitchen that looks as if it's been picked up and shaken like a snow globe, with nothing fallen where it should have. There are saucepans on the floor and gumboots on the table. The cat is eating the remains of a child's dinner up on the kitchen counter.

Tom looks repelled. I shoo it off while he opens one of our own bottles and finds glasses. I take two and make my way upstairs to find Jen who is in their bathroom changing the nappy on the Duke (real name Andrew). I hand her the glass and she glugs it down in one.

'Lovely,' she says and passes it back to me, gets on with wiping her child's backside. Her hand has left a smear of something on the glass and I put it down quickly.

'It's a good thing Tom didn't see you knock it back like that. It's vintage something or other. It came all the way from Joaquin's vineyard.'

'Oh, Charlie will appreciate it. Poor thing – all he ever gets is plonk. Me, I don't care.'

'Is there anything I can do?'

'No – unless you feel like cooking supper, cleaning up the kitchen, ironing a shirt for Charlie...the usual.' She looks up from what she's doing and smiles. 'By the way, Sara, you look lovely tonight. Really lovely.'

Jen herself is not looking particularly lovely tonight. Her hair is still wet and she's wearing the same clothes she wore when she was pregnant. She hasn't managed to get into her old ones yet. But she pays me the compliment gravely and seriously, without a hint of bitterness – or comparison, even. It's part of a secret language she's developed just for me, as if it's something I need to hear. We both know what she's saying: I may not have a baby, but I do have a waist. Small consolation, for which read: no consolation at all.

Because this is how Jen sees me: Sara who grew up without parents and who now will grow old without children. Nothing before me and nothing to come after me. A full stop stamped in Time. Human punctuation.

Often I catch her – friend since we were eleven – looking at me over the heads of her babies with eyes gone soft with pity. She thinks I'm grieving. It's as if we have gone back in time, to when we were children and she couldn't imagine a fate worse than losing one's parents. Expecting me to cry at any moment for people I never knew.

It's happening again. Jen thinks I am grieving now – not for parents this time, but children I also have never known. I've tried telling her she's wrong, but she just smiles, convinced I'm being brave, that it's nothing to do with choice. She's a daughter who has grown into a mother. She can't think there's any other way to be. It's not her fault. I'm just not like her, that's all.

Besides, if I had a child, who would look after it if anything happened to Tom and me? There would be no Marietta, no proper family, no matter how grudging. Just care homes and orphanages and social workers. I put that to her once, exasperated. Finished up by saying:

'Would you take on our children then, if something happened to us?'

She flushed and said lightly, 'Oh but Sara, nothing would happen.'

But she was wrong, she knew that. Things do happen. And no one knows it as well as us, Tom and me. We know how things go wrong. And how, sometimes, things go right.

Lucky to have found each other. That's what Jen can't understand. But still she watches me, eyes soft, as if seeing something I can't even see myself.

Tom and Charlie are working their way through the wine. Charlie, an anaesthetist, isn't on call tonight so he can afford to. And Tom – well Tom is exactly the way I knew he would be when Joaquin's in town.

'So what does Joaquin actually do, Tom?' This is Jen asking. 'I mean, does he make you take back decisions? Does he fire people without asking you?'

'I'd like to see him try.'

'So...what? Does he sit at your desk? Play with your executive toys? Finger the secretaries?'

'We don't have secretaries. We're a paperless office.'

'I know the problem.' This is Charlie. 'It's to do with authority. If he's there, it means Tom isn't the boss any more. Joaquin, just by walking into the building, is showing who's in charge. Suddenly there's a lid on everything. Doesn't matter if he never opens his mouth. He's there, and it changes everything.'

Tom winces. Which means Charlie has hit the spot.

'You know...' Tom says. And I do know. I know exactly what's coming next. 'I don't know how much more I can stand.'

Charlie and Jen groan. They've heard it too. Countless times.

'Seriously. I want a house and a few acres of land. Have a stream, make our own power. Grow enough vegetables to feed ourselves...'

'...This from the man who apparently doesn't like vegetables.' Jen points to the mound left on his plate. She's overcooked them and Tom is fastidious that way.

I laugh, but Tom doesn't. He says, 'Well look at us. Look at the noise, the pollution. And traffic, and crime. Look at the way we live.'

'I like the way we live.' I say it quietly. Otherwise it sounds as if I'm picking an argument. Which I'm not.

It doesn't matter because Tom hasn't heard me anyway. He says, 'Ask Sara, she'll tell you the same. She can't even drive for a pint of milk without someone getting road rage.'

But that's not true. I drive in London the same way I swim in our local pool: giving way to the men with pumping arms and the women whose heads plunge forward as if searching for children lost beneath the waves. Do anything else and they will plough right into you, jerk you through the water like the victim of a shark attack. Leave you bobbing in eddies of disturbed chlorine. Better to let them go, tread water, watch the patterns of the tiles moving peaceably fifteen feet below. Don't even try to compete. That's how I drive in London.

Except I scarcely ever drive. And definitely not for milk, not when I only have to step out of our front door and into Mr Georghiu's shop, and take it off the shelf. And anything else I need.

'Well personally,' says Jen, 'I don't see how you could ever want to leave. How many couples do you know have a three-storey house on the top of Highgate Hill? And the wherewithal to live in it?'

Tom looks blank suddenly. When his parents died there was nothing left to cushion their infant son. They were young, had lived in a council flat and every penny of the insurance policy was used by his aunt to keep him in shoes. But with me it was different. Probably the car my parents drove to destruction was worth more than the house Tom grew up in, which is a clue in itself. Then there was Marietta. Marietta who loved me in her dry, clear-eyed way. And she left everything to me, including the house I grew up in.

It's as if every time people disappear they give me money. I'd rather have Marietta still alive.

But it's something Tom prefers not to think about. It makes him uncomfortable. And it casts an uncomfortable silence around us now. Maybe Jen was being faintly malicious, taking a small poke at Tom who thinks life is hard in his white-walled office and his Highgate house. A reminder that others are working all the hours at a hospital, paying a mortgage that would buy a small castle in Scotland while their wives juggle two children and bills and ...

From upstairs comes the sound of crying. The Duke has woken up, is summoning her with all the might in his lungs. Straight away Jen is on her feet.

'Sorry,' she says, but she's not. She loves that sound.

But she has upset Tom. He doesn't say as much, but it's there later in our bedroom, as he watches me undress, considering what he sees. Comparing and contrasting.

'It's really nice,' he says finally. 'The way you haven't let yourself go. You're as skinny as the day I met you. Not like some.' He means Jen.

'It's nothing to do with not letting myself go. Skinny is how we are in our family. Remember Marietta. She was like a stick.'

'You're not a stick.' He pulls at the covers so I can climb in beside him. For a moment he lies stroking my breast, then he laughs out loud.

'What?'

'I'm just feeling sorry for poor old Charlie. One thing you can guarantee he's not doing is lying with a woman in his arms. You know what he told me? If the younger kid... what do they call him? The Bloody Red Baron...?'

'The Duke.'

'If the Duke squawks in the night, Charlie's kicked out of the double bed and into the spare room. Jen makes sure the baby is happy if no one else. Ugly bugger he is too. Built like a panzer tank, that one. Fuck that – not being allowed in your own bed with your own wife. God, Sara! Imagine being like them.'

He laughs and stretches. 'She's going to carry on, isn't she? Having kid after kid. Pushing them out as fast as Charlie can push one in.'

'No. She likes what she's got. This is as far as it goes for her. Pig and the Duke – they're all she needs and all she wants. She doesn't want any more children.'

He rolls his eyes, but then he's quiet and it's over, his one small act of revenge. He likes Jen and now that he's commented on her size and her devotion and the baby's looks, he'll let it lie. Won't hold it against her.

But I think he's wrong about Charlie feeling mistreated about the spare room – or anything. When he waved us off he was drunk and slightly ruffled, with his shirt hanging out. He had his arm around Jen, pulling her in close. Big grin on his face.

We make love and drift off to sleep. Soon Tom, who ploughs through his day, telling people what to think, telling people what I think, will cling to me again. Like that man drowning, clutching at the thing that saves him.

On the edge of sleep myself, I'm anxious now. Wondering if she will be back, the little girl. If again I'll have to watch her, helpless, knowing what must happen next.

But it's all right. Instead I sink into a dream of water. I am swimming in our local pool. This time I have solved the problem of people pumping and plunging in the race to the shallow end. I am down here instead, beneath them. Swimming deep underwater where it's clear and blue and empty. I can swoop and turn somersaults, don't even have to breathe. Above me their legs and arms are waving and kicking like people struggling not to drown.

Down here it's peaceful. A much better place to be.

# CHAPTER TWO

'Wake up, Sara.'

Tom is leaning over me in the bed. He looks excited, younger even than he does normally. Outside, morning has barely lightened the windows. It's Saturday. Is he going running this early?

'Rise and shine, I've got an idea.' He kisses my shoulder then leaps out of bed. Stares down at me expectantly. Clearly part of the idea is that I jump out of bed too.

'But it's only six o' clock...'

'Never mind that, come on.' He pulls the duvet off me and flings it on the floor. Too determined just to be playful.

Bewildered, I swing my legs over the side.

'What do you think of a weekend away? Find a hotel, walk, look for some good pubs. Have some time to ourselves.'

'I don't know. Where?'

'South. Follow the sun. Devon, Cornwall. Land of the cream tea.'

'It's already Saturday. We'll only manage a night, then we'll have to drive all the way back.'

'That's why we've got to head off now. But what I'm

thinking is that I take Monday off. Maybe Tuesday. Why not bloody Wednesday while we're at it.' The excited look fades. 'Look, I'm serious. I can't handle it, Sara, not when Joaquin is there. We talked about it long enough last night, you heard me.' And I did.

'You know what he's doing, Sara. He's trying to undermine me. Kick the legs out from under me. Rob, Shirley – they talk to me, but they're looking at him, making sure they've got his approval. He's staying on to make a point. There's nothing he needs to be here for. This is just to get at me.

'So I'll leave them to it. Joaquin will be able to see the shit that goes down when I'm not there and I won't be around to put up with it.'

'What about me? What about the museum?'

He smiles and rubs my head. 'Like you're their most important member.' The irony is meant to be affectionate.

And there's nothing I can say. I'm only supposed to be doing them a favour, helping with the packing. Keeping the spirit of Marietta there till the end, until they move and forget all about her. The end of an era. The end of me.

Tom takes my hand in his. 'Please, Sara. I mean it. Let's just get away.'

We grab a few things and jump into the car.

As he drives, Tom formulates a plan. 'We'll get as far as we can before lunch. Seven o'clock now. That's five, six hours. Let's see if we can get right into the south of Devon. Meanwhile, you flick through that.' He tosses a guidebook into my lap. 'See if you can find us a hotel. Something fancy. No wait, I've got a better idea. Look for one of those places that have gone alternative. Hemp bedspreads, organic food.

That sort of thing. Let's get a proper taste of the country, try and get real for once.'

So I do my best. As we're driving through Wiltshire I phone ahead to a small hotel in Devon that promises organic everything, and locally sourced. Except for the cotton sheets on the bed, which are woven in Egypt. But they are organic too.

Tom is pleased. With every mile away from London he gets more and more cheerful.

And maybe he's right. It's May, and this is England. Beyond the margins of the hard shoulder, the fields are green and the hedges white with petals – just like the lawns in Dartmouth Park and the sprays of may blossom draped across the stone angels in Highgate Cemetery. Trees are coming into full leaf – exactly like the lime tree outside our house, making our bedroom green and glowing when the sun shines through in the morning.

If we were at home now, we would be making our way to our favourite cafe for strong coffee and croissants. But we're not home and, instead, we stop in a motorway service station for flabby rolls and pretend cappuccino. Normally Tom would prefer to go thirsty, but he knocks back the 'coffee' as if it really were coffee and beams at me. So naturally, I'm happy too, and even the rolls taste all right with the little pot of fancy jam he's picked out of the basket by the till and slipped into his pocket. I don't suppose he even remembered to pay for it. He tends to assume these things come for free. One of life's givens.

Too little sleep. I've nodded off when Tom nudges me. 'Look, Sara. Stonehenge.'

I sit up and there it is in the distance. Small from where we are speeding past, not as impressive as I'd expect. It looks like something Jen's little girl, Claudia (aka Pig), would put together out of toilet rolls. I'd need to see it up close. Tom is more easily pleased. 'Incredible!' he says. 'Like the heads on Easter Island. You can't begin to imagine how they could even dream of getting them up. You just have to look and think how the fuck did they do that? Makes you wonder if there wasn't something in it, all that stuff about extraterrestrials.'

If Marietta were here she would tell him the process was probably the same – in Wiltshire and Polynesia. Build a platform and gradually increase the height under the top part of the stone until it's upright. Difficult, but perfectly do-able, witness the fact that they're here. No need for talk of spacemen or helpless speculation. Marietta had trust in Man's ingenuity, on people's willingness to depend on each other. And she could be quite snippy when she wanted.

Suddenly Tom frowns from across the steering wheel. 'Why are you doing that?'

I give a start. 'Doing what? I wasn't doing anything

'You were looking at me just now, I don't know – the way Marietta used to. It's something you've started doing lately. Like the only thoughts worth having are your own.'

I blush and turn my face to the window.

The hotel is on the edge of Dartmoor.

It turns out to be small, with a honey stone exterior that inside gives way to white walls and muted colours. The owners greet us in person with glasses of organic champagne and kisses on both cheeks. The first thing they do is invite us to sign a guest book which contains the names of at least three rock stars. They congratulate us on discovering them at such a quiet time, when they can relax, enjoy their guests. Once the season starts, they say, the Primrose Hill brigade will descend as a pack and keep them busy all summer.

'Mayhem, darling,' says the woman, smiling at me. 'Absolute bloody mayhem. They eat us out of house and home. It's just so lucky that Johnny Archer's estate has gone organic. We can outsource it all to him.'

Tom grins. This must be what he means by real. Already, he and the owners are talking waterwheels and carbon footprints, and the man is offering to take him outside to have a look at their reed bed sewerage system. He goes and leaves me with the woman who smiles warmly. She's wearing MaxMara under her striped butcher's apron. 'I'm about to start making your supper for tonight. Do you want to come and keep me company in the kitchen?'

I smile with equal warmth. 'Can you believe it? I just need to sleep for a bit. You know what it's like; never a moment just to – take a breath.'

'Darling,' she says. 'Of course. Go and catch up. Breathe. We'll see you at supper.'

She shows me to a room with grainy walls and hardwood floors. There's a fall of Egyptian cotton at the window, and lilies in a vase, beautifully arranged. She sighs with pleasure at her own good taste, waits for me to do the same. Instead I step to the window. Here is a genuine reason to be surprised: a few hundred yards away another building rises out of the moor to make a silhouette of soaring roofs and crenulations. Massive walls that seem to swallow up the sun. It had been invisible from the other side of the hotel.

'What's that place?' I ask. 'A prison?'

'Good grief no.' She is quick to correct me. 'It's Benton. Perhaps you've heard of it. It's famous enough. It was built in Victorian times, as an asylum for women declared criminally insane. Hopeless cases only, mothers who had murdered their own babies. Child killers, that sort of thing.'

For some reason, I am taken aback. Perhaps because it was only yesterday I was with Jen, watching her swing between tenderness and fury for her children, hot and flustered with love. Almost unwilling, I look again.

'Actually, the regime there was rather enlightened for its day. They even used to hold balls there, and soirées. The women were encouraged to dress up and dance, pretend they were still civilised, and weren't all mad as birds. Not the best place to be. But by no means the worst. Of course, it would have been the stuff of freak shows – people used to come from miles around just to watch the Mad Balls. They still do, in a way. It's just a boring old mental hospital now, but you wouldn't believe how many writers and historians travel here to look at the place. I must get you to look at our guest book.'

She leaves and I sink onto a bed which is as wide as it's long – only to find myself getting up again to close the curtains, shutting out the sight of the building and its walls, swallowing the sun.

Dinner is exactly as I knew it would be. We all end up eating together as if we are their invited guests and you would never dream we will be handing over three hundred pounds in the morning. And Tom...Tom is saying he doesn't know how much longer he can stand it in the city, the noise, the pollution etcetera, and they are shaking their heads and saying we know, we know. It happened to them, but they took the plunge and they haven't looked back. And really it's what everyone should do, we should just get out now while we're still young and our children are flexible.

'We don't have any children,' I say.

And they beam at both of us then. Even better, they exclaim. No ties. How wonderful.

That night Tom sleeps on his back with his arms flung out on either side. He has forgotten the need to cling. Maybe it's the sheer size of the bed, bearing our weight like a raft on the surface of the sea, making him feel safe. And for once I have no dreams – or none that I remember. I just...sleep. It's as if even our brainwaves have been stilled and smoothed into a state of where nothing happens.

Too much sleep now. In the morning I feel drugged by it, foggy. Heart sinking at the thought of the couple downstairs waiting for us with pots of organic honey and stoneground toast. An endless capacity for talk. Tom kisses me.

'Stay there, I'll bring you up a tray.'

Somehow it doesn't occur to him to phone down and order one.

When he comes back up, it's obvious he's been talking to them. Now he wants to stay here, round and about the hotel. 'I just want to see how people go about it, Sara.'

'About what?'

'Making a go of things. He was in advertising, and she was – well, I don't know what she did exactly. They didn't know a thing about being self-sufficient, let alone running a hotel. But they've made it work for them. And they've never looked back…'

'Actually,' I say. 'I don't want to stay here. I want to go walking like you said. Find a pub, and eat cake in cafes. I don't want her talking to me and calling me darling.' I look at him. 'Is that all right?'

He hesitates. Then nods.

Is it because it's so rarely it happens? That I dig in my heels and tell him what I want. When I do, he always gives in. Sometimes quickly – or else reluctantly as now. Slightly sullen. It comes to the same thing. We don't argue. An unspoken preference for agreement.

But it's ruined Tom's mood. This time it's me that drives, while he sits staring at the scenery out of the passenger window. Meanwhile, Dartmoor pays out more and more green, as if from an unending swatch; it furls and unfurls in hills and valleys picked out with bobbles of sheep with their lambs stitched close. Here and there are clumps of abandoned mine workings and trees crouching in hollows, the rocks laid bare as if a giant hand has been scooping out fistfuls of earth.

Surely, this is what we came down for. Yet Tom is dull-eyed as he takes it all in. He wants to be in the honey-coloured hotel with its organic owners and locally sourced everything. He wants to be sitting close to their Aga in the kitchen, with mugs of good coffee talking about what's real and rooted. He wants to show them he's on the same wavelength; that he's just like them.

In Tavistock we stop because he says he needs a coffee. So we find a cafe and, despite breakfast, order big slices of walnut cake. He eats his, half of mine, and starts to cheer up again. Make plans again. When we wander back out onto the high street he has almost forgiven me for dragging him away. Things are turning out well after all. He even takes my hand as we walk along. We are friends again, strolling through this town with a Sunday morning quiet to it.

It's still early in the year for tourists, and most of the shops are closed. Only the cafes and antique shops are open, and the occasional estate agent. Inevitably Tom gets snagged by the window of one. It's the London preoccupation. You stare at what's on offer, and compare what you can buy here for the price of your own home. Sometimes – looking at a converted barn, say – you even get the sense of a life, branching off from your actual life. One that's lived here, in this barn, with this much land, so that suddenly you're living two lives: one where you belong and one where you might belong. Just for those few seconds, forgetting where it is you actually do belong, casting doubt over everything.

But always I remember our house and the lime tree coming into leaf. Rooms where Marietta let me roll African gourds along the floor while she made patient descriptions of amulets and fetishes at her big oak desk with its photograph of my mother and, next to Marietta's pens, a china cat that smiled to itself. The other life vanishes and you can step past the window, knowing exactly where you belong. In fact, Tom has already moved on. There's nothing here that's caught his eye.

But he hasn't seen what I've seen.

Down in the corner of the window; a photograph of a house. Unlike the rest of the photographs of properties, the house itself barely takes up any space in the picture. What you see is small – a couple of pink gables. It's what else is in the picture that matters: a deep, dark background of lawns and trees and river. A strip of blue sky overhead.

The caption reads – House in own secluded valley, bordering the Tamar River. Nine acres.

'Tom, look at this.'

... And bite my tongue.

But it's too late. He is turning round, attention already moving from my face to the corner of the window he missed before.

Hurriedly I step away, as if somehow this will make him follow me, distract him. But he's closing in, frowning, bending down to see better. Long seconds of staring, his entire body rigid. Finally he stands up.

'Let's go inside.'

He takes my hand and pushes open the door.

So here we are, driving with a map spread out on my knee, Tom at the wheel. The day has turned serious.

Inside the estate agent's, they had been doubtful they could contact the owners at such short notice. If we were to come back in the week? But Tom was adamant, and so all attempts were made.

And the result was that Mr Marsh would expect us in an hour. He is going out with his family after that and we have promised to be on time.

Except that was an hour and fifteen minutes ago and we are still driving. We crossed the Tamar River, so we are just inside Cornwall now, according to our book. So close. But somewhere between a farm track and a church we missed our turning. There's a village we have to find, and after that, a track that's not even drawn on the map. Tom's hands clutching the wheel are showing white at the knuckles.

I know him so well. He has had a glimpse of the possible. Now he has the sense of it already slipping away.

A bend and then a row of houses. A pub, a shop. More houses, then – nothing. We are looking for an unsigned road half a mile after a bend. But there's nothing there. Only more road. I'm almost ready to let myself think we will never find it. The place doesn't even exist. It was just an estate agent's dream. We have escaped.

I open my mouth to say we can go back to the hotel, spend the next two days mucking out the couple's pigs, or whatever it takes to show we really, really are on the same wavelength, and I won't mind when she calls me darling...

Then Tom jams his foot on the brakes, and the car stops, throwing me hard against my belt.

'That's it.'

He crunches the gears and puts the car into reverse, so fast the engine strains, high-pitched, everything working in the wrong direction.

'There.'

A lane that was invisible from the other direction, hidden by the bend in the road. He turns the car into the mouth of it – and stops again. This lane, barely the width of our small car, plunges down in front of us, so narrow – and so steep – you have to pause just to consider it. Sunk in the fabric of the surrounding earth, its banks are brown and exposed. But out of them, trees are growing, reaching up from either side of the road, branches meeting and clasping in a never-ending apex above our heads. In full leaf, they make a long, green, descending tube.

Tom winds down his window. Indicates for me to do the same. He breathes deep.

'Smell that?'

'Yes.'

And it's true. I smell something that makes me think of colours. Brown and green. The scent you'd imagine finding on your fingers if you've been weeding, or pulling off muddy wellingtons. But richer than that. Greener. Browner.

'Loam,' says Tom decisively.

He could be right. What is loam? I've no idea.

'Let's hope there's nothing coming up,' says Tom. He puts the car into gear and eases forward, and we begin to go down.

And down.

At first we go slowly.

Inching past the roots of trees protruding out of the banks. Here, it seems, the tangled limbs of things that belong underground have broken cover. Coiling and gnarled, they are velvety to the touch. And I do touch them, through the open window so that they slide under my fingers as if they are the things moving, not us. Then there are the ferns, unfurling with the energy of springs. They catch at the door handles, find their way into the car, brushing my arm, and occasionally my cheek, with a feathery, curious touch of their own.

Faster. Already Tom is convinced that this is a place where no one else comes. There will be no other car, no danger of collision. The only motion is down. So much so, it's tempting to switch off the engine, and see if we don't just keep on going, like a rabbit in the body of a snake, a kind of peristaltic action.

But inside a snake there is no sunshine. And there is sunshine here, filtered through the trees, dappled – and green, like the smell. And still we go down. I have to close the window now. At speed, the ferns' touch has turned into a slap, almost an assault.

Just once, I turn and look behind us. The sides of the lane have converged, running together into a closed V. A vanishing point.

Then suddenly we are on the level and the world flattens out. We are driving through trees and rhododendron bushes, clumps of them on either side of the road, with great heads of blossom nodding as we pass. Behind them are more trees, but they are set back and dense, casting a net of shadows on the floor between them. Tom tilts the wheel, and the house itself comes into view. Square with pink gables, it has decking running round it under a wide porch, somehow incongruous. An add-on. These people watch the makeover programmes.

But then, you understand why you might want a porch, a wide space in which to sit and simply stare. Where the road stops, lawns carry on, sweeping down to a bank of undergrowth. A bank that acts like a margin between us and the river. Because here, the river runs, brown and rushing, in a valley that belongs to it and the house, and nothing else. On the far side of the river, rising high above us, there are cliffs of trees, a great solid wall of green.

'My God,' breathes Tom. 'It really is a valley. The place is its own fucking valley.'

He turns off the engine. There is a silence. There is nothing. Not until your ears become attuned. Then you hear it. The sound of the river moving over stones. And birds calling out, giving warning that we are here. Bees buzzing in the snapdragons lining the path to the house, where the owners have been waiting for us.

Now I remember, and glance at my watch.

Before I can say anything, the door to the house opens and a man is stepping out. He walks quickly, like someone with a chip on his shoulder, an axe to grind. It's because we are late. We have kept him waiting.

Beside me, Tom is reading the same signs.

'Shit.'

For this is someone who would turn us away simply for not being on time, I can tell. It's clear in the way he lets his arms swing, in the precise placing of his feet, and as he gets nearer, it's clearer still. He's one of those short men who seem to be short for a reason, every cell in their bodies being compacted together, making them harder, stronger, more tensile than other men. A man with no patience for the lax. The late.

He comes and stands in front of us, but keeps his distance. He is wearing a red T-shirt too small for the muscles in his arms. Dark hair cropped short. Now he waits.

'Look, we're so sorry we're late. Really we are. In fact we're incredibly sorry, words can't express, etcetera. Isn't that right, Sara?'

This is Tom, not making a good job. He doesn't have the experience. He's having to apologise for something that's almost a virtue where he comes from. Now he's only managing to sound abject and patronising in equal measure.

Sure enough, the man – Marsh – just looks at him. Looks at both of us. But then, without any warning, he smiles. Adjusting the muscles of his face into a beam that seems to come straight from the manual. A landlord's grin, slapped on till last orders, until it can be whipped off and thrown away. He takes three more steps with his hand stretched out to shake Tom's, then mine.

'Mr and Mrs Lewis? Not at all, no problem. Just glad you found us. Come on, this way. Let's make sure you see everything.' He speaks and smiles at the same time, with the same assumed beam. His vowels are wide, slightly lingering.

He turns and leads us past the snapdragons towards the house.

Tom looks at me, triumphant. He thinks he has won him over. But I find myself watching the back of the man leading the way. It remains set, muscle-bound. Now that we can't see his face, I would swear the smile has disappeared. Hidden from us, it would have fallen away. Instantly, like ice cubes sliding off a plate.

But he's fooled Tom, who catches hold of my hand and grins.

On the porch with its brand new decking, Marsh pauses and calls out: 'Carole.'

There's a pause, then slowly a woman appears, holding a baby, about the age of the Duke. Nine months, maybe less. She is small with a thin face that seems pinched somehow. Makes me think suddenly of Jen with her hot red cheeks, glowing as if the heat of her pregnancy never really left her.

This woman looks cold, shivering even on a sunny day.

Marsh says, 'This is my wife, Carole.' He waits for her to say hello. But she says nothing. And I catch my breath, because I see him as a man who expects much – of himself and others. And he would not expect his wife to stand speechless in front of visitors, like a child who's not quite right.

But I'm wrong. Instead he says softly, 'The baby needs changing. You want to take him into the conservatory? I'll show them round.'

She nods. And then she's gone. But the tone of his voice will stay with me now. Gentle. Unforced. Not what I expected. Suddenly makes me like him more.

But then he turns back to us, and there it is again, the switch. The smile.

He shows us the kitchen first, tells us about the house.

'It's an old miner's cottage. A ruin when we came. We did it up ourselves. Everything from scratch.'

'Like the TV programmes,' says Tom helpfully. The man looks blank.

We look round us at the kitchen, at what he's done here. There's the slightest of pauses. I say, 'It's great, you did a great job.'

Tom says nothing. He'll be thinking of Marietta's kitchen, with its original butler's sink and butcher's block, and its range. This kitchen is laminate and MDF, every corner sealed with Artex. Grouting shines between the patterned tiles behind the stove. There are horse brasses and samplers and dried flowers, and everything sparkles.

'Country style,' I say, to make up for Tom.

'Thought we'd keep to the character of the place.'

But in Tom's view, the character is gone, vanished beneath borders and friezes. It's the same in the rest of the house. Marsh takes us from room to room, each wall papered up to the fake dado, with matching paint above that. Dark carpets, the shades chosen to go with any colour scheme. They've kept some of the original fireplaces, but filled them with gas, coal-effect fires. Their furniture shines and is set just so, nothing out of place. We navigate between sofas, almost awed by the tidiness of everything. No one we know keeps house like this. Jen and Charlie spring to mind again, living in a mess only this side of squalor.

I need to keep an eye on Tom. Watch out for wincing or gurning, or just the sideways glance at me. Sometimes, he just feels honour bound...

But he's being good, and gradually I remember: this is how his aunt kept house. Shoes off when you come in. Coasters for every cup of coffee that's drunk. In rooms where any mirror or polished surface could give him away, Tom is staying careful, to the point of being cowed.

Besides, he is doing what I am doing. Can't help himself. In every room, we are drawn to the window, to the green of the outside. To the river and the rising cliffs and the blue strip of sky above. The real attraction.

The baby's room is less tidy. The cot blankets are tossed and there's his last change of clothes still on the floor. Marsh frowns and picks them up, but it's almost a relief to be here. There's the faintest smell of juice and the cream that Jen smears on the Duke's bottom.

Out on the landing, I ask the question everyone asks. 'So... why are you moving?'

He must have expected it, yet for the space of seconds, he seems thrown. Then he finds his groove again. 'This place, it was a project. We've done everything we can with it. Besides, there's my job. I work unsocial hours, which leaves my wife by herself a lot. If we move, she can see more of her mother, not be so alone.'

'OK,' says Tom, 'so what do you do?'

'Police. Uniformed.'

And unconsciously we both nod, because now it just seems obvious. Marsh opens the last door on the landing. Pushes it wide, then steps back. A different way of showing a room. Before, he has led the way, master of his house. This time, he is inviting us to enter by ourselves.

It's a little girl's room. Smaller than the baby's, which maybe is why he stays on the landing. It has pink walls, pink bed. Dolls lined up tidily on a shelf. A pink rug laid just so. So tidy, so clean, so untouched you almost feel sorry for her, the child whose room this is. As if she never comes in here.

Mandy. Her name is Mandy. I know because it's on the wall. Her name spelt out in wooden letters and stuck there. M A N D Y. Letters so large they invite you to say them out loud. Tom is busy frowning at the pink walls, so I move to the window without him, drawn as always to the green and the river, where trees make shadows that in turn make shapes, solid figures out of light and shade.

One small figure. 'That must be your daughter I can see down there,' I say.

'Where?' Marsh's voice reaches me, so sharp, I jump.

'There, by the water.'

Why does this man sound so surprised? If I were a child,

this is where I'd want to stand all the time, making the same small white shape I am looking at now, half hidden by green and the dazzle of sun on water. Scarcely more than a glimmer amongst the trees. A child watching the river flow.

But the answer is a movement behind me, so abrupt, I turn.

And there, I've seen it. Marsh's face stripped of the smile. Expressionless. Every line closing it down. Mouth sealed, eyes shuttered so there's no looking past them.

There's a pause. Then: 'You're mistaken. Mandy's not here.'

Tom has taken my place by the window. 'There's no one there, Sara. You're seeing things.'

I look again. And he's right. There's no sign of a child now. Just water chopping up the light from the sun. 'Oh,' I say in surprise. 'Oh...'

But both men are ignoring me. Marsh has turned on his heel, and eager to be outside, Tom is following.

Outside, next to the river, Marsh suddenly seems tired of us.

'Why don't you just look round for yourselves? I won't be under your feet, and you can save up any questions for after. We'll be in the conservatory when you want us.'

He wants to get back to his wife, with her silent stare. Alone, almost daunted, we pick our way along a path, with the river to our right. With every step, we leave a footprint, pressed into the grass. Scents of green rise where we walk, birds call out warning of our approach.

And yet nothing seems quite real.

Here is the river running beside us; and there, rising above us, are cliffs hidden by trees so extravagantly tall we could be in one of Marietta's jungles. This is not like any garden I have ever known. It's not like anywhere. Even the air is different. Heavier, claggier. So dense and so green you could imagine moss forming in your lungs.

And all of it for sale. Whoever buys this place will have this river and this air, when it never even occurred to me that such things could be owned.

Tom must want it. He has to. It's everything he has ever dreamt of. More. He's looking at fruit trees as we pass them, cherry trees that have only now stopped flowering. Stretches of lawn that could be turned over to vegetables. He could even build a wheel beside the river and turn water into energy. He could do anything here. And I am afraid that he will.

Suddenly the air seems too heavy. The sides of the valley too high. I feel like something fallen into a deep trench, and it makes me want to leave before it becomes the end of everything I've ever known. My life. Days spent in the rooms where I grew up. Places, people, work.

I want to return to the pink house and say our goodbyes, climb into the car and drive away. Back to where we came from. Where we belong.

But Tom has grabbed hold of my hand, is holding it tight. His skin is hot with excitement. I can feel the pulse throbbing in the wrist pressed against mine. He says, 'Let's go and look at the river.'

But when we look for a way down to the water's edge, we can't find one. Where you would expect a broad and gentle sweep, there is only a swathe of brambles knee high.

I'm wearing sandals and it would tear my feet apart trying to pick a way through. No easy way to the water. No way down at all.

'Never mind,' says Tom. He has his eyes on the outbuildings, imagining shedfuls of gleaming machinery. Vague imaginings because he doesn't actually know what they would be for. Neither of us do. The only mechanical thing we own is our car, small enough to slot into traffic and city parking spaces.

We make our way back to the house, the river on our left now. And hard as I try, I still can't see a way that would let us close to the water.

The conservatory adjoins the house, overlooking the river. Three sides of glass and there the Marshes are waiting. We can see them from the path, careful not to be caught watching us. But their eyes will have followed us all the time we have been outside.

They would have marked the excitement that hovers over Tom like a swarm of invisible bees. They would have seen me looking, again and again, for a way down to the river.

And though they do their best to hide it, when we step into the conservatory, they are more watchful still. Even the woman, who before looked only tired. She is holding the baby on her knee, pretending to show him a toy. But like her husband she is watching us.

They want to sell this house so badly. You can feel it. Almost touch it. Someone needs to say something to prick the air of waiting. Wanting.

It's Tom who speaks first. 'What a place! What an incredible place. You think so too, don't you, Sara?'

I nod. But it's the woman I watch. I even manage to catch her eye, just for a moment. A tiny space of time, but it's long enough. In that brief second it is all there to see:

She hates this place. Every green blade, every bending leaf. Hates it so much she blushes and looks away, because she has to hide it. Has to. To leave, she needs to find someone to replace her. Someone like me.

Tom sees none of this. He is talking about mains drainage and gas supplies and water. Faintly proud that he knows the questions to ask. In London, everything comes to you, without anyone even stopping to think. Now he wants to know what the soil is like, and nods when Marsh says he could grow anything and everything – if only he had the time.

'Not everything.' Without warning his wife has spoken. 'Sun's all wrong.'

Marsh frowns.

But Tom looks out of the window. Doesn't know what she's talking about. The sun is shining down hard from that strip of sky, polishing the grass, glancing off the surface of the water in flashing shards of broken light.

'Sun looks all right to me.' He smiles.

It's time to go.

Now we are back in the car. Neither of us is speaking.

Again we drive slowly – not because the car is finding it difficult up the lane but because Tom wants to. Back at the house they will be talking about us, wondering how serious we were. I'd say it was a relief, having us gone. He can wipe the smile off his face. She can allow the baby to gurgle and crawl where he wants. And the little girl…

We never did see the little girl. The closest we got was her room, pristine, as if she was never there.

Just before the top of the lane, where the trees are still a green vault above us, Tom stops the car.

'So, what did you think, Sara? Really.'

I've been waiting for this. I have my answer ready.

'I think it would change our lives. Completely.'

As I speak a fern nods at the window, a feathery ear bending to catch what's said.

'I'm ready for change, Sara. Change is what I want.'

When I don't answer, he sighs. So I say, 'I also think it was the most beautiful place I've ever seen. It's just I can't imagine us there.'

'You mean you can't imagine yourself there.' Tom opens the window again. 'Breathe in, Sara. Put your head out and take a proper breath. Try and remember that when we're home and you're sitting in a stinking carriage on the Northern Line. This is what you could be breathing, all the time. We both could.'

He starts up the car. As we go through the village we pass the shop again. This time I see its name. Tremaine's.

'Want to stop?' I say.

Tom shakes his head, and we press on. But a few yards later, he jams his foot on the brake. We are by the church. Older than all the houses surrounding, it has a small, stunted tower and a roof sinking at one end. Reminds me of a ship taking in water. But Tom is smitten, is already getting out of the car.

'Coming?'

He pushes open the gate and leads the way into the

churchyard, goes and waits for me amongst the stones, taller than any of them, looking uncannily like a man about to address a crowd.

A crowd. For that's what the graves bring to mind. It's the flip side of the village we have just passed through, the houses quiet, lulled by the warmth of a May Sunday. And yet... and yet behind the windows and doors you knew there were people, probably watching us as we passed.

Well, here there are also people. They just happen to be dead.

Tom is thinking; staring up at the sky latticed by trees, listening to the birdsong. He turns to me. 'If we bought that house, this is where we would end up. This would be where we belong.'

But all it does is make me shiver, the thought of having to die to belong somewhere.

Tom shrugs and wanders off amongst the graves. I follow at a distance. I don't enjoy graveyards. A long way from here, my parents lie, crumpled bones laid into straight lines side by side. I don't go to where they are. It's Marietta I miss, and still miss. Lately I've missed her more than ever. Missed the dry, clear-eyed way she loved me.

Close to my feet, though, something catches me by surprise. Flashes once and disappears. The tail end of a tail. A moment ago there must have been a cat, probably sunning itself at the base of a headstone – until we came along and disturbed it.

This is where it was. By this stone.

Slightly set back, this one. Covered in moss and impossible to read. Tom has walked straight past. But I stay, fascinated by a vegetable growth so dense it reminds me of the soft pelt of an animal, the sort that makes your fingers long to stroke it. Which, as if of their own accord, is what my own fingers do now...

'Oh!'

I pull my hand away. The stone is warm. It rippled under my fingers like something alive, fur smoothed over flesh.

'What?' calls out Tom.

'Nothing.'

I put my hand back to stone that doesn't feel like stone at all, half expecting it to breathe as automatically I probe the green growth. Gradually, from under my fingers, letters take shape. An R...an A...a V.

'Oh!' Again I have cried out.

'What?'

'Nothing. Honestly.'

I step away from the grave, but it's too late. Tom frowns and walks over to me. Fortunately the moss gleams and covers what's underneath, so even though he looks, he can't see.

A name. Only my fingers could read.

Ravenscroft.

My name – and Marietta's; and all the people who came before us. All those wicked railroaders and financiers and arms dealers, whose wealth would buy the pink house for us, though Tom won't like to admit it. A name I don't want him to see. Because I know exactly what he'd do. He'd turn to me in triumph, beaming.

'Look Sara, it's a sign! You've got to move here. Even the gravestones have your name on them. You'd be coming home!'

And it wouldn't matter that we Ravenscrofts never stepped foot in Cornwall. The first John Ravenscroft – first of the robber barons – came from Fife in Scotland. A Kirkcaldy man, he bought a ticket to America and never looked back. It's all written down in a book somewhere – a potted history of money and the pursuit of it.

There's nothing to connect that Ravenscroft with this one.

Yet it would make no difference. Tom is looking for signs. If he saw this, his eyes would gleam and then narrow, determined to make it mean something. But he didn't see and, grateful, I step away from the stone with its surprising warmth and the name that has nothing to do with me.

In the hotel, over supper, over copious wine, which they drink and we will pay for, Tom tells the owners about the house in the valley.

They examine the estate agent's details. Shake their heads in wonder. Amazing, incredible. We would be mad to let this slip through our hands. Tom swallows his wine, looks at me in triumph. The man starts to draw up plans for asparagus beds, writing down the name of the best organic seed suppliers. She does thumbnail sketches of how we could turn the house around, banish all trace of 'improvements'.

I sit and say nothing. Watch them drink the wine they will be charging us for in the morning. Watch Tom.

Upstairs he holds me in his arms. He is vibrating with energy, excitement. 'You see, Sara? You see how it could be?'

* * *

His eyes are shining, his face lit up and handsome. It's the reason *she* watched him all evening, hung on his every word. Older women often seem drawn to Tom.

I murmur, 'I'd miss people, Tom. I'd miss Charlie and Jen and—'

'But they'd come down! Everyone would. We wouldn't be able to keep them away. We could make a go of the place all the week, grow things. The weekends we'd spend hanging out. You could see everyone you want.'

Again we fall asleep in the bed that is big as a boat. This time, when he throws his arm across me, he is awake. Not drowning as he does in his sleep, but drifting, with me in his arms, imagining a life that bears no resemblance to the one we have.

~

# Chapter Three

Back in London, though, the fever subsides.

The night we got back, Joaquin held a dinner party in a restaurant for the magazine. Made sure I was sitting next to him. Joaquin is about fifty, dark, a little overweight. Or perhaps it's just the largeness of him, making him seem overweight next to Tom with his lean, light limbs. He has a crooked nose, broken as a boxer's and a mouth that makes me think of a Renaissance prince.

And I know exactly why he flusters Tom. Joaquin fills a room, not just with his bulk, but with things that are intangible. Heat, scents of Acqua di Parma, a gaze that lingers then moves on. Mocking. Observant.

Another thing I have noticed – and then tried not to notice: he observes me. Last year, perhaps because of that observation, I dreamt I lay in a bed with him. Dreamt I lay against his stomach, which was firm and covered with a pelt of fine grey hairs that tickled the length of my body.

And I loved it. I could have lain there for ever, buoyed up by flesh; his body a springboard as well as a bulwark. Hard to imagine him clinging to another person as if to a ship's spar. It's a dream that makes me blush, one I try to forget and yet wish I could have again.

Tonight he sat, watching me eat. Through the amuse-gueules, four courses and ice cream.

'Good,' he murmured. 'I love to watch a thin woman eat.'

'Oh?' I smile. 'Why is that?'

'It tells me something. When a thin woman is greedy – as you are – and yet never grows fat, it means she needs something more than food.'

'But I'm not greedy,' I protested.

'No,' he said slowly. 'No, you are not greedy, Sara. Rather, I'd say you were hungry. Terribly hungry. Pitifully, ravenously so.'

A pause. All round us, the conversation seemed to die away. I put my spoon down. Joaquin nodded.

'So...what are you hungry for, Sara? Is it something a man could give you, I wonder? Something I could possibly offer.'

Hearing this, I felt disappointment wash over me – tinged with relief. I had never thought Joaquin would be so crude in his approach. Now I would forget the dream. I picked up my spoon again.

'I'm not hungry for anything you could offer, Joaquin.' My voice had the sudden clipped edge of Marietta's.

Joaquin's smile faded

'Ah, no, no, Sara. You think I am flirting with you. You think this is a conversation about sex. No, forgive me. This is much more...intimate.' He sighed, flicked his forehead. 'My clumsiness. I thought I would learn about you if I sat with you, asked you important questions, but I should have realised. You are not a woman who gives away her secrets easily. I must assume Tom is content not to know. Happy to live with a mystery.'

'There's no mystery about me,' I countered lightly. 'Tom would be the first to tell you that.'

Simultaneously we glanced across the table where Tom was talking to a young woman. He looked serious and she looked impressed.

And when I looked at Joaquin, he was laughing.

'Ah yes. I do believe you're right. I believe he would tell me that.' He leant to pour wine into my glass. 'He doesn't like me very much, does he? Your Tom.'

I began to protest.

'No, Sara! Don't trouble yourself. Besides, I know exactly the reason, and it seems to me he cannot help himself. This husband of yours, he is good at his job. He makes my magazine run like...how might you say it in English? A clock. A wonderful, expensive clock. But he does not trust himself. He needs me to tell him he is this, he is that. He needs praise, like a little boy. And when he does not get it, he becomes angry. Why is that, Sara? Why should a grown man need another man to tell him what he should know for himself? Didn't his father do that for him? Is that why?'

'His father died. And his mother. Both together when he was a baby.'

Joaquin looked at me then, eyes half closed. Then said, 'Aaah.' Opening his mouth wide. 'So...yes. Now I see. Tell me, Sara, do you plan to have children?'

I shook my head.

'No. It was silly of me to ask. How could you possibly have a child? Tom could not allow it. He would lose your gaze, your attention to his needs – which are deep and real. It would make him an orphan all over again. It takes much,

I think, to keep a man like him happy. Sacrifices have to be made. Hard choices.'

'I really don't see how you—'

I stopped. Joaquin had moved his hand, laid it beside mine. And now there they were, our two hands, his skin touching my skin. A touch so unexpected, so strangely intimate, my cheeks burnt.

A moment passed. I took my hand away.

Just in time. Tom looked up, as he so often does when we are together but apart, his eyes in search of mine, testing the thread that keeps us connected. The briefest glance before, reassured, he turned back to his own conversation.

Such a small thing. No one would notice, not even the woman he was talking to. No one – except the man sitting next to me, whose shoulders again were shaking with mirth, and who was bending to whisper in my ear:

'But it must be tiring for you, Sara! I must find some way to help you. You will let me help, will you not?'

He leant across for a bottle, poured the last of its wine into my glass, more attentive to my needs than his own.

I told Tom about the magazine running like a big expensive clock. He said nothing, but looked pleased. After that, I waited for him to mention the pink house in the Valley. But he didn't. A week went by, and then another. After a fortnight, the estate agents stopped phoning. And now it's been a whole month and Tom seems to have forgotten all about it.

Instead he talks about Joaquin who, it seems, has suddenly become extravagant in his praise. Telling him the *this* and the *that*. Things Tom should have known for himself. Last week Tom came home with a briefcase made out of tooled leather, a parting gift from Joaquin who finally has gone back to Portugal. It looked and smelt magnificent, somehow like Joaquin himself. And Tom is happy, full of plans. None of them include a house in the country.

This must be what Joaquin means by help. Making Tom want what he has. A clever man. I should be grateful.

But last night I dreamt again. I was back where she was, the little girl. Little white dress, little red shoes.

She stood, as she always stands, next to the river. But the dream had changed. The river clattered and chattered over stones. Birds sang and insects buzzed. And I knew if I could only turn, if I could only look away, exactly what I would see. A house with pink walls. Trees. A strip of blue sky.

I woke and Tom was lying with his arms across me, pinning me to the bed. A dead weight to keep me in place, keep me from reaching her before she took the step.

He was humming this morning, as he disappeared into the Underground.

'Smile,' he said. 'It's a lovely day.' He was swinging the briefcase as he walked.

Smile? Unlike him, I had nowhere to go. At the museum, they have finished packing. Now they don't need me for anything. I have become something left behind.

An hour later, though, it began.

I didn't know at first. It was only when I went to Mr Georghiu's to buy milk and he waved me away as I tried to give him the money. 'Later, darling.'

He was listening to the radio, pushing his large face

against the dial. It made me stop and listen too. Then I ran home and switched on the TV.

The Underground was shut down and in chaos. There had been explosions. People trapped. People dead. Like Tom, they had gone down, out of the sunshine. Now only some of them would ever make their way back up.

I rang the magazine. Rob had arrived and so had Shirley. But not Tom.

I phoned his mobile, but the network was down. All I could do was watch the television. Scan the faces of people stumbling on to pavements, their faces blackened, some helping each other, others completely by themselves. No one helping them.

The same images all day. The same faces over and over, people making their way out. None of the faces was Tom's. I phoned Charlie, and he said stay away from the hospitals, there was too much going on. Tom would come home, he said. He would be all right.

But I waited and Tom didn't come home.

Midday came and went. There was silence in the house. Outside the sun continued to shine, but I pulled a quilt from our bed and wrapped it round me as I wandered between rooms. At my heels, a train of memories: of Tom falling asleep the first time. His arm a weight I thought I could carry for ever; the warmth of his breath, the scent of his neck. Remembering a night of laughing and crying because it was the end of being alone.

Then I remembered Joaquin; his hand touching my hand, and my cheeks burnt with shame. As if it were a crime, and now it was time to pay.

Everyone who loved me lies under stone. Now it was Tom's turn, disappeared under many thicknesses of stone, layers of concrete and earth and brick. Gone deeper than my parents, deeper than Marietta.

No one to pray to, but still I prayed. Just let him come home. If there were promises to be made, a way to pay, I would make any promise. Pay anything.

Finally, towards evening, comes the sound of the front door, softly closing.

'Tom?'

'Sara?'

And there he is. The last one in. Still carrying the briefcase, Joaquin's parting gift. He is dirty and scuffed, but otherwise he looks as he did when he left this morning. At the same time, different. Smaller. His collars and cuffs seem too roomy, his shoes too large. He stands in the doorway, looks like a boy in man's clothing.

Then I hold out my arms and he comes to me. Frantically I touch him, searching his skin under his clothes, looking for marks, for damage. There's nothing. Beneath my fingers, he is whole, intact. But he's shaking. Shaking all over.

'Tom,' I whisper, and he begins to cry.

He was on a train that stopped because all the trains had stopped – although he hadn't known it then. After an hour of waiting in the dark, he had been told to get out and walk with all the other passengers. And so they had walked along the tracks in the dark, breathing air that burnt their mouths and made their lungs raw. No one knew what had happened. No one knew anything.

Then they had come across another train. All lit up, its carriages were mangled, debris filling up the tunnel. Inside, shapes of men and women were toiling like ants, like insects that click and cluster and glow in the dark.

'Did you see…?'

He shook his head.

All the same, behind him a woman had begun to scream, and having started she never stopped, not even after, when they had stepped back into the world. People had led her away, still screaming. And Tom…

Tom had stepped out of the Underground and kept on walking. Heading for home with no idea how to get there, stumbling over himself in shock. He had walked without even knowing where he was walking from or to. Landmarks useless to him because he couldn't make sense of them, not when the world was like this.

Even now I can't understand how it took him so long. 'All this time,' I whisper. 'You've been walking all this time?'

It's as if he hasn't heard me. Then he stirs. 'I found a pub. Sat there for a while. An hour, maybe two.'

Or three or four. There is alcohol on his breath. He could have contacted me. He could have found a way to keep going, let me know he was safe. Instead of leaving me to…

Suddenly there's a taste in my mouth, bitter, hot.

He looks at me, sensing a mistake has been made. Puts his hands around my face, whispers, 'I just needed to find a way home. To you.'

I nod. Then swallow.

Nothing matters. He is home. I take his hand and lead

him to the sofa. Here we lie under the quilt, and here we stay, watching the TV play and replay its images.

He says:

'Down there, while it was happening, I found a way to shut it out – the dark, the train all screwed up. The woman screaming. Shall I tell you how I did it, Sara? I put myself in that place, in the valley with the pink house. I made myself feel the sunshine and smell the grass. I imagined the sound of the river and the birds. It was the only thing that kept me going.'

He stops.

'Do you understand what I'm saying, Sara? I can't live here anymore. Not when this could all happen again next year, or next week. Or tomorrow. I have to get out. I have to get out of the city. Do you understand, Sara? Do you?'

He finds my hand under the quilt. And I try. I try to understand. Make myself see that we are lucky; I am lucky. I could have been one of the people sitting by their phones, who are still waiting. Who will wait for ever now.

It could have been us, and it wasn't. Meanwhile Tom wraps his hand tighter around mine. 'Sara,' he whispers. 'Help me do this.'

Around me is Marietta's house. Walls I have known since I was a child. And beyond them, streets, pavements, people. Distant traffic that makes the city sound as if it's breathing, a person in its own right.

It's everything I know.

'Sara...' Tom's voice is imploring. A reminder that he is here. He came home.

I make a noise. It's caught in my throat, so I make it come

again, louder. It could mean anything, but it's enough for Tom. He falls towards me, kisses my face, my neck, his hands warm with gratitude.

'Thank you,' he whispers. 'Watch us now. Watch us both be happy.'

He laughs against my neck. Certain that whatever makes him happy must make me happy too.

~

# Chapter Four

Tom's fear was that the pink house would have been sold, but I knew better. If it had been so easy, the Marshes wouldn't have welcomed us and watched us so intently. How long had they been trying to sell their house? We never thought to ask.

We didn't even haggle. Tom emailed his resignation to Joaquin and stayed away from the magazine after that. The only thing keeping us was selling Marietta's – our – house. But that was no problem either. It went on the market for one day, and before we showed anyone around we had a cash buyer.

When I told Jen, she stared at me in disbelief. Horror.

'But this is your home, Sara. You're happy here. Why are you doing this?'

I looked at the Duke who was lying in my arms. For some reason he likes it when I hold him. Butts his head against my chest and dribbles as he sleeps. Doesn't seem to care that I am nothing like as soft as Jen.

'Tom…'

Jen rolled her eyes. 'Tom!'

'He can't sleep, Jen. Even now. He was there, underground. He saw too much…'

'So did lots of people! But the next day they left their houses and they did what they always do. They carried on. Just to show they could. Or because they had to.' She shook her head. Started again. 'He's talked you into this. He's told you this is all it takes to make him happy. I bet I'm right?'

'Something like that.'

'And you believed him!'

'I want him to be happy, Jen.'

She frowned. 'Then you're a fool. You know we love Tom – maybe not as much as he thinks he deserves – but we love him. He's charming and boyish and funny, but...'

'But...?'

'He's never going to be happy with what he's got. It doesn't matter where he is. He could be here or Timbuctu. He's always going to think someone's got something better. The man needs to grow up.'

With this we both fell silent. We had come to the edge of something. A quarrel, something worse. To be avoided at all costs.

She sighed. Quietly she said, 'What about you? What do you want?'

My answer was instant. 'For you to come and visit as often as you can.'

I tried to dazzle her with a smile. On my lap, the baby's nappy had begun to leak. Wet was seeping into my jeans. But unlike his mother, he was peaceful and serene, a warm, wet weight.

She grunted and put out her arms to take him. Immediately he began to cry, distressed at being disturbed. Giving voice to something we both felt, and refused to put into words.

Now, two weeks later, I close the door on Marietta's house for the very last time. Do it quickly, and without looking back. I am afraid of the ache that one last look would bring. Closing it fast like this, without a second glance, it doesn't seem real. I can walk away to join Tom waiting at the kerbside in our car and half believe I'll be coming back.

It's the end of July and summer is at its height. London lies hushed and dirty under a layer of hot, heavy dust. A good time to move, says Tom.

As we cross into Devon, he has an idea. He turns the car from the motorway and heads for the organic hotel.

'Let's surprise them. Show them we had the balls to do it.'

But at the hotel, they don't even recognise us. The entrance hall is full of bodies. Stylists and PR people, gofers and photographers, and photographers' assistants. Tom fights his way through to the owner – who frowns at the interruption.

'Look here, old chap, can't accommodate you at the mo. Got the Primrose Hill Brigade down with their kids. We're in the middle of a photo shoot. There's a Novotel up the road if that's what you're after.'

'It's me,' says Tom. 'We did it. We chucked in the city and bought the house.' He stands, waiting for praise.

The man does a small double take. 'Ah, recognise you now. Well, good show. Best of luck and all that. Sorry, got to get on.'

And he turns his back, leaving Tom to stand, looking lost. We drive away, and when I look behind, it isn't the hotel I see, but the asylum – Benton – crouching against the sky, swallowing the sun.

But soon Tom regains his spirits. We are coming closer. Crossing the Tamar into Cornwall, coming to the village. Past the houses, past the shop. Past the church. And as before, nothing is moving. Only the gravestones in the churchyard seem to stand a little taller to catch sight of us passing.

The single exception is a car, reversing out of a small, tidy drive, and inside it an elderly man and a woman with a head of steely-grey curls. On impulse, I wave – to see the woman passenger look startled, then purse her lips and look the other way.

Tom takes his foot off the accelerator. 'Don't want to miss our own turning!'

But the turning turns out to be unmissable. In front of us, wedged like a cork into the top of the lane, is our removal van. A car is trying to get past. Finally it succeeds – just – and roars off, revving up as if in irritation.

Tom gets out of our car. 'What's the matter?'

One of the removal men shrugs.

'It's the lane, isn't it. You should have said. It's so narrow we can't get the van down. Impossible. Absolutely no bloody way.'

Tom looks at me in dismay. Waiting for someone to come up with the answer.

The solution was a couple of smaller vans, hired at some expense from Tavistock.

It took all the rest of the day to unload everything off the bigger lorry and into the smaller ones. And being so much smaller, it took them three, four journeys, up and down the lane. Tom went down to supervise the unloading, while I stayed at the top. He was afraid the men would be careless, break things just because we'd made life difficult.

But now finally he comes for me, and it's our turn to make our way down.

Dark by this time. Darker than ever it is in the town. Trees blocking out the stars. Tom stares straight ahead, his face white in the headlamps. He looks tired, done in. I reach across and touch his cheek, and this revives him. He catches my hand in his own and says, 'Wait for the morning, Sara. Wait till you wake up in your own bed, in your own valley.'

At the bottom, the second of the small vans is about to leave, its headlights on full glare, blinding us to the pitch dark left behind.

Tom is the first to stir, get out of the car. He goes and stands by the front door with the hall light shining round him. Waits for me. But even then I don't move.

What am I doing?

I am listening. Waiting for a sound to make itself heard under the cover of other sounds – wind in the trees, the chug of the van still making its way up the lane, Tom's voice urging me from the door.

'Come on, Sara. I'm not going in without you.'

But even now I stay put. Not moving until I hear it and have it secure, lodged in the senses; a sound that underlies all the rest. Here it comes – the hiss of water in gullies, trickling over stones, slapping against branches. Water that sounds like words.

Now, now I have it. The river.

Only then do I move, join Tom at our new front door, and walk into the house.

# Chapter Five

And there she is again. Little white dress, little red shoes. She stands on the bank, her small body poised, while below her the river runs, brown and rushing.

She stands and she listens. To the river, to water racing over stones, elbowing its way between rocks. The sound of a thousand voices urging each other on. Louder now, crashing against stones, spluttering in gullies. Louder and louder...

At which point Tom rolls over in his sleep, throws his arm about my neck. Instantly I'm awake. She's gone. There is no child, no little white dress, no little red shoes.

And I know where we are. We are here, in the house in the Valley, with the river running by, only a murmur below the window.

And Tom, he's still asleep. Doesn't know it yet.

Outside, the sky is blue, light filled. My watch says it is almost nine. We have slept for hours, helped by the champagne that we drank before we came to bed.

Yet the bedroom is still in shadow. There is no sun – not directly. I slip out from under his arm, tiptoe to the window. There is the river, of course. And there are the trees. But still the sun hasn't risen above the rim of the cliffs – and it changes everything. The same trees, the same Valley. The same strip of blue, yet without the sun, nothing like the same.

Green. It's the difference the sun makes. Or the lack of sun. Without sun, Green lies in blocks. Green meeting in the shadows of more green. There are no boundaries here, no separations. Beyond the walls of our house, Green lies powerful as an unbroken force, a country without borders.

But it's only for a moment. Tom murmurs out of his sleep and, in the time it takes to turn round, everything changes. Everything. The sun has appeared.

'Sara.'

He smiles at me from the bed, his hand already moving to shade his eyes. Sunshine is pouring into our room, filling it with light, making sunbeams dance on the wall. Outside, Green has broken down into a multitude of shades, fractured and jostling. Not powerful after all.

He beckons me back to bed; and of course we make love, knowing exactly what we are doing. We are marking the start of something, a new beginning. Afterwards, Tom leans over me, his face flushed and his eyes alight.

'You see, Sara? Dreams do come true. You just have to make them.' Then he jumps out of bed and throws the window wider. As if it had been waiting, the sound of the river pours into the room.

The river. Yesterday we belonged over there, on the other side. Today we belong here.

Tom has gone to stand in the shower. He's happy. I imagine the water catching the shine off him and bouncing off his body in golden drops. It makes me throw off my nightdress and step in beside him, let the water light over us both.

Tom puts down his coffee, points to the ceiling in its coat of Artex.

'First thing I'm going to do is strip down this bloody kitchen.'

'Aren't we supposed to be getting to work? Outside.'

I can't call it garden, what lies beyond our door. A garden is what Marietta had. A small courtyard with walls covered in clematis that lived in pots. Now we are here, in our nine acres of land – where Tom is going to make things grow, make us self-sufficient, depriving the supermarkets of their profit.

It doesn't seem real. Not yet. It doesn't even seem possible.

Tom shrugs. 'We've only just arrived. Let's give ourselves a few days to settle in, then we'll start. One step at a time.'

So instead we go for a stroll around what's ours. Beating the bounds Tom calls it, except that neither of us is sure what those bounds are. Beyond the path, the trees carry on growing in all directions. Who knows where the property ends exactly? And where will we actually grow things? It seems to me that every inch of this land is already growing, is alive with growth. Trees, ferns, bushes, bracken, briars. Down by the river, great fleshy leaves sway, sprouting out of thick blotchy stalks, tall as a man. Only the lawn with its trimmed edges is clear, under control. But it looks like an island sinking into a sea of deeper green.

Yet Tom has plans. He points to the woods. 'We'll keep the lawns, but clear all the trees from there, and there. Rotovate it, get it ready for soft fruit. Right there we'll have asparagus beds. Artichokes over here, kohlrabi there…'

Artichoke, asparagus, kohlrabi – the only sort of vegetables he ever eats. The kind you order in restaurants. He walks beside me, a spring in his step, unfazed by trees standing ten times his height, giants he intends to kill. They whisper behind our backs. He's using up valuable energy just talking.

I interrupt. 'The first thing I'm going to do is clear a path down to the river. A proper track.'

He hasn't heard me. Busy with plans for organic compost, he has more important things on his mind. We have arrived at the outbuildings now. The largest stands with its bright-blue doors heavily padlocked. He feels in his pockets for a key and opens up.

'Ah,' says Tom, and steps back. His voice has gone soft, reverential even. 'Now that's what I call hardware.'

Because the shed is full of machines, gleaming scarlet and green: a sit-upon lawnmower, a rotovator, a chainsaw, a leaf blower. Others with wires and teeth that I don't even recognise. There's a smell of clean oil and petrol. All along one wall is a bracket hung with rows of machetes and hatchets and knives.

None of this is ours. The Marshes have left it here by agreement, to be collected later. All we brought with us was spades and forks and trowels. Tom's face falls at the thought of all of it going. Then it brightens.

'What's the betting he's left all this here deliberately, hoping we'd want to buy it off him? I'm going to give him a ring, Sara. See if I can interest him in an offer.' He pulls out his mobile. 'No signal. Whole place is probably a blind spot. I'll have to go inside and use the landline. You wait here. Don't do anything without me.'

When he disappears, my first instinct is to run after him. Childish. It must be because even now it feels like trespassing. As if we were poking around in somebody else's sheds on somebody else's land. I have no sense of ownership yet. I can't believe this is where we belong.

Minutes pass. There is no sign of him coming back. I'm about to go in search when I notice the sun, glancing off the edge of something sharp hanging on the wall. A hatchet. It gives me an idea, a way to be like Tom.

I'm going to clear a path to the river.

Except I've never done anything like this before.

An amateur, I do my best – aiming and chopping the only way I know how. But it's no good, the hatchet flies back at me as if I were hacking at springs, ends up shredding nothing but a few leaves. The undergrowth stays thick as ever, reminds me of the trees silently mocking Tom with his plans for their downfall. Already my arms ache.

So I stop. Think. And little by little, I remember.

Marietta. I remember Marietta – a young Marietta who, before there was me, used to hack her way through entire jungles to reach the ruins of her precious Mayans. How would she have gone about this?

I know: she would have attacked with firm, controlled strokes; her skinny arms expending only as much effort as was necessary, until she had a path in front of her. No fuss. The way she did everything.

And that's what I do. Find control, find a rhythm; hacking, chopping, pruning and trimming, until I have what I want – a narrow path leading straight to the water's edge. Finally, I put the hatchet down.

My arms aren't aching anymore. They feel loose in their sockets, as if they could have kept this up all morning. But they don't have to; the job is done.

For beneath my feet, the river runs. Our river. If I wanted, I could dip my toes right in, let the water cool them. Instead I pick up some broken stems and toss them into the water. Then leaves, twigs – anything – just to watch the current carry them away. It's like being a child again, bent over the streams in Waterlow Park, while behind me Marietta read her book. Never interfered.

Down by my feet, though, something catches my eye – a curl, a twist in the undergrowth. Flickers, then is gone.

A snake? Unlikely, despite surprise having raised a small slick of goosebumps along my arms, tearing an extra beat out of my heart. Not a snake. A tail?

The tail end of a tail. A cat? Maybe.

But now there's something else to think about. Another movement. This time it's behind me, and this time I know exactly what it is. It's Tom. He's finally finished with the phone and now, quiet as a mouse, he has crept up on me, thinking he can catch me by surprise.

I don't even have to turn round. Call it sixth sense, although you know what it really is – just the body sending messages to the brain. Breath on the back of the neck, the slightest stirring of the surrounding air – sooner or later you know when you are not alone. Like now, when I can almost hear the silent gasp of suppressed laughter. All I have to do is spin round on my toes. Quickly. Show him he can't surprise me so easily.

Turning and smiling, to be the one who surprises him instead...

And he's not there. No one is there. All the same, I've turned so quickly, my own momentum throws me forward, as if still expecting that somebody will catch me. But of course there's no one, just empty space, and instead I begin to fall, into the void where I would have sworn there was Tom.

But then I stop falling. Pull myself together and stand up straight, feel the ground sure beneath my feet. No one here but me.

A moment as my head clears. After confusion, disappointment. I wanted Tom to be here. I wanted him to see what I've done. Tom may be the one with all the plans, but look – it's me who's made the first mark, cleared the first space. Not such a city girl after all.

But this too is a deception. When I move away from the river, a long strand of briar reaches out and catches my toes, snags the skin to leave a speckled line of blood, bright like a fresh tattoo. And it stings. So it turns out I was wrong about that too. I didn't clear the path as well as I thought.

I find Tom upstairs, lying on the bed. He is fast asleep.

A surge of irritation, then I remember. This is the man who saw too much. Who spent these last weeks unable to sleep because of it. Now he looks relaxed, utterly happy. A man who finally has got what he wanted. Let him sleep.

Downstairs, the fridge is switched on but empty. I need to get in the car to go shopping, which in turn means bumbling around the bedroom to find the keys. And even then Tom doesn't wake.

Everything is asleep, it seems. Or absent in some other way. Up in the village nothing is moving. I drive slowly through the heat of the day, half expecting curtains to twitch, faces to glance. I thought that's what people did in the country. But no, doors remain closed, windows unoccupied. Nobody is interested in us.

It's the same in the shop, Tremaine's. Behind the counter a young woman is reading a copy of *Hello*, sees no reason to put it down.

'Hi,' I say.

Only then does she look up.

I try to think what we need, realise I should have brought a list. 'Do you have any coffee?'

Slowly she points. I'm standing right next to shelves of Nescafé Instant. She must think I can't read.

'No, sorry. Fresh coffee. For espressos.'

It is as if I have asked for rocket fuel. It's the same when I ask if she has unsalted butter. Better not to ask. Simply look for what I'm after. And if it's not there, then...

Go without.

The door jingles. An elderly woman has entered the shop, and at once I recognise her as the woman I waved to in the car. She ignores me now as she ignored me then; walks straight past, leaving behind traces of face powder and cold cream, the kind that stands for years on shelves in chilly bathrooms.

'Hello, Mary,' says the girl. Her voice welcomes her as it had signally failed to welcome me. 'Turned out hot again, hasn't it?'

I put my basket on the counter. There's not much in it. Instant coffee, milk, a packet of biscuits; broccoli, its branches already limp and yellowing. Sliced white bread which is simply going to make Tom's lip curl. A bright slab of orange cheese wrapped up in polythene.

As I pay, the girl makes an effort. 'Down for a holiday, are you?' The question is automatic, reserved for tourists and strangers.

'No. Actually we've just moved here to live. We're at the bottom of the Old Lane...'

The bored look disappears. Suddenly she is wide awake, finally taking me in. She has large blue eyes and pale lashes. Thin blonde hair that gives up the ghost before reaching her shoulders. 'What, in the Marshes' place?'

Her hands that a second ago were flying over the keys of her till have become still. Her eyes have darted towards the woman. But she is bent over the packets of peas in the frozen food cabinet, isn't looking at us.

'We moved there yesterday, my husband and me.'

The girl waits a moment. Then says, 'Kids?' I notice she puts the question carefully. Watches me.

'No,' I tell her. 'No children.'

Something odd happens then. She seems to relax. Her hands move again and she closes the till with a friendly bang. Hands me my change, smiling. 'Be seeing you again soon, then, won't we, Mary?' This is thrown at the woman behind us. Who nods curtly.

I climb back into the car, but for a moment I don't go anywhere. It's as if I've forgotten something. Something I would normally have picked up without even thinking. It's not coffee, or unsalted butter. It's not even cheese that hasn't been suffocated inside a plastic shroud. It's something else, but now it's missing and I can't think what it is. Not straight away. Then I remember.

Warmth.

On a hot day, with the sun shining, suddenly I'm missing warmth. The smile Mr Georghiu produced every time I walked into his shop. Which was every day. Smile at Mr Georghiu, and he would smile right back at you. Didn't matter who you were, although sometimes, because it was me, he would beckon me close. Pop a piece of Turkish delight into my hand, or some sugared almonds. Always something sweet, to go with the smile.

I lean forward and turn the key. The girl did smile – eventually. Maybe things just take longer here.

At home Tom is off the bed and busy stripping wallpaper in the kitchen.

'You might want to change your mind about not using the supermarket.' I show him the cheese, the jar of instant coffee.

'Never mind, we can drink tea.'

Tea. I forgot tea. I think about the long winding lane and could kick myself.

Tom says, 'I spoke to the cop – Marsh. He'll sell us the entire shedload. Makes you wonder what sort of place they've moved to. He didn't want to keep anything.'

He's rubbing his hands with sheer glee, thinking about riding the lawnmower, toppling trees with the chainsaw. So I don't tell him about the shop, and the women who can barely summon a smile. I don't want anything to interfere with the way he is now – bouncing, shining with an energy that pours straight out of him and into me.

And it's the same later, even when he tells me that his head aches, blames it on the dyes in the cheese. Nothing stops him. Having started on the kitchen, he wants to keep going, sanding down the walls, levering out nails, springing from task to task. He makes coffee and says sometimes instant hits the spot better than freshly brewed. Then puts his mug down and grabs me. Pushes me up against the bare plaster and kisses me. Tickles me till I laugh out loud.

If Jen, if Joaquin could only see him now, they would understand. This is Tom as he is meant to be. This is all it takes. Happiness. For this, promises are made and kept.

Night comes. He stands by the bedroom window and says softly, 'Sara, come over here.'

I step up to join him. He looks at me a moment, then swoops down, catches my nightdress by the hem and pulls it over my head.

'The window…no curtains.'

He laughs. 'There's no one to see. Look, you can stand here stark naked and there's not a soul to know about it. We're by ourselves, Sara. Listen to the silence – we could be the only people left alive.'

He nuzzles his face against my neck, his hands starting to move over my body. For a moment I respond, begin to warm to his touch – but then what I notice are the currents of air, reaching in through the open window. They move where his hands have already been, raising goosebumps on my belly, lifting the hairs on my arms.

Listen to the silence, he said. I do listen, and for a moment

I hear it – silence. But then it disappears and what I hear instead is the river. Below the window, it uses the silence simply so it can make itself heard. In any number of voices, like a crowd of people gathered in the dark.

It's only Tom who hears silence.

'Hey, give me a hand with this.'

It's the next day, and all morning and afternoon Tom has been struggling with the units in the kitchen, prising them away from the walls, one by one. Soon there won't be a cupboard or a workspace to store or chop a carrot. I would protest, but he says he knows what he is doing: taking apart what was a perfectly good room, bit by bit. He has dust all over him, greying his hair, making him look older. Closer to the age he is.

I like it that he knows what he's doing. I like the grey in his hair.

All that's left is a tall cupboard that's defeating him now. It stands next to the back door in prime condition, looking as if it had never been used. Makes me think we could use it, just till we have cupboards of our own.

'No,' says Tom when I suggest it. 'It's nasty. All it's fit for is kindling, like everything else they put here. When it's colder we'll have proper fires, and this can be the first thing we burn.'

So I step forward to help while he manhandles the cupboard out of the back door and on to the path, leaving me to clear up the mess.

But when he comes back I am still there, dustpan in hand, staring at the bare wall.

'What's the matter?'

I point. There's a vertical line of marks inked on the wall. A date written in by each one.

'It's the little girl,' I say. 'This must be where they measured her.'

'What little girl?'

'Mandy.'

'Who's Mandy?'

'The Marshes' little girl. We saw her that first time we came, down by the river. Remember?'

He frowns. Already it's so long ago to him. 'Don't know what you're talking about. I never saw a girl. Just some thumping fat baby.'

'Yes you did. She was standing right by the river. She had a white dress on, and little red shoes. We saw her from the window.'

'Well there you are,' he breaks in triumphantly. 'We couldn't have seen her because there was no way to the river. No path. You kept going on about it.'

I open my mouth, then close it. Feel the colour sweep into my cheeks. And begin to laugh.

'What's so funny?'

But I'm too embarrassed to tell. Of course we didn't see her. We didn't see anyone. As for the little white dress, little red shoes – they belong to a dream, an old, old dream nothing to do with real life.

Suddenly I need to be touching something solid. A chair, a wall. Tom frowns. 'What's the matter with you?'

'Nothing...dizzy all of a sudden. I don't know why.'

'Dust probably.' Tom is still looking at the wall. 'Seems they got bored,' he says.

'Bored?'

'With measuring. They stopped, look. Months ago. Long before we got here. Apparently they couldn't be bothered after. They went and put that bloody great cupboard there instead.'

Somehow, that surprises me. They didn't look the sort of people to get bored, not to finish what they started. But there it is, the very last mark, a date written into the wall. December the tenth. Then nothing. As if time stopped there on the tenth of December. As if a child had simply stopped growing.

Four o'clock, and although it's light, the sun has disappeared, quietly sunk below the level of the cliffs. I leave Tom to put on the kettle and slip upstairs, to the bedroom window. I want to see if it has happened again.

And it has. Without the sun, all the colours of the day, all the different shades of green, have made their peace and come together. Powerful again. Our house now stands in the middle of something bigger than itself. Besieged by Green.

Downstairs Tom swears noisily. We've run out of milk.

~

# Chapter Six

Again I hear it – the noise of the river, driving and thrashing, filling my head. I am awake, but I haven't opened my eyes yet.

Then I do open them, and the noise dies and falls away, is nothing but a murmur through the open window. Three days and I've learnt what to expect – the river, filling then emptying in my ears. Sun that hovers below the rim of the cliff, while the Valley – and our bedroom – stays in shadow.

I hold my breath and…

A sunbeam slants on Tom's eyelids. Followed by a myriad of others. The room fills with light. Immediately he wakes, smiles across the pillow. Ready to start his day.

After breakfast, he pushes aside his mug and reaches into his trouser pocket. Takes out a key and holds it up for me to see.

'It's time,' he pronounces.

'Time for what?'

But he's already gone.

Ten minutes later, I know. From outside, a motor explodes into life, sends the birds spinning from the trees. Tom is driving the sit-upon lawnmower out of the shed, his face lit up with the noise and the power he imagines to lie under the gleaming red bonnet. It's a huge sound, louder than anything a car would make. Reminds me that hanging from the wall in the shed had been a pair of ear defenders.

I run up to the shed and find them, then hurry in the tracks of Tom's machine. Of course, he doesn't hear me when I shout. I have to run round in front waving them as I go. But Tom looks at me and shakes his head. Gestures that he has no need for them. Then he pushes another gear and roars away.

The noise drives me indoors, back to the kitchen and its wrecked walls. One man has gone to mow – but I'm not even sure where, or why. The lawn is already clean-shaven, the one thing growing that's under control. Marsh must have done it the day he left.

Now Tom is there, mowing it all over again, just to show he can, so in love with his own noise, he won't even cover his ears. And even though it's hot and all the air is still, I have to close the doors, then the windows. The noise of the machines is too much for me.

Yet I've always liked it before – the *krrrum* of working metal. There must be something about this machine that's different. Maybe it's just the way he's using it, not so much for the job it does, but the noise it makes.

Tom stays outside all day, tries all the machines in turn. Does the same the next day and all the days after. Machines keep him busy till suppertime when reluctantly he comes inside, dizzy and elated. Eats like a man who is famished, then he's ready for bed, impatient for me to come too. Sun and wine and toil combine to make him aroused. In bed he reaches for me, his skin vibrating and buzzing to the touch as if some rogue energy of the motors has leaked into him.

We make love and even before we fall apart he is asleep, too tired to talk. Happens every night. Me, I stay awake, listening to the river through the open window.

These are our days and nights – the best Tom has ever known.

'So, how long is it now? Since you moved in?'

She looks too young to lose track of time, this young girl who sits in her shop, minding the shelves of condensed soup, the hairgrips and the arrowroot biscuits I didn't know people ate anymore. Looks up sleepily each time I walk in, but is fast when totting up my bill, fingers darting over the till. Her name is Evie.

I answer her question. 'Two weeks. Nearly.'

Two weeks tomorrow to be exact. If we were on holiday, we would be on the point of going home, back to Marietta's house, to the lime tree and the shapes on our bedroom wall. Outside the shop, a family with children have just driven away, the back window of their car filled with buckets and spades and bathing towels. People who really are on holiday, with homes to go to. People I try not to envy.

Of course, Evie's not really interested in how long it's been. She was just being polite. She only comes to life when there are other people in the shop – people like Mary who seems to spend all day here. Farm workers who stop by for cigarettes and rolling tobacco, children who run in and out to swap pennies for handfuls of chews – she'll talk to them, her soft voice sounding warm. Talks nineteen to the dozen. But she barely talks to me.

Two weeks and I'm beginning to understand: it's not true what they say – that in the country everyone wants to know your business. It's an urban myth people tell each other in the town. In the country, no one is interested in you, not if you don't belong.

It wouldn't matter if we were going home. But we're not. Two weeks is about to stretch into forever. We need to belong. So I make an effort; I say, 'My husband – Tom – he's never been happier.'

Yet Evie's smile, already vague, grows vaguer still. Only becomes a real smile when the shop's bell tinkles.

'Morning, Mary.'

My heart sinks. Evie is distant but polite; Mary isn't even that. Today she is more forbidding than ever, has a head steely with tight, unforgiving curls. She must have come straight from the mobile hairdresser's whose van is still outside; there's the sting of perming chemicals in the air, like the traces of gunpowder prior to battle. And Mary makes no bones about who the enemy is.

But why? What have we ever done to her? I stand a little straighter and smile at Evie. Try to make it look as if we're in the middle of an animated conversation we've both been enjoying.

'You should see how hard he's been working. He's clearing land at the moment, then he's going to start planting.'

Evie nods. 'Got your newspaper here, Mary.' The words are addressed over my shoulder.

'It's a labour of love, you see. Something he's always wanted to do. He hasn't taken a break since the day he started. You should see what he's got planned.'

Hopeful, I look from one to the other. Surely they'll bend. Find something to approve of in a man who would give himself up, body and soul, to a project. But they simply stand, wait for me to pick up my shopping and go.

I turn to Mary.

'Maybe you could give us an idea what we should sow.'

And now – at long last – it comes, the flicker of a response. Mary smiles thinly; then answers the question.

'Nothing. Because there's nothing that would grow where you are. Copper mines it all was down there, right till I was a girl. Trees – that's all will grow in a place like yours. Take for ever to change that. No one would have the time for it.'

I leap on this. 'We've got the time! All the time we need. It's the reason we're here. To change things.'

But I should never have spoken. She's smiling again.

'Oh you don't have to tell me what you're up to. You're one of those – what do they call them, Evie? Downgraders.'

Evie giggles. 'You mean, downsizers, Mary.'

But Mary knows exactly what she means. 'There's plenty of people would like to downsize round here. What about you, Evie? You'd like to down*size* out of your mum and dad's house into somewhere of your own. How long have you and Gary been wed now? Two, three years? Found anywhere for yourselves yet?'

Evie has gone scarlet. 'You don't need to worry about us, Mary,' she murmurs. 'We're all right.'

'Course you haven't found anywhere. There's nowhere you can afford, is there? Not nowadays. Not with all the folk coming with their money, downsizing into every house going. Buying their holiday homes, snapping up every last bit of land so they can plant their fancy bits of veg.'

'Mary,' says Evie. ' I don't think—'

'Paying three times what a house is worth, and never mind the effect it has on the locals. What about you and Gary? What are you going to do when you want kiddies?'

'Something will turn up...'

'Oh will it indeed? You're talking daydreams now, my girl.'

'Maybe.' Evie breaks in, flashes a sudden, surprising smile at me. 'But it's done the Marshes a favour. If it hadn't been for folk coming in, willing to buy, they'd have been stuck in that house for ever. Do you think anyone round here would have wanted the place after what ...'

But now the older woman is staring at her. Hard. There's a silence.

Which I break. 'After...what? Did something happen there?'

But woman and girl suddenly have become busy. Mary with her shopping bag. Evie with the till.

Mary clears her throat. 'Well, I don't know what I'm doing chatting all day. Reg will be back from the club and he'll be wanting his dinner.'

'Can't keep Reg waiting,' agrees Evie.

The older woman nods, then hurries out of the shop. Hasn't even stopped to buy anything. I turn to Evie. 'So what was that about?'

Evie shrugs, flicks dust from the top of her till. 'Oh you don't want to take any notice of Mary Coryn. It's the old folk, all got the same bee in their bonnet. Incomers – it's all they ever talk about. You'd think it was the Germans invading.'

'But you were talking about our house. You said no one local would have wanted it. Why not?'

Pale cheeks suddenly gone pink. 'No reason. It's a lovely house, yours. Anyone would have bought it.'

'Not anyone round here. That's what you said.'

A pause. Her hands fly over the counter, rearranging packets of sweets, lottery tickets. This girl is thinking, considering her answer. Finally she has one:

'It's so far away from anywhere, that's what I meant. People round here, they like having folk nice and close. It's different when you're from the city. You want to be alone. You don't want people breathing down your necks. That's why you all end up coming here, isn't it?'

The smile returns, brilliant and vague. She's happy with her answer. Her face is friendly, yet tells me nothing. Perhaps she's not quite so young after all.

Tom rolls his eyes.

'It'll be flooding or something. The sort of thing people never tell you when they want to flog you a home.'

'But we're here now. If something happened, why wouldn't Evie say? Or Mary Coryn? Why won't they talk to me?'

He snorts. 'I'd have thought that was obvious. We're the evil outsiders taking over. Why make life easier by dropping us a word of warning?'

'I don't think Evie is like that.'

'Well maybe she's trying to save his face – Marsh's. What's the betting he's her uncle or brother or second cousin twice removed? She's watching his back. I bet everyone round here is related some way or other. Inbred. It's that sort of place.'

'But what if something terrible happened? What if it happens again? Doesn't that worry you?'

Tom shrugs. He has his feet in my lap, and a full glass of wine by his head. 'How bad can it be? The house is still standing. And we have insurance.'

'But they think we're ruining things for everyone else, buying all the houses and paying too much. Making it so people like Evie never get to have homes of their own.'

He shrugs. 'She should try London if she thinks it's any cheaper. Anyway, it's swings and roundabouts. Take that shop. I bet we spend more in one day than most people would in a week. I've seen them all up there, jumping into their cars to load up at the supermarket. Shops like Tremaine's couldn't survive without people like us.'

He reaches for his glass, smiles into my eyes, happy.

'It's lazy thinking, Sara. Everyone wants someone to blame. So they turn around and blame us.'

He picks up the remote, switches on the TV. Tom's world begins and ends exactly where he chooses. He's spent all day on a machine. Tired out, half deaf, he'll lose no sleep over what Mary Coryn thinks of him or why no one local would want to buy this house. Can't see why I shouldn't do the same.

Morning arrives the same way it always does.

Tom dozes beside me, twitching in the last throes of a dream. In a moment sunbeams will touch his eyes and he'll wake up. It will be just another day for him.

Different for me. Two weeks. If this were a holiday, today's the day we would be going home. But it's not. This is where we live now. Far away other people are waking to the shadows of the lime tree moving across the wall. A child wanders across the landing in search of company. A woman carries a cup of coffee through rooms where Marietta worked and I rolled gourds across the floor. Bewildered I watch them, a ghost in my own house...

Tom stirs and I wake again. And those other, familiar rooms disappear.

Meanwhile Tom gives a jerk beside me, hands twitching against the sheets. He's moaning. Instead of waking, he's been sucked back into sleep, and into dreams.

'Tom...'

It doesn't rouse him. A moment later he moans again, in thrall to the dream that's snared him.

'Sara!'

He shouts my name, and wakes. For a moment he stares at me, frozen. Then his body loosens, and collapses against mine.

'I thought I was underground. I couldn't find a way out. I was looking for you, Sara. I needed you, but I couldn't find you. Oh God, Sara.'

Sweat pours out of his body, drenching the sheets, making them into transparent shrouds. I put my arms around him, hold him close as he clings and murmurs in my ear:

'Thank God we came away. Thank God, Sara. Thank God.'

I hold him and rock him and wait for the murmuring to stop. I forget about the other place. This is where we live now. I roll up the ache for home, memories of other rooms. Put it all away.

* * *

But the day is ruined before it's even begun.

After breakfast he strode outside with extra determination in his step. Started up the machines, increasing the torque so that they split the air of the Valley, louder than they have ever been.

It was the dream that made him do it. Made him pit the lawnmower against holly bushes, and the rotovator against the tree roots as if he was setting up a battle, a gladiatorial contest. The noise told me what he was about. Machines protesting, screaming at him; he was using them all wrong.

But when I went outside, I could see from his face: noise was what he was after. The screaming told him he was in control. Yet he wasn't in control. I came away frightened for him. Machines have a power of their own. A jagged wheel might fly off the rotovator. The mower might tip over, pinning him underneath. Something. If he uses them like this, he'll break them.

Or they might break him.

But after a while, the noise stopped. I looked out of the window and he was lying on the grass staring at the sky. His body was relaxed, all tension gone. And I relaxed too.

Later still, a van arrives at the bottom of the lane.

Tom walks over to see what is going on. His hair is falling into his eyes and there are leaves and grass clippings clinging to the sweat on his shoulders.

'What's this?'

Two men are heaving boxes – tea chests – out of the back of the van and onto the path.

'Marietta's things,' I tell him. 'Her private collection. The museum has sent them on to us.'

It takes a moment for him to make sense of this. He still refuses to wear the ear defenders and consequently the machines have begun seriously to deafen him. But then...

'Oh.' He scowls, and turns away. And that's that. The day is ruined again.

It's because of what's inside the boxes. African heads and fetishes; Mayan statues and amulets. Bones and stones and jangling claws she'd found and kept for herself.

I grew up with them. I thought every child did. Masks with eyes to watch you as you played. Bundles of feathers and skin, gnarled and beaded with dried blood. Things that rattled and rolled with the strange percussion of bones.

When I was a girl, it was Jen's house that amazed me, with its china shepherdesses and balloon sellers, pictures of ruined churches or dogs. Shiny objects with eyes that looked straight past you. Jen's house bewildered me completely. I didn't know what any of her things were for.

I knew what Marietta's masks were for.

Marietta had explained it all. It was the way the Dead looked back at the Living. Looked after the Living. In the jungle, life was too dangerous to be lived alone, she said. You needed the Dead on your side. Sometimes you needed the Dead to ward off the Dead.

So who looked after the living in Jen's house? Who looked after Jen? That's what I wanted to know. What were the shepherdesses for?

I tried to explain to Tom about Marietta's things, but I never could make him see. Tom hated them – the masks, the knuckle bones, the puppets and the fly switches. Hated being alone with them. When Marietta died and we moved in, I let him pack them all up and send them to the museum to be stored. By then I had forgotten myself what they were for. Now they have followed us here.

He flinches when he hears me tell the men to carry the boxes upstairs, to the pink room that used to be Mandy's; stomps back to his chainsaw, revs up the motor louder than ever, sends the birds spiralling from the trees to escape the shattered peace. If he had his way, he'd put it all on the bonfire. Set the match to it himself.

Later I go outside with a mug of tea I've made for him, but he shakes his head. Says he doesn't want it. Turns his back on me.

I truly had forgotten how much he hated them. Marietta's things.

'And Tom?' says Jen. 'Is Tom happy?'

'Oh yes,' I tell her. 'Tom's very, very happy.'

Over the phone, across the long distance that separates us, there comes the hint of a snort. But all she does is to add crisply. 'Well, good. Because what would be the point of being there if Tom wasn't very, very happy?'

The baby starts to cry in the background, which means we have to say our goodbyes. I would like to have talked longer, until Jen forgets to be snippy. It's always like this when we phone nowadays. She's angry with me because she thinks I've indulged Tom, and won't let me forget it. Two minutes of talk though, and invariably she turns soft, and the snippiness goes away. As happens now:

'I worry about you, Sara. I worry about you being alone down there.'

'I have Tom.'

'Tom,' she snorts again and puts down the phone. Like a true friend, she thinks there is no substitute for herself.

But it's true, what I told her. Three weeks since we came and Tom is still very, very happy. Goes to sleep happy, wakes up happy with a head full of plans.

It's just that he's not quite so very happy as he was. He's getting tired. Maybe he never was quite as fit as he thought. He sighs as he eases off his boots, his head rings from the noise of the machines.

He's run across a problem. It threatens to take the Shine off things, getting in the way of the important stuff – the asparagus, the artichokes and the kohlrabi. I want to help, but he says there's nothing I can do. He says the task is something only someone with a machine can handle.

The problem was there from the start. He just never realised how much it was there. It lies under the ground, stopping him doing what he wants. Stopping his plans.

Roots. His problem lies in the roots.

They branch in all directions under the lawn, hidden like the foundations of an ancient city. They are the reason the trees stand so tall, anchored in the earth. You can't see them, you wouldn't even know they were there. It's only when the rotovator judders and stops, its blades trapped, embedded in woody growth, you realise. Each time it happens you hear it, the grinding scream of machinery protesting.

Yet Tom drives on, spraying sparks, churning up soil which is nothing like the rich red earth at the top of the lane. And that's another problem – the soil itself. Down here, by the river, it's stained, filled with rubble and bits of metal that make whichever machine Tom is using scream and spark harder still.

If I could stop anything, change anything, it would be Tom's way with the machines.

'It'll come good,' Tom pronounces. The energy is still there, the plans still fomenting. 'We just have to work with what we've got. Marsh said he could grow anything. It just takes the right equipment.'

Yesterday, though, I thought about Mary Coryn's words, and went and looked up copper mines on the Web. Discovered they can leave a legacy long after they've been closed: land that is tainted, good for nothing but trees. I went outside to where Tom was at work with a Strimmer, and told him what I had found out.

He frowned. Listened with an impatience that grew.

Finally he interrupted me. 'So what are you saying, Sara? That we've come to the wrong place, that nothing will grow? Look around you. Does it look like some blasted heath here, a place where nothing will ever thrive?'

'No, I—'

'Or are you saying I'm some kind of idiot who can't work out a problem when he sees it?'

'No, I just thought—'

'Well don't. Don't think. Watch and learn.'

He forced himself to smile with these last words, pretending there was humour in them. I watched him go back to his task beneath the trees bending and swaying above him. Mocking.

Trees – just like Mary Coryn said.

He'd started up the Strimmer again, with its sound of a

dental drill, high-pitched and piercing. Bent over, trailing the electric lead like some long unwieldy tail, he was chasing something fibrous along the ground. Making a slow circle, coming ever closer back to the wire at his feet. And suddenly I realised: Tom was taking his own advice. He wasn't thinking.

In a moment the circle would be complete. Then what? The blade of the Strimmer would cut the wire, the circuit would be broken. A child could tell what would happen next. An electric current would sear through his body. Heat would burn the nerves that held him together. Shock would stop his heart...

Then what? Watch and learn, he said. The jolt ran through me first, making me scream.

'Tom!'

A sound more piercing even than the Strimmer. Tom stopped the motor. I pointed to the lead next to the blade and watched as he failed to understand. Then he did understand and the blood rushed into his face.

He turned and kicked the wire out from under his feet, flicked the hair out of his eyes. Then carried on, his body stiff and set, keeping his back squarely to me. Making it clear that somehow it was my fault, what nearly happened. Not his fault that he couldn't see the danger between his feet. Just like everyone else, Tom needs someone to blame.

Later – much later – he came inside. Put his arms around me.

'Don't get so worked up about things, Sara. Stick to what you know. You're doing a good job inside. Just carry on with that, yeah?'

He didn't say a word about the Strimmer and the lead.

Instead he wants me to keep on with what he started. Pulling the house apart, ripping wallpaper, chipping away tiles. Making ordinary rooms look as if someone has gone mad with rage, leaving the walls stripped and trembling beneath a film of dust. I have to remember to pick up the nails that have kept everything together, otherwise the house would have its revenge, drive holes into our feet every time we walked.

And Tom approves. Wants to know when I will start on the upstairs. Not for a while, I tell him. Too much to do downstairs. So the baby's room keeps its faint smell of ointment and cream. And Mandy's room stays as it's always been. Pink walls, pink carpet. Empty except for Marietta's boxes.

Although I think there may be mice in there. Last night I heard a rustling through the door, like the scraping of tiny claws. Things moving in the dark.

Tom has come to stand behind me, is watching me paint a wall in the kitchen.

'Here,' he says finally. 'You want to do it like this.'

He takes the roller and begins to paint over where I have already painted. I look on, wait for him to hand the roller back. But it doesn't happen. Already he's become immersed in the job; he's found what he calls 'flow'.

Flow. Tom hasn't mentioned it for a while, although back in London he talked about it all the time.

Flow. The unconscious enjoyment of the moment, when mind and body are united in an action, not thinking of anything else. Creative people have it, he says. And gardeners.

He says it's something everyone should achieve. A life with flow is a life made up of perfect moments, one moment after the other.

I don't think Tom has achieved a single moment of flow since the roots started to show, since he began to understand what he is up against. The machines are beginning to break down, the roots are defeating him. Just as before, up in London, Tom's problems lie underground.

But now that he has taken my roller and is covering the wall with clean broad strokes of cream, he has finally achieved flow.

It means I have to look for something else to do.

I tell him I'm going outside, but his mind and body are so united I don't think he's heard a word I said.

I go down to the patch of land that's been causing all the problems, sent him trailing inside with the mud weighing down his steps. Four weeks since we came. Surely he'll have something to show for the strain, the slight lowering of spirits threatening to take the edge off the Shine.

But you only have to look. Now I see the trouble. Now I can see exactly where the Shine has gone.

On the very edge of the lawn, he has cut down two of the smallest trees. And that's all right. There are their stumps, small and round and neat as coffee tables, their growth rings so clear you can count them. Young compared to the giants around them. Perhaps twenty years old.

But there his success ends. Having dealt with the trees, he has tried to attack what kept them upright. Tried and failed. The trouble remains where it's always been, underground.

Crushed in some places, scraped and bleeding sap, but still there, indomitable.

Roots.

Roots everywhere, still growing, still delivering life to where it's needed. There are leaves already beginning to sprout again from the sides of the stumps. So much work, so much noise and all he's done is scratch the surface.

Who will he blame this time then, for roots that won't be uprooted, for Shine that threatens to be rubbed away? Doesn't Tom always look for someone to blame?

I can't stand to look at them anymore – these roots that will undermine us. Turn my back on them, to find myself facing the river instead. Glinting between banks, more glamorous than churned earth, it beckons. A living example of flow.

So I come to where my toes are almost in the water, close to where dragonflies dip and hover; and where dandelions bend, dipping their petals in the stream. River runs, soothes me with sound. This is better, much better. Why haven't I been coming here all these weeks? Why have we both not been coming here, together, Tom and I? Just taking time to be still, while the river washes everything away.

Close my eyes. Nothing in my head but sunlight – and the vague wish that Tom was with me here, now. Happy just to stand and listen, and let the river flow.

It's then I feel it – a change in the air. Comes like the last time I stood here – the prick that tells me I'm not alone. Breath lighting on my neck, inviting me to turn. Making me think there is someone here. Close, close enough to...

But this time I know. It's a trick of the air; breeze flying off the surface of the river. Breeze. It's what I tell myself, but still I don't quite believe. It feels as if somebody is here, with me. Right next to me...

I can't help myself. I spin on my heel, fast...

And I was right. There is no one. River runs. Trees sway. Insects buzz and birds sing. But there is no one here except me.

Yet it happens again anyway: the feeling that comes after – of falling, of being sucked into empty space, a rent torn into the fabric of things. Again I have to pull myself together, make myself stand up straight. Knowing I have been fooled not once now, but twice. Foolish.

So foolish, it's no wonder that from close by I hear it – laughter. High-pitched, it spills through the registers, sounds like water falling over steps. It's a child. Somewhere a child is laughing at the silly woman who keeps thinking she's not alone...

Then sense returns and I realise it's not laughter but birdsong. One I don't recognise and no wonder because I'm from the city and what do city folk know about birds?

Yet when I listen for it again, there is only silence.

Nothing but silence. In fact, a silence like no other. A moment ago the air had been filled with noise: noise of water and unknown birds, wind and bugs. Now there's only this – a silence that is sudden and absolute. Pregnant, charged with waiting. Everything waiting.

Then it stops. The silence breaks, and every noise returns. Every insect buzz, every note under the sky. But now it comes as a roar, like the crunching of gears, as if Nature itself had slid into reverse. This, surely, is the noise that comes after an explosion; when things that have flown apart defy physics and come back together with a crash, like a jigsaw reassembling. I want to close my eyes, block my ears, but still it would be there. The sound of life exploding. Life giving life to more life.

Green. All of it Green. No boundaries. Nothing but Green.

And beneath the Green, a harder, brighter note again. Cuts through everything else. The river. It's the river that is brighter, louder. It's the river that snatches its own surface dazzle and hurls it at me.

Right at me.

The backs of my eyes flare, then turn to jelly. I stand, assaulted by light. Stand in the centre of everything. Blinded, deafened, not Sara anymore, because it's my own cells that have been exploding. Part of this. And deep, deep inside me, the feeling of something come alive.

As quickly as it began, it's over.

I am able to breath again. See again. The Valley snaps back to normal. The sounds die back to their former hum. Only the sunlight tears a last wicked flash across my eyes – then returns to the water.

Everything back to the way it was. As if it never happened. Except for me, ears numbed, arms and legs and eyes throbbing. And inside me, a warmth, a heat that remains.

Unsteady, I step away from the river, walk back to the house, where in the kitchen Tom has started on another wall.

He takes one look at me; then looks again, more closely. 'Hey, what's the matter?'

I open my mouth – and discover I have no words. He

puts down the roller, touches my face as if to check that it is actually me. 'Maybe you need to lie down for a bit. You don't look like yourself.'

And when I look in the mirror, I discover that he's right. Not only do I not look like myself. I can't even see myself. The savaging by the sun has left me purblind. In the glass, my reflection is just a mosaic of light and dark. And my ears – not numb anymore – my ears are singing.

I climb into bed, pull my knees in close and immediately fall asleep, only to dream of light that glances off the river like shards, like slivers of hot ice. And one shard has become embedded deep in the centre of me. There it stays, and glows. Part of me now.

'Migraine,' says Tom later – much later. 'It'll be the paint. Fumes getting to you. To be honest, I feel a bit headachy myself. I just ignored it and carried on,' he adds.

I swing my legs off the bed. My head feels empty and achy, but otherwise I'm normal. The strange, centred feeling has lessened. Is nothing but a warmth in the pit of my stomach. 'It's getting dark!'

'You've been up here for hours,' says Tom with only a hint of reproach. 'Lucky one of us was up and about.'

He's made it sound as if something has happened, and I have slept through it. He hands me the cup of tea he's brought for me. 'Did you hear the phone a while back?'

'No.'

He smiles. 'Thought not. It was Charlie and Jen. They're coming down on the weekend. Couldn't wait any longer.'

He is looking at me in triumph. Because it shows he was right. People will make the journey. They will come all this way to see us. Envy us. I look at him again and see it's come back. The Shine.

'That's...wonderful.'

He frowns. 'You could sound as if you think so.'

'But of course I do.' I have to make an effort, for the sake of the Shine. 'We'll need to get the house into shape.'

Tom laughs, then kisses me. 'For Charlie and Jen? You are joking.'

He goes out, still sniggering at the idea of tidying up for them, of all people.

~

# Chapter Seven

They're coming on Friday. Bank holiday, the last weekend of summer.

Before then, for five, six days, the sun shines. Never lets up. Each day hotter than the day before, arriving on the heels of nights that have felt like some vast animal fallen asleep on your chest. We wilt, but other things thrive. Those vast sprouting plants by the river have grown even more huge, their leaves swollen as if with dropsy. And that's not all. Yesterday Tom gave a shout from outside.

'Sara. Come here! Come and see this.'

He was standing in his shorts beneath a tree. When I arrived he pointed upwards. Cherries, deep red. Cherries everywhere. Neither of us had noticed them. I've been inside and Tom has had his eyes cast down, locked in unequal combat with what's beneath his feet. It's only the buzz of insects that has drawn his attention to them now.

'Oh wait!' he exulted. 'Just wait till Jen and Charlie see this.'

As if there was nothing like this to be found up there in London. Not a single fruiting tree.

He disappeared inside the house to find a recipe that

would use cherries. Meanwhile the machines stayed quiet and the roots settled even deeper into the earth. Remembering that children were coming, I checked the floors for nails. Stayed away from the river.

And enjoyed the silence, the peace that comes after all engines have been switched off.

Now they're on their way. First thing this morning, the phone rang. I reached across a sleeping Tom, to hear Charlie's voice.

'Just putting the kids in the car. Anything you want from civilisation? Cornflakes? Baked beans? Or do the natives keep you supplied?'

'You're leaving very early, Charlie.'

'You think? Our crew have been up since break of day. We're on our way. Better kill that fatted calf.'

In Tremaine's, Evie glances over my groceries.

'Expecting visitors, then?'

I nod. 'They're coming down from London. They should arrive around lunchtime.'

'Oh yes? Leave at dawn, did they?'

'Well not quite...'

She shakes her head over the vacuum-packed ham she's ringing on the till. So much added water there you could dowse for it. Fortunately Charlie and Jen won't mind.

'Well you can put your feet up in the meantime. You won't be seeing hide nor hair of them till after tea.'

'But surely...'

'Bank holiday, isn't it? And the sun is shining. They'll be on the road all day. It's what always happens. Folk never learn. They'll sit in their car and boil, just like everybody else.'

She's right. Lunchtime comes and goes, and here it just gets hotter. Flies buzz over the salads I've made and gorge on the sugar smears Tom has left after assembling a cherry crumble. Lots of flies. Huge ones that don't look like any I've ever seen, their bodies so fat and glistening, their wings so heavy, you can actually hear the thud as they land.

'Where the hell are they coming from?' grumbles Tom in disgust, swatting at one that's landed next to him. 'Oh...shit!' The fly has disintegrated under his hand into an oozing glob, only its wings intact.

'It'll be the cherry trees,' I tell him. 'They're feeding off the fruit. We should have picked it all yesterday.'

'Fuck that,' says Tom, annoyed. 'That's our fucking fruit.'

He stumps off outside like a farmer all set to deal with poachers. But he comes back minutes later looking slightly pale.

'There's thousands of them. Millions. The trees are swarming with them. Try getting near and they just crawl all over you.'

'I suppose it's the weather. It's very...close.'

Close is an understatement. The air is heavier than ever, almost viscous, something you could stir with a spoon. I think of Jen – large and billowing – someone who feels the heat. Wonder what she'll say about it. Only the river keeps flowing freely.

Finally, round about six, we hear the car inching down the lane.

'At last,' mutters Tom.

We wait at the end of the path, next to the snapdragons, still going after all these weeks – although dusty now and wilting in the heat. Tom takes my hand so that the picture looks complete, and what they see is Tom and Sara standing hand in hand at the bottom of their valley. Like children from a fairy tale.

But Charlie and Jen have real children, and are not impressed. Behind the wheel Charlie's face is scarlet and Jen's the same. Even with the car doors closed we can hear the racket. The Duke is screaming and Pig is sitting, rigid in her seat, her face set in a rictus of rage.

They turn off the engine, but for a moment, they just sit, as if in shock. Then slowly Charlie opens his door, but still he doesn't get out. Looks at us.

'Tom. Sara. We seem to be...er...later than expected.'

He pauses then leans back into his seat, turns to Jen.

'Will you get that fucking child out of his fucking seat and make him fucking stop crying?'

And only then does Jen move.

'Ten hours,' says Charlie. 'Ten bloody hours. We could have flown to Chicago in the time it's taken us to get here from London.'

Jen has disappeared. She is seeing to the children upstairs, in the baby's room. I've already been up with the usual glass of wine, and all she did was drink it down before handing it back to me with the one hoarse word.

'More.'

'I didn't know it was possible. That you could just sit and go nowhere for four solid hours. That's how long we were stuck outside – where was it? Wadebridge? Some bloody place like that.' Charlie is on his third glass of wine. Has his eye on the bottle as if afraid someone will take it away. 'And here's you saying you moved to get away from traffic.'

'Maybe you left at the wrong time,' suggests Tom, a touch of acid in his voice. 'Planned it wrong.'

I see Charlie bristle – then let it go. Because under the high colour and the fatigue, he is still Charlie. Easy going. Instead he reaches for the wine.

'The Duke started bawling at Swindon. After that he didn't stop. Not once. Didn't matter what we did. So bloody hot, you see, and nowhere to let off steam. Mind you...' He smiles. Finally, finally the alcohol is kicking in. 'You have to admire the lungs on the little bastard.'

Jen comes into the room, her shoulders sagging. Charlie looks up.

'You hear that, Jen? I said you have to admire the lungs on it.'

And Jen, hearing praise – any praise, from any quarter – for her child, smiles and perks up.

Everything is better after that. Charlie and Tom finish one bottle and open another. And another. Although Jen, after those two glasses upstairs, seems to prefer water. Maybe the heat is having the same effect on her as it has on me. Makes me thirsty, but not for wine, which after the first sip, seems heavy, not to my taste.

By the time I set the cherry crumble in front of them, Tom and Charlie are raucous, while Jen is almost asleep. So it's only me, sliding the first spoonful into my mouth, that notices: the shock of cherry, jolting me awake. Cherries grown in our valley, their sweet sourness cutting through the sugar of the crumble.

Our cherries.

I glance at Tom, thinking we could share the moment. But it's passed him by. He has spooned his up and pushed his plate aside. Now he's back on the wine. Charlie is guffawing and Jen is scolding him in case the children wake up.

But there's no fear of that. They are sleeping soundly upstairs, both of them in the baby's room, worn out. I could have put just the Duke in there, and Pig in Mandy's room, but I didn't. That room has stayed empty, the way it seems meant to be. Only Marietta's boxes to cast a shadow on the clean pink carpet.

The taste of the cherries stays on my tongue. Makes me feel wide awake, nothing like sleepy.

Next morning, I'm already up and dressed when the children start to grizzle, and meet Jen on the landing. She looks terrible. The night has been hot again and her face is covered with a greasy sheen of sweat.

'Go back to bed,' I offer. 'I can look after them.'

But she pushes me aside impatiently.

'That's terribly sweet of you, Sara. But what do you know about kids?'

She joins me downstairs. The Duke arrives bringing a reek of ammonia seeping from his pyjamas.

'It's the heat in this place,' says Jen. 'He had to drink gallons, so he's peed gallons. It's got all over the travel cot.'

'I'm sorry,' I say as if I were responsible for the weather, for the heat, for the Duke peeing.

Jen grunts.

The little girl, Pig, says, 'I want to go home.'

Jen shakes her head at her and Pig goes back to stirring her Weetabix round her bowl, too listless to eat.

It looks set to get worse when Charlie and Tom appear. The combination of heat and hangover makes them move like invalids, old men careful not to tax themselves.

But Charlie rises to the occasion. Puts down his tea with a bang and declares, 'We're in Cornwall, folks. We'll be all right once we've had a bit of sea and sand. Good long stint on a beach, couple of ice creams, slap of wind. Lovely.'

Jen says, 'Where do you recommend, Tom? Perranporth? Or we could go back into Devon, try Croyde...?'

'You could try anywhere you like,' says Tom. Coldly. 'If you want to go to a beach, go to a beach. I mean, we'd sort of hoped you'd want to stick around here, see what we're up to, but it's your choice.'

'Tom...' I begin.

But Charlie is quicker than me. 'Absolutely. Forget the beach. This is exactly where we planned to be. Right here. Don't want to miss a thing. Do we, Jen?'

Jen nods. Doesn't look at us.

But it's a mistake, anyone can see that. After breakfast, we decant ourselves outside, just as the sun climbs up over the cliff, appearing with a sudden flare as if it has just rent another hole in the ozone layer.

Straight away the Duke begins to cry.

Jen rocks him, makes both her and him hotter still.

'He's one of those babies who prefer the cold,' she explains to anyone who cares to listen. 'He likes it in the winter when

I wrap him up and take him out. He loves the wind on his face.'

And it's true. I've seen Jen wheel him up and down in howling gales round Dartmouth Park, his cheeks ballooning red under his bobble hat, and grinning. But we sit down on a blanket under a cherry tree and, cooler now, Duke stops crying while Pig plays with her doll. Even Jen looks happier.

Then she says, 'What's that noise?'

Simultaneously we look up and there are the flies again, swarming in the branches above our heads, their buzzing suddenly a cacophony, as if it had taken the sun rising above the cliffs to wake them.

'Ugh,' says Jen. Gathers up baby and child and flees.

Finally we find a place in the shade, away from the cherries, away from the flies.

I'm carrying the Duke for Jen who has armfuls of blankets and drinks, and as soon as I'm able, I set him down on his front. Immediately his arms and legs float up around him like a set of tentacles. His belly is so large, nothing else can make contact with the ground. I'm afraid that he will start to suffocate under his own weight, like those fat men who expire, thrown on their stomachs into the backs of police vans. I would turn him over, but Jen snaps:

'Leave him. He's happy that way.'

And sure enough he lies the way I put him. Contented. Lowering his head to graze the hairs on the blanket like a baby animal put out to pasture, dribbling and talking to himself. Pig wanders off.

'Oh thank God,' says Jen. 'Peace at last.'

She closes her eyes, too exhausted to talk and I watch them a moment – mother and child laid out on the blanket under the trees. She and the baby seem to be made out of the same stuff. Both of them noisy and red cheeked, elsewhere their flesh soft and white and billowing.

Pig, aka Claudia, is cut from a different cloth. I watch her beneath the trees, bending over things in the undergrowth, frowning to herself. She is small for her age, with bony arms and legs and long, untidy hair. Anything less resembling a pig could hardly be imagined. You wonder if Pig is the name they'll be calling her when she's thirteen, in front of friends, people she needs to impress. Or will they explain they called her that because she used to snort when she slept, like a piglet snuffling for acorns? Jen and Charlie love their children with a passion that makes Tom go pale, but they are not sentimental. Sometimes they are not even kind.

Not knowing she's being watched, she looks up at the sky jigsawed by trees – and down again in what can only be discontent. Probably they kept her happy during that long, long drive with promises of sea and sand, ice creams and waves to tickle her toes. Now she's been told she has to stay here, where it's hot, and the adults too listless to play with her.

'Jen.'

'Mmm?'

'Pig's all by herself. She looks a little – well, bored. Shall I...?'

Jen sighs. 'Leave her be. Children need to be bored every now and then. Does them good.'

So I say nothing. Do nothing. Tom is showing off his

armoury of machines – the chainsaws, the rotovator, the sit-upon mower. Charlie stands nodding, probably only half listening, his head protected by a panama hat so battered I imagine it belonged to his father. Meanwhile, Pig – Claudia – continues to wander by herself from tree to tree, in and out of shadows.

Jen says sleepily, 'So is it all working out, now Tom's got what he wanted?'

'Yes. He's happy. Really, really happy. Look at him.'

Jen opens one eye. Tom is talking, pointing to areas of wilderness that he intends to tame, just the way he did when we first came. Happy as the day we moved here now there is someone to impress.

'And what about you?'

'Me?'

'Are you really, really happy?'

'Of course.'

She smiles. 'Yes, of course. So long as Tom is happy. I forgot.' Closes her eyes again, and doesn't look at me.

Irritated without knowing why, I search for Claudia once more. She has wandered a good way off now, her little white sundress flashing between the trees, sun glancing off her hair.

'Jen,' I say uncertainly. 'Claudia's going rather far.'

'She's four years old, Sara. She's allowed to go far. People spend all their lives standing over their kids, not letting them off their apron strings. They smother them.' She stretches, feels automatically for the Duke. 'So...how long will it be before you and Tom get to eat your first carrot?'

'I don't know. But you ate our cherries last night.'

'Did we? Oh, you mean in the crumble! Sorry, I just

assumed they'd come out of a tin. Or frozen. Still, aren't the cherries the reason for the flies? You'd be better off without them, to be honest.'

'Maybe.' But I don't agree with her. I can still taste the shock of them in my mouth. Sweet sour. Our cherries. Then I blink. As hard as I stare, I can't see Pig in the trees any more. No flash of white dress, no glance of sun off her hair.

'Jen?'

'What?'

'Jen!'

This time I scream, because I've found her. Found Pig. She is there, where I hacked a path through thorns, at the river's edge. Grass green beneath her feet. Little white dress, little red shoes. She has her back to us, watches the river as it runs, brown and rushing, waits for no one.

Except for one person. For Pig stands poised to take a step. Little red shoes to carry her over the edge…

Jen sits bolt upright beside me. 'Jesus, what? What's happening?'

I point. My hand moves, but the rest of me is paralysed, speechless, like in my dream. Unable to stop what happens next.

And around us a pause, a catch in the air. The insects have gone quiet, the trees have stopped swaying…

'Oh for God's sake,' says Jen impatiently. She raises her voice. 'Pig, come here. Now.'

Unbelievably, Pig turns round. Slowly. Steps away from the water. Walks back towards us, but reluctantly, resentful of the summons. Despite her tiny size, the boniness of her arms and legs, there is a bullishness about her now, in the way she moves. Shows she is Jen's child, after all.

'What were you doing?' says Jen.

'Looking at the river.'

'And what have I said about rivers?'

Pig's answer is instant. 'Don't stand too close.'

'And how close were you standing?'

Pig thinks, then spreads out her arms, as far as she can.

'Good girl,' says Jen. 'You never forget, do you?'

Pig shakes her head. Hair swings about her face, and off she goes. Doesn't look at me.

Jen turns to me. 'What was that about? You scared the daylights out of me, Sara. Screaming like that.'

'I'm sorry.'

'Did you think I wasn't watching her?'

'No...'

'Did you think I don't know where my kids are, every minute, every moment?'

'No, but...you had your eyes closed.'

Jen's mouth narrows. 'Well that's what you think.' She pauses, then says softly, 'You know, Sara, you should stick to mothering Tom. It's what you're used to, and it's not as if you haven't got your work cut out. After all, real kids grow up.'

When I don't answer, she glares at me. Then something changes. Her face becomes soft. Soft as when she's hugging a child of her own.

'Oh God, Sara, what's wrong with me? I'm so sorry. You're shaking. Shaking all over. You honestly thought she was going to drown, that brat of mine. You were just frightened for her.'

She falls towards me, arms open, doesn't seem to care that

the Duke is squashed and pinned beneath her. 'Look at me, I'm a hag. Horrible. A horrible, horrible woman. I got so frazzled yesterday and never seemed to shake it off. But I'm better now, sweet Sara. Lovely Sara.'

And I let her hold me. Because I feel like a child, unable to know what's real and what's not. I saw a little girl standing on the riverbank, poised to take that one step. I saw the river flow, and the waters about to close above her head.

And this time I wasn't dreaming.

It's the reason I let Jen hold me, and rock me, as I would after a nightmare. Let her voice soothe me until gradually I hear what she's saying.

'I'm pregnant again, Sara, that's what's the matter with me. Stupid of us, it's our own fault. It took so long to get the Duke after having Pig, somehow we never thought it would happen. And now look at me. I've turned into a monster, shouting at you, shouting at everyone. It's like I've been possessed, Sara. Hijacked.'

'Jen...' It's my turn to put my arms around her, startled to find her large body is shaking. She's crying. Jen is crying.

'We didn't ask for this, Sara.'

'Shh, Jen!'

'Everyone thinks I'm one of those women that just wants kid after kid, like some big, fat dairy cow with hanging udders. But I'm not. I want my children. The ones I asked for, prayed for. Not this. A stranger. And I hate it, Sara. I hate it.'

I hold her more tightly still, until I feel her relax, and her limbs melt into mine. We stay like this for a long moment. Then she draws away. Blows her nose on the toilet paper she keeps to catch the Duke's dribble.

'Well there you are. That's me. Not such a good mother after all.'

'That's not true.'

She forces a laugh that is still perilously close to a sob. 'Don't worry. I'll come round. I'll get used to the idea. Women have to, don't they? When they have no choice.'

'Don't you have a choice?' I am cautious as I speak.

'Choice? Maybe I did, once upon a time.' She sighs and points to the Duke forming spit bubbles on the blanket. 'That's what kills choice – the kids you have already. Not morals, not God. Just a sense of fair play. I gave space to him, and Pig. I got what I wanted. So now...'

'So now...?'

'Now it means I have to give space to something I don't want. It's what having babies does to you. It makes you need to be fair, no matter what. It's payback time. Can you understand that?'

I shrug, unplaced to argue about such a thing. Not sure I do understand.

The men are strolling over towards us. Pig is holding Charlie's hand. 'What was all the fuss about?' says Charlie.

'Sara thought Pig was going to fall in the river.'

Charlie looks down. 'Fat chance of that, isn't there, Pig? First you'd drown, then your mother would beat you for getting too close to the water. What did you want there anyway?'

'I was talking to the little girl.' Pig's voice is matter of fact.

'Girl?' says Tom. 'There's no girl here.'

Pig shrugs. Sees no more point in arguing with him than with the Duke.

* * *

'Not drinking, Sara?' says Charlie.

It's the next evening. He has offered me wine and I have said no.

'Don't feel like it. The heat probably.' I reach for the bottle of water on the table – and catch Jen watching me. Her eyes are questioning. Frowning. Then suddenly it's as though a light's gone on.

She leans and takes the bottle away from Charlie. 'We all should go easy tonight. Long drive tomorrow.'

Charlie groans. 'Ah yes, a delight in store. I vote we drug the children.'

'I'll miss you,' I tell them. And it's true. After the bad mood of the morning, yesterday was lovely. And today, despite Tom, we went to the beach. Slathered suncream over the children and slotted into the bank holiday crowds on the sand. Even Tom enjoyed himself, if only because crowds remind him of what he has escaped.

'Never mind,' says Tom to me. 'They'll be back soon.'

'Absolutely,' agrees Charlie. 'Bad pennies and all that.'

But already I've caught the look that passes between him and Jen. They'll come back – of course they will. But it won't be soon, not after the journey they had on Friday, and will have tomorrow.

Jen sees what I'm thinking, catches my hand. 'Come up and stay with us. Come as often as you like.' Her eyes are still lit up, flashing signals at me. Signals I'm not sure I understand.

'Too busy,' says Tom, answering for both of us. 'Too much to do.'

'Bollocks,' says Charlie, and smiles at me.

I smile at them all.

I'm still smiling as I fall asleep. Happy until I dream.

The little girl stands by the river. Little white dress, little red shoes. I stand behind her, while behind me stands the house; and behind us all, the trees. All the world in one place, waiting for that one step.

Different this time. All the years I have watched her, I have been dream-paralysed, unable to move. But as I watch her now, my limbs are free and easy. There's even a path that would take me to her, one I have cut myself. Yet still I don't move. It's because of the river. It runs, it rushes. If I go to her it will have me, have us both. The waters will take us and cover us and carry us away.

She lifts one foot higher, poised now, ready to step away, disappear for ever. And still I do nothing...

I wake with a scream, making Tom start and jerk his arms from me as if I was timber that has shivered and split. He rolls away from me in the bed, leaving me to lie, eyes staring at the dark until they ache, till the blue lightens the sky and the children begin to stir.

Hours later, ready to go, Jen looks at me.

'God, you look pale, Sara. Come here.'

She reaches and pinches my cheeks to bring the blood back. 'It won't last, you know,' she says softly, so only I can hear. 'It stops, you know, after a while.'

I stare at her. Is she talking about the dream? How can she possibly know?

'What, Jen? What won't last?'

'The tiredness, the general oddness. The body adapts. Although this weather doesn't help.' She stops and a look of mischief comes into her face. 'So when were you planning on telling us?'

Again I can only look at her, bewildered. 'Tell you what?'

'That you're pregnant, of course.'

I take a step back from her. Feel what colour there was drain from my face. Jen sees me and lets out a small scream of dismay.

'Oh my God. Oh Sara.' Her face twists. 'I'm so sorry. I thought... It's just you weren't drinking, and you were looking so...stretched. And Tom, he was telling us about you getting ill with the paint fumes. It all seemed to add up. Then just now, with you so pale... Oh look, forgive me. This is just wishful thinking. Stupid and wrong. Wrong of me.'

She stops. 'Forgive me,' she says again.

There's a sound behind us. It's Tom. 'Charlie's got the children in the car. He says to get a move on.'

Tom.

All the colour Jen missed is pouring back into my cheeks.

~

# CHAPTER EIGHT

Jen was right, of course.

I got a pregnancy kit from Tavistock and brought it home. The tester stick turned blue almost on contact. Blue as the strip of sky above our valley.

That was an hour ago. I haven't told Tom.

'Sara.' His voice reaches in from outside the front door, throbs as if he's furious at something. Maybe he knows.

I go out to find him heaving the rotovator into the car.

'I'm taking this to the machinist's. Fucking thing's packed in for good this time. Useless. The fucking policeman ripped me off.'

He doesn't know.

He drives off, revving up the engine the way he does with the machines. For a minute I wait, listening until the sound of it has died away.

Then gradually, by degrees, I allow myself to breathe. And tell myself what I have not told Tom: I am pregnant. Something has taken root inside me, something neither of us wanted. Now it's there.

I want to think, but I have no thoughts worthy of the name. One strip of blue, and I've become less substantial than a pile of feathers. I couldn't be lighter if I was made of straw. If a wind came now, it would blow me into a thousand pieces. Yet still it would leave something behind – small and dense and hot. I imagine it, glowing like a piece of coal. Comes from the centre of me, alive. It's been there since the river hurt my eyes. Hurt me.

Did the river do this to me? Is that what happened that day when the light attacked me, left me trembling, half blind?

Stupid thought. Comes from nowhere. I shake it away and do the only thing I can do. I walk. One foot in front of the other.

But within yards I've stopped. I have come to Tom's patch of tumbled earth, where he thinks his problems lie. It looks like the corner of a battlefield here, his tools lying abandoned in defeat. This is where the Shine is rubbed away, more and more each day. When he comes home, I will tell him about the strip of blue, and the Shine will disappear completely.

Yet Tom cannot live without Shine.

The lightness disappears. So fast I sink under my own weight – down into the scraped earth. I can't even look up. All I can see is what is here between my two hands pressed into the ground. A weight inside me.

But here the weight shifts. It's outside me now – a hand, come to settle on my neck and push me even further into the ground. Lower. Lower than the stumps of trees, the small hillocks of churned earth.

So now I have it – a worm's-eye view of Tom's trouble. Roots and rocks and messed-up soil. And, tossed into the middle of it, a hand fork that I've seen Tom using to prise stones out from between the blades of the rotovator. I recognise it – one of the few tools we brought with us, before we had ever heard of rotovators.

I remember the day we got it, in a designer garden shop in London. Tom picked it up and tested the broad wooden handle in his palm. I could see the image that came to him as he held it: of himself kneeling, patiently probing the soil, pressing seeds into the compliant earth. Patiently? Tom's patience wore off long ago, along with the Shine.

The dead hand on my neck pushes me down, lower still. Even so, as if of its own accord, my own hand reaches out.

It wants the fork. Reaching for it as it might reach for a photograph of earlier, easier days. Now my fingers close around it, the way Tom's did that day while he smiled at the image of himself: Tom as he wanted to be. And it's like a memory of what never happened. Tom never uses anything not driven by machine.

So this is all it is – a tool that has never been used, and which I am now holding. And it's absurd. Absurd how, even with the weight on my neck, I feel sorry for it; and feeling sorry, push it into the ground, into the earth. It's nothing – only a gesture, a salute to what might have been. A kind of apology.

Yet something curious happens.

For immediately the fork snags, like a comb caught in a tangle. I pull, and the ground pulls back, tugs me towards it. So I stop pulling and work the fork gently out instead. The earth shakes back into the ground, and the fork is free again.

Now, though, there's a morsel of earth clinging to one of the tines. Dark and crumbly, like a piece of fruit cake. I suppose it means I've christened it, this tool that has never touched soil. I could put it down now, but I don't. Instead I push it into the earth a second time.

And for a second time the earth catches and tugs. Again I have to work it free. But what I notice now is that the handle has grown warm and the smooth curve of the wood has taken on the curve of my hand. It's what makes me keep hold, push it a third time into the ground.

And keep pushing. Tunnelling and loosening the soil until I see what is possible. Smaller roots and stones that can be picked out and thrown aside. The soil sifted and softened until it falls through my fingers like pastry, nothing like the scraped earth left by Tom's blades and boots.

Finally, in about a square foot, only one big tree root remains, de-fleshed and bare, like a limb pared down to the bone. A fork couldn't do any more here. A rotovator even less. But I know what could. I run up to the shed and come back with the hatchet I used to make the path.

It's easier than clearing the undergrowth. The root only needs to be hacked halfway through before I can stamp on it. Two attempts, and it snaps, giving way so my foot plunges into the soil beneath. Now I have a perfect square of earth, broken up and free of stones and roots. Glancing at my watch, I discover an hour has gone by. I hadn't even noticed.

There's something else: incredibly, I forgot about the weight on my neck, the strip of blue. One moment flowing into the next – I forgot everything.

Not anymore. There's the sound of a car and Tom pulls up. He gets out and walks towards me. I know that way of walking. Slow, kicking out his feet as if aiming for invisible stones, like a boy sullenly making his way to school. He used to walk this way in London all the time, to the Underground, and home again. He looks at me. And frowns.

'What have you been up to?'

'Nothing.'

All the same, I stand aside, so he can see what I've done here.

But he doesn't seem to notice. Not the mound of broken roots, or the patch of clean brown soil. His eyes slide away into the middle distance where nothing is pleasing.

'The rotovator's shot. They need to get a part up from Truro or some place. I'm not going to see it again for days.' He heaves a sigh. 'Look – I'm going to do some work in the house. Maybe make a start on the dining room.'

The truth is, he doesn't care which room he changes. Just so long as he changes something, makes a difference. I watch him go, then I pick up the fork once more.

When I look up again it's almost dark. There are lights on in the house. No doubt Tom's still pulling wallpaper off the walls, finding flow. Inside, it's easy to change things. It's outside that it's difficult. Everything wants to stay the same. Roots are too deep.

I'm tired, but I don't want to go in, not yet.

He won't believe it at first. We've done nothing out of the ordinary, taken all the usual precautions. Yet here we are. Maybe it happened that first morning we arrived – in bed, marking our new beginning. Did we begin something else that day?

It was an accident, though. Accidents happen. After the first shock, that's what Tom will say. And accidents can be put right. That's what he'll say, too. And he'll be right, of course. Nothing has been done that can't be undone. Nothing has changed. That's what he'll say.

But it's not true. The moment I stand up I know. Things have settled inside me, like opposing forces after a collision. The weight has shifted from my neck. It's inside me now.

I need to go back to the house. Tell him what has happened.

Inside, the scene is different from what I expected.

Tom is not scraping wallpaper. He is here in the kitchen, with the table laid and candles flickering on the bare walls. There's the smell of cooking in the air, herbs and butter bubbling on the stove.

'Hey,' I say softly.

He looks round from the stove and his face lights up. He's wearing a big woollen jumper, his legs long and lean beneath. His hair flops over his forehead. He looks young. Younger than when I first met him.

'Hey. I'm sorry about the scene with the rotovator. It's just I wanted to get so much done and—'

'I know.' I go and put myself beside him. Busy stirring a pan with one hand, he hugs me with his free arm.

'I thought you'd need fuel. Go and pour yourself some wine.'

But I don't move.

'Oh look, you're shivering,' he observes with concern. 'Are you cold?'

I nod and he hugs me closer still. And for the first time I feel the difference in his arm. It's harder, stronger. There are workman's muscles under the wool of his sweater. Does he know? The roots may have defeated him, but the battle has done more for him than all those hours in the Soho gyms. Tom's arms are strong.

Strong enough for anything. A thought flies into my head.

'Sara?' He smiles into my eyes, and I stare back into his, studying what I see.

My husband has become a gardener. Not a very good one. He struggles with forces greater than he is – trees that rise above him and sink their roots like claws, deep into the ground. But he wants to be better than he is. He reads manuals, he imagines plants grown tall. What if I told him that there was something else we could grow? Unplanned, blown in like the seed of something we'd never heard of. But here now. Ready to grow – if we let it.

What if I tell him, and his face changes – but not the way I imagined? What if...?

Tom's arm stays warm and strong. I have never felt the strength in it till now. I pull away to look at him even more closely. He's still smiling. And now I see. Something has changed since we were outside. The Shine is back. Tom looks happy. As happy as it's possible to be.

What could have changed? Nothing. Unless it's this: he knows. The tester strip is upstairs in the bathroom cabinet. He could have found it. Is this what has brought back the Shine?

Suddenly I stagger slightly, despite his arm around me.

'Hey,' he says and his arm tightens. 'What's this. Tired already?'

Not tired, but dizzy. I am dizzy at the thought of a future different from any I thought possible – with Tom, this man who is glowing with contentment beside me, and with a kind of excitement I haven't seen for weeks.

He reaches across me for his glass of wine. 'Something happened when you were outside.' His voice throbs with his eagerness to let me know.

I wait, almost ready to say *I know.*

'I had a phone call from Joaquin.'

A fall inside me. I didn't know this. But still I wait.

'He wants me to come back to work. Not full-time, I had to put him clear on that – just on a consultancy basis. The thing is, the magazine is heading south without me. The guy who's meant to be editing knows sod all about anything, but he's willing to accept "guidance". Joaquin wants me to go up there and do just that. Really, really wants me. Just a few days a month. It means we get the best of all worlds, Sara. I can be here, doing what I want. And I can be there, still making a difference. Still making a mark.'

We? I?

'How long?' My voice is flat but he doesn't seem to notice. 'How long will you be away?'

'I told you – a few days out of every month. Hardly any time. But he's practically begging.'

'Where would you stay?'

'At his place. Joaquin won't be there, that's the beauty of it.' Tom pauses and looks at me, his face earnest. 'Tell me honestly, Sara. Are you OK with that? It would mean you having to hold the fort here. Do you think you'd be all right?'

He waits for my answer, confident of knowing what it will be. Then little by little, his face changes as seconds pass and no answer arrives.

'Sara?'

'I'm pregnant.'

There's a silence. His arm falls away from me.

In the middle of the kitchen floor, he watches me sway. Something without roots or branches. Nothing to keep me up, easy to cut down.

~

# Chapter Nine

Tom sits in the passenger seat and waits for me to drive him to the station. We make the journey in silence. We have said everything it was possible to say.

At first he had been patient. Stating what we both know to be true. That we do not tamper with something that is good. That we are happy with what we have. We are not Charlie and Jen. We are orphans, lucky to have found each other. We do not need to pass on our selves to others. Content to be full stops marked in time.

And when finally he believed it was safe to ask, confident of the answer, he said, 'So, do you want this child?'

'No,' I told him. And it was the truth.

The sun returned to Tom's world. He strode across the room and took me in his arms. But then he felt me stiffen.

'Sara?' Cautious now. 'You're going to deal with this, right?'

When I didn't answer, his face became sharper, chin grown pointed, like a child's. Forcing the calm into his voice, he said, 'So...tell me again. You don't want this kid?'

And again I shook my head. 'No. I don't want it.'

He looked at me, bewildered. 'So what's the problem?'

Finally they came. Words I'd been looking for from the moment the tester stick had turned blue: 'I could want it. I could if you wanted it too.'

His eyes narrowed. Then he smiled slowly, brilliantly. Like a toddler who has triumphed in logic. 'Well I don't want it, so that's simple, isn't it?'

He waited for me to agree. Waited for a full minute. And when I didn't agree, he turned away. Ignored my hand searching for his. Later, in bed, I reached out to touch him again, and he flung himself over to his side and stayed there, the sheets a chill, wide margin between us.

But in the small hours I woke to find him clinging to me. Desperate, like a man drowning in his sleep.

And now he's going away. He gets out of the car, reaches for his bag. His train is due in five minutes, leaving no time to talk, even if we wanted to. Tom walks away.

But then he turns back. Comes to the window and tilts my face to his. 'Look, we can sort this out, you know. We want the same things, Sara. We always have. Just remember that.'

And I nod. He nods back, then turns for his train.

I was going to stop off in Tremaine's, but as I'm slowing the car, Mary Coryn appears in the door of the shop making me decide to do without cheese and disapproval. I put my foot down and carry on.

Back in the house I make a mug of tea and take it on to the veranda, and there I stand, searching for something, without knowing what. Only aware that something has changed. Something is missing.

It's the noise of the machines. After six weeks of protest, suddenly there's nothing. Even the river seems to run more quietly. Tom goes away and, as a result, the entire Valley seems to sigh with relief. Glad to see him go. Relaxes like some large animal no longer under attack.

In the trees, a bird releases an arpeggio of notes. If Tom had been here, the machines would have drowned it out. Now it's a summons. Draws me from the veranda down to the patch of soil with all its roots and trailing things. Picking up tools as I go, the trowel, the fork. Following where it leads.

Later, much later, the telephone rings by the bed.

'You weren't asleep, were you?'

'No.'

But it's a lie. Midnight and I had been dead to the world. Not even dreaming.

He clears his throat. 'So...are you OK? Alone, I mean?'

'Of course. Why shouldn't I be?'

'I don't know. You might start hearing things that go bump in the night. Freak you out a bit.'

He says this because he knows it wouldn't happen. Not to a child brought up in Marietta's house, surrounded by skulls and bones, things that rattled and rolled.

'No. I'm OK.'

There's a pause, which neither of us quite knows how to fill.

'So, have you done anything yet? About the...the Other Thing.'

'Done?' I repeat after him, stupidly.

'Don't you need to make an appointment or something? See somebody. A doctor.'

'And tell them what?'

He sighs. 'What you told me. That you don't want this kid. Neither of us wants it. Am I right?'

'Yes...'

He waits for me to say more, then sighs again. 'Sara. You need to get your head round this. Have to. We've got to do something. Soon.'

'I know.'

Another pause, even longer than the first.

'OK. I'll ring you tomorrow.'

He rings off. Immediately I want to try again, go back to those silences and this time fill them with talk. I tap in his number, but an automated voice tells me he is unavailable to take my call. Tom has turned off his phone.

I lie back against the pillows, turn off the light. But now, as if of their own accord my fingers have begun to move. Restless, curious, they wander over skin, grazing the traces of old suntan, a faded appendix scar. Familiar landscape of a body I thought I knew.

It turns out I never knew it all. My body - a stranger to me.

And Tom, who has never been a stranger, has turned off his phone, can't bring himself to speak to me.

This is not a night for sleeping. Sleep lies a thousand miles away, on another continent.

Eventually I climb out of bed and go downstairs. Make tea, switch on the radio. Thinking if I sit long enough, surely sleep will seep from above, usher me back to bed.

It doesn't. I stare at the kitchen walls, still fresh with the smell of paint. The only wall not covered is the one by the door where Tom ran out of paint. So there they are still – the marks of a little girl growing. Then stopping. I stare at them until my eyes become dry.

And give up waiting for sleep. I turn off the radio, put down my tea and go back upstairs, to bed.

But rooms change when no one is there to see them. In my absence, something has stolen into this room, slipped through the windowpanes like a ghost. Now it lies stretched along the bedroom floor, pale and sharp-edged.

Moonlight. It beckons me from the door, points to a milk-white path below my feet. Leads me, moonbound, past the bed towards the cold glass of the window that let it in. There it invites me stand and cast my eyes.

And what has it brought me here to see? This – a valley, honed by a scalpel light, all the green flesh cut away, lying gutted and glowing below the window. A different valley, nothing like the day.

It's the trees. All you have to do is look at the trees.

Flayed by moonlight, they have bones that shine and leaves that crackle. Drained by moonlight they are sapless and tinder dry. Gathered on the lawn's edge, they look like giants, ready to catch and burn in a burst of cold white flame.

*Is it safe here?*

I have never thought to wonder. Now, tonight, it seems the one question we should have asked. I've seen the trees throng by day. I've seen the way they whisper behind our backs, mocking Tom's desire to lay them low.

Moonlight shows what we should have guessed for ourselves: these trees have no intention of staying where they are. They want to come close, and closer still, until the pink walls of the house disappear and the windows are blinded by leaves. The lawn stands in their way, but it's only a question of time. The roots that have defied Tom are there, underground, burrowing all the way to the house. A woven reticulated bridge to take them where they want to be.

We should be frightened of the trees. Tom should be careful...

But that's nonsense, of course. It's just the moon having its effects. If Tom were here now he would laugh at such wild imaginings. Worse – he would be alarmed, unsettled. Not by the moonlight or the trees, but my reaction to them. Like a child spotting a weakness in a parent, he wouldn't like it, the effect of the moon on me.

And he wouldn't like the way I turn from the trees to something else. Or the sharp catch of my breath as for the first time I notice.

The river.

Oh Tom – if you could see what the moon has done here...

For the river has become a fissure of light, a crack in the mantle of the Earth. Nothing like the day, it's a shining flow of mercury, a spate of liquid metal. Listen, it even has a different sound. Harder. Water clinking against stones like endless coins falling on a road.

And beautiful. All of this is beautiful – the strangeness of the trees, the quicksilver of the river. The cold glittering light that frosts the Valley. But I have seen enough. Here are my hands on the windowsill – moonlight has turned them white as bones, veined with ink. Hardly human.

I have seen more than enough. I will steal away from so much beauty and climb into bed, pull the covers over my head. Wishing and wishing that Tom were here…

But it's as I turn, I see – a shape that catches my eye. Softer, much softer than the trees, a small, pale figure stands close to the river's edge. A fall of hair. Little white dress, little red shoes. Although, of course, not red, not by moonlight.

I freeze.

Freeze and blink. An instant later when I open my eyes my breath has misted the glass pane in front of me. Frantically I rub. All the Valley is there, cold in the moonlight. But she isn't, the little girl I saw just now.

Thought I saw. I saw nothing.

~

# Chapter Ten

I wake, and even before I remember the Other Thing, I remember something else completely. A small white shape by the river. Soft. *Is she there now?* I swing my legs out of the bed and...

*Now* I remember the Other Thing. The movement becomes a race to the lavatory to retch. Clear, scalding liquid rising as if there's a hot spring inside me.

Sickness. Nausea. It means it's begun: the long daisy chain of changes. Cells dividing, triggering more changes – unless we stop it, Tom and I. Stop it all before it's too late.

When at last I look outside, the Valley has changed again. After the shock of last night's moon, rain has come, soft and persistent. It falls through the trees, patters between a thousand floors of leaves. And, of course, she's not there, child of my mind's eye. It was the moon blurring the line between what's real and what's not. Playing tricks with an old dream.

What's real is this, my body a stranger to me. One that, weak from retching, moves from room to room on legs that feel not my own. In the kitchen I am unsteady, so unsure of myself I have to sink into a chair, forced to stare again at a wall.

Yet even here, the world stays uncertain, threatens to wake the nausea. Only this is worse than any sickness. For as the minutes pass, I become aware of a new feeling. Begins in a small way, then grows. Bands of tightness reaching around my chest, gripping my ribs, and closing round my lungs. Squeezing. Tighter with every breath, so I try not to breathe at all.

While in front of me the wall billows slightly. Pencilled marks rippling like numbers on a sail.

The wall...

A final squeeze...

Then the band snaps; the tightness is gone. With a gasp, I breathe easy as, falling back into the chair, I gaze at the wall. And understand.

Look at the marks. Look where they stop. There's a reason they stopped. A little girl grew, and then she stopped growing.

I fetch a coat and go down to the river. There, in the rain, I allow her to take shape again.

Mandy. She stands at the water's edge. Waits for imagination to instruct her.

Although how could she have stood here? There was no way to be close to the water. A spread of thorny undergrowth would have kept her – and everyone – at bay.

Briefly she wavers, this child who has taken shape before my mind's eye, and I am not certain.

But of course, the thorns grew afterwards, after it happened. They – the Marshes – would have chosen to let them grow. Mandy's shape becomes solid again, stands on a smooth, bare slope where there's not a single thorn.

This is what happened here. This is why the Marshes had to leave. Their little girl went down to the water and there they lost her. The river took her and never gave her back. After that, no more measuring.

And now she stands. I can't bear to imagine what comes next. I blink, and Mandy vanishes. Where she stood is nothing but thorns and briar. Yet all I had to do was imagine. The truth was there all the time.

Tom listens with all the patience he can muster over the phone. But it's hard for him. Several times I hear him about to interrupt, only to bite his tongue. But when I come to the end, he can't stop himself.

'Oh Sara, for God's sake.'

He hasn't believed a word.

'No Tom, think. Remember what they said in the shop, "Who'd want to live there after?" '

'That could have been anything. Flooding, drains.'

'But don't you see? The place has been telling us. It's why the Marshes were so desperate to sell. We should have realised that the very first day. All the clues were there. We just refused to look.'

'You've lost me, Sara.' He clicks his pen against the phone. 'There was nothing to see.'

'Think back, Tom. It was in their faces. Remember the way they watched us. They wanted us to take this place so badly. Remember how the baby was there, but *she* wasn't. There was no sign of her.'

'Well so what? She could have been out for tea – or

whatever people do with kids to keep them out of the way.'

I interrupt. 'It's why no one local would buy the house, Tom. It's why they couldn't sell it at all, because something terrible happened. Everybody would have known it. Don't you see?'

'So you think just because of a few nettles and an empty room, she died?' He's exasperated now.

'Then there are the marks. For years they measured her, then they stopped, just like that.'

He thinks, then sighs. 'All right, let's say for a minute that you're right. Why wouldn't they tell you, your friends in the shop? If it was so very terrible, and it wasn't drains, why go all silent?'

'Because they're not my friends. We're incomers, remember. They think it's none of our business. Mary Coryn doesn't think anything is our business. They're not going to tell us.'

There's a silence at Tom's end, as if he's totting up facts in his head. 'OK.' His voice is matter-of-fact. 'All right, maybe. I suppose it sort of adds up.'

'You believe me?'

'I'm saying you might be right. Maybe the kid did drown. It wouldn't be the first time. But I don't see why you should get so worked up about it.'

'But doesn't it make you sad? Don't you think it's terrible, awful?'

'Well...yeah. Of course it's sad – if it's true. But I'm not going to lose sleep over it, if that's what you mean. It just proves we did them a favour taking the house off their hands. They got what they wanted, didn't even have to lower their price.' He pauses. 'Are you still there?'

'Yes.'

'You've gone quiet.' He waits, then adds impatiently. 'Oh look, you're not going to dwell on this, are you? A kid falls in the water. That's awful, terrible. But it's not our loss. It's something for the parents to deal with. None of our business.'

And when still I don't answer, he has an inspiration. 'If you want to make something out of this, see it as a sign. The place is no good for children, not with the river there. Accidents happen, Sara. If you have a kid, it's the last place you want to be.'

This time, he's so pleased with his own logic, he doesn't even need me to reply.

Rain falls on the river, muddies the water.

I've come back. This is where she would have stood. Mandy.

Now I know.

And so does Tom. And it doesn't bother him at all. If it had been drains, he might have been upset, depressed even. A little girl lost doesn't touch him.

But it touches me. She stood here and the river took her. Never gave her back. Now I look at where we live, and the world seems smeared by loss.

Jen would understand. She'd stand where I am standing now and it's Pig she would see – bony and bullish, hair falling across her face. She'd imagine it was her they pulled from the water. Little hands cold, nothing Jen could do to warm them, not now. Somebody else's child, somebody else's loss, but in her mind's eye Jen would see, feel, Pig. She'd weep if she knew what I know now.

And I...

I see the little girl who has been in my dreams for as long as I remember. Little white dress, little red shoes. The closest I have ever had to a child of my own. When I see Mandy, I see her.

It's the difference between Tom and me.

Back in the house, the phone is ringing. I hear it from the path, but by the time I reach the front door, it has stopped.

Only to ring again, suggesting an urgency on the part of the caller, a need to speak. This time I pick up.

'Sara?'

A voice that is like an answer to a prayer.

'Jen.'

I sink onto the stairs. Jen will understand. I will tell her about Mandy and she will know exactly why the world has become smeared.

Yet for the moment, all I hear is silence.

'Jen?' I pause. 'Are you there?'

'Yes.'

Just one word. But it tells me to put away thoughts of little girls and rivers. 'What's the matter? Something's wrong. You sound, I don't know...'

'I sound pregnant, that's what. Ignore me. I'm tired. And sick, same as the last time I was up the duff. And the time before. You remember.'

I do remember. But last time, Jen laughed when she was sick. Retched and yawned like a big, contented cat. Glowed with a warmth that made her cheeks and hands hot.

'Jen? There's something else, isn't there?'

'No. I told you. Ignore me.' But then she starts to talk again. 'You know, they should be shot, those people.'

'What people?'

'Those fucking people who stand outside the clinics, trying to frighten women into giving birth. Screaming at them. Those so-called priests with their beards and their dog collars – if something came and took over their bodies, they'd go straight to their archbishops. Get it driven out with whips and bells. But when it's a woman who needs help – proper help – they scream at her and call it murder. Hypocrites.'

'Jen! Is that what's going to happen? Are you...?'

'No,' she snaps. 'But it's what I want. I want it to go away, Sara. I can't bear it.' Her voice has broken. 'Ignore me,' she says a third time.

And what I hear now is Jen crying. Huge broken-hearted sobs, making her sound like a little girl. Weeping over the state she's in.

The state we're both in. But she doesn't know that.

A moment later she stops. Blows her nose. 'Ignore me,' she says again.

'Jen,' I say softly. 'I can't do that.'

There's a pause, a swallowed sob. Then, 'You know what this is, don't you Sara? It's a punishment.'

'Punishment?' I am startled.

'For being smug and stupid. Telling myself – and you – that what you really needed was a child. For never listening when you said that all you and Tom wanted was each other, and how a child would ruin everything. Now I understand.

I'm going to have a child I never wanted and it's going to ruin every good thing we have.'

'Jen, how do you know that?'

'Because it's there now, inside me. Like a parasite, something you catch from not washing your hands. No control, no choice. I have to carry it around, getting fatter and fatter. Then I'll have to give birth to it and look after it and try and feel the same way about it as I do with Pig and the Duke. But I won't feel the same, Sara. I won't, because I already hate it.'

She stops, fighting the drive to keep talking. And loses.

'And don't tell me you know how I feel, because you can't. You can't understand this, not without it happening to you.'

'Jen,' I murmur. 'Maybe I—'

'No! Don't even try, Sara. This is the one thing you can't pretend to know. No one can.' She sounds fierce as she tells me.

'And Charlie?' I say softly.

'Charlie? I can't talk to Charlie. He thinks I've gone mad. I'm Jen, his great, fat laughing cow. He says I'll end up wanting it, but I won't. I'm like you. I just want what I've got, which is a whole world. A whole perfect world we made for ourselves – and it worked. The world of Charlie and Pig and the Duke and me. Now it's all going to be destroyed.' She pauses. 'Sara?'

'Yes?'

'What would you do – if you were me?'

My answer is ready. Swiftly I say, 'If it was a whole world I was saving, I'd make it go away. I'd have to. I see that now.'

There's a silence. Then Jen says, 'You know I couldn't do that.'

'I know.'

'It's a question of fair play. I told you about fair play, didn't I?' she adds anxiously.

'You did, Jen.'

'It's not that I would stop anyone else. I just couldn't do it myself.'

We fall into a silence.

'Sara?' Jen's voice is wistful. 'I wish I'd been right about you last week. Being pregnant.'

My heart skips a beat. 'Why?'

'It would have changed everything. It would have brought it all back – what a miracle it is, life starting over. I wouldn't have felt like this. I'd be happy, I know I would be. Everything would be different. Selfish of me, I know.' She breaks off. 'Sara?'

There's a note in her voice. It tells me what's coming.

'Would you come up and stay, just for a couple of days? Help me get through this. Please.'

I wince and close my eyes. Across the miles that separate us, I can feel her need for me – shy, reaching out. It's the closest Jen has ever come to asking for anything. Always the one eager to be the mother, the one who looks after me. I try, I try to not think of this as I answer her, as gently as I know how:

'I'm so sorry, Jen. I can't. Not right now.'

There's a silence. She's waiting for me to explain, but I can't think of any explanation to offer – except for the true one. That I am pregnant too.

'I'm sorry,' I say again. 'I'll come soon. I promise you – as soon as I possibly can. Just not now.'

Again I cast around for an excuse, a lie. But nothing comes. My mind has become a blank with only the truth stamped on it. Yet my hand is steady as I replace the phone. Already guilt is settling on my shoulders, I can feel the weight of it. But gratitude outweighs even guilt. I can't help Jen, but Jen has helped me, more than she could ever know. She has made me see that I am lucky. Luckier than she is.

I can't go to Jen because she doesn't have a choice. But I do. And I choose the world that Tom and I have made for ourselves. Our world. These last few days it has been hanging in the balance. No wonder Tom is haggard, can hardly bear to look at me. Later, I phone him again.

'I've made an appointment – with the doctor.'

'And...?'

'I'm going to ask to get it sorted.'

'Darling,' he says. 'My darling. I'll be back tomorrow.'

Suddenly it seems he didn't have to stay away so long after all.

He arrives in the evening with a bottle of champagne, and I drink it with him. It's important to drink. He sees it as a celebration. He watches me, his eyes warm, happy. A weight has disappeared from his shoulders, left him lit up with love, with Shine. In bed he holds me, presses his lips against my hair.

I'm so happy, Sara. So very, very happy.

Afterwards my sleep is dreamless, empty. Without shape or content.

# Chapter Eleven

In the morning he drives me to town and goes to wait in the cafe not far from the doctor's surgery.

'Tea and cake for when you come back.' He has a seed magazine to while away the time.

In the surgery, the doctor nods when I tell her I'm pregnant.

'They're pretty reliable, these home tests, so there's not going to be much doubt.' She smiles. She'll have read my notes, noted that I am thirty-five, ten-years married. Older than me, she has pictures of children on her desk, presumably all grown-up now. She'll assume I'm over the moon.

'What the kits don't tell us is how far you are along. You say your periods are sometimes irregular. Have you any idea when you may have conceived?'

I am about to tell her yes. I have every idea: it was that morning we arrived. Starting something – which I am about to finish. Instead I say, 'Is there any way you can find out?'

I want to know for sure. So that it's clear, making a beginning and an end; otherwise it will seem like a dream. And dreams have a tendency to return, never leave you in peace.

'We would scan you. Assuming...' The doctor looks at me – more keenly now. 'Assuming, of course, you want to go ahead with the pregnancy.'

There must be something in my face that warns her. Tells her to assume nothing. She waits for me to say something, confirm that I am what my notes suggest I should be. Thankful. Ready to be a mother.

Now, of course, is the time to tell her I haven't come here to be a mother. But then she might not scan me and I will never know. Nothing will be real. The strip of blue will have come and gone, evidence of nothing but itself.

So I smile and say nothing. If I keep quiet, I don't even have to lie. But still she watches me closely. All it would take is a slight trembling of my mouth to give me away, show her I have no intention of having this child.

After a moment she picks up the phone, says a few words, then stands up. 'We're in luck. We can do the scan right now. The advantages of working out of a polyclinic.' She takes me to another part of the clinic, to a room with a bed and VDU screen beside it. And there I undress, quickly, drearily.

'Hop on the bed for me.'

She smears gel on my naked belly. 'Flat as a pancake,' she observes. 'You girls nowadays – you don't eat enough.'

I could tell her about Marietta, and my mother the same. About thin being the hallmark of my family. But none of them exists anymore. Tom is my family, sitting outside with a catalogue of seeds, determined to make them grow.

But then I forget about Tom. She has slid a hand piece over my belly and a sound has filled the room – pulses, fast and echoey. Somehow watery, as if reaching us from a place that has been flooded. The doctor says:

'That's the heartbeat you can hear. And there...' she turns to the VDU which has flickered into life '...is what we are looking for.'

At first I don't know what she's talking about. I look at the screen and all I can see are moving shades of black and white, like an artist's impression of water. A riverbed, with shapes that drift in the current, in a swaying watery world. But then one shape catches my attention.

'There.' I point to the one shape clinging, limpet-like, fast to the bottom of the screen while around it everything moves. 'What's that?'

'That's your baby.'

Suddenly heavy, my hand drops. She takes a closer look and says:

'I'd say it was six, maybe seven weeks. Somewhere in between. We can book you in with that date in mind. I'd have to work it out on a calendar, but I'd make a guess for about the first of May next year.'

She smiles at me, waits for me to say something. But all I do is stare. I am counting back, adding days to other days. Six and a half weeks ago we came to the Valley and made love. So it's true, it began then. And this is the result.

'It's quite a thing, isn't it?' She has turned back to the screen. 'Being able to see it there. Sometimes I wonder how we managed before. How did we ever convince ourselves they were real, these little bits of things that were invisible? I swear there must have been women who went right up to the hour and the minute they gave birth, never quite believing.'

I watch the screen, the strange watery world which is me. This, I believe this.

But it's only me that believes. I am here while Tom sits in his cafe, waiting. Turning the pages of a seed catalogue, choosing between what he wants to grow and doesn't want. Waiting for me to come back so that life can carry on, just the two of us. All the family we could ever need.

I open my mouth to tell the doctor the truth: this is as far as it goes. There will be no baby. I need to ask what happens now.

On the screen, though, there's a blip. A fault? Or something else, worse. For an instant it all disappears. No movement, no shape. Nothing to see but black.

'Where's it gone?'

A voice has cried out, swallowed by the empty screen. My voice. My words. At the same time my heart has begun to pound, thrown against the sides of my ribs as if something has alarmed it. As if something has been lost.

She smiles, this doctor – and in a flash, it's back, the swish of sound and the swirl of shapes. And the limpet thing, still attached, hooked into the river's bed, begins to pulse again.

My heart stops its pounding, lies down again. I breathe once more.

'Mrs Lewis?'

I don't answer. I have lain back onto the couch and closed my eyes. I am trying to blot out what I have seen, trying to remember what came before. When I stepped into this room, I was intact. I was Sara – everything about me was mine. I had a choice.

But now...?

I close my eyes harder, screw them up tight. But there's nothing I can do. I can still see it, the small dense shape, clinging in its watery place. Meanwhile, what belonged to me, the choice I had, is slipping away like something the river has taken. In my mind, I reach after it, trying to catch it. But it won't stay. It won't be caught. It twists and it turns, like a shoe floating away downstream, lost to its owner. Pauses once. Then drifts away, all the choice I ever had. Leaving only the Other Thing, here to stay now.

I have no choice, not anymore. My body lies back, satisfied; while my head reels, appalled. I had no part in this. A decision has been made without me, and now everything is turned upside down.

What do I do now?

'Mrs Lewis?' says the doctor again. 'Are you all right?'

This time I reply. 'Nothing,' I say. 'Nothing.' Answering not her question but my own.

And this is the truth. There is nothing to be done. My body has decided. Before my very eyes, it peeled away to become a stranger to me. Made a decision while all I could do was watch.

In the cafe, Tom sees me coming, puts down his catalogue with a smile. He's expecting me to tell him a date, a time, somewhere else I will need to be. He's ready to be helpful, to be tender.

Then he reads my face and the smile disappears, and I see how it will be. There will be no more tenderness now.

'What have you done?' He sounds fearful.

'Nothing.' I say the word again, gently.

He stares at me and instantly understands. 'I thought you didn't want it. I thought you wanted us to stay the same.'

His voice is unsteady. I believe he is about to cry. I want to take him and hold him, comfort him somehow. I need him to see that I don't want it either. I need to tell him how it was, how my body became a robber, a stranger. Robbed me of choice. Robbed us both. But when my hand reaches to touch his across the table, he snatches it away.

For a long while after that, we sit, not talking. When at last we find the energy to move, the seed catalogue gets left behind.

He has a right to be angry. Tom fought all his battles decades ago, at an age when most are having their battles fought for them. He survived death and loss, and – worse than anything else – other people's families. He thought – he truly thought – he was safe from all that. Safe with me.

And now I've shown him he's wrong. I'm not safe at all.

I look at Tom as he drives – hunched, angry and grief-stricken over the wheel. Hating me. I want to blame him for it and I can't. I've changed the rules, broken our promise to be everything to each other. Broken our world. Now I am going to turn him into something he never had himself. A father.

And at the same time, make him an orphan, all over again. Just like Joaquin said.

~

# Chapter Twelve

The first thing he does when we get home is to go outside, start up a machine. Now he's out there, tearing up the ground, sharpening the air with the sound of blades. I stay inside and wait.

Eventually, he comes. Stands at the kitchen door, looking at me. Then he walks to where I'm sitting and lays his head in my lap. He has nowhere else to go. I stroke the back of his neck, his shoulders, his arms, while he says nothing. He's waiting for me to speak.

He wants me to tell him that despite everything, nothing will change. That somehow we will stay like this, as we are this moment. It's what I want to say, but I can't. I have seen the creature in its swirl of water. Pulsing, hooked into its riverbed. And I know what will happen. It will grow, taking over what used to be ours, using it for itself. Has to. Everything will change, nothing can be the same. To say anything else would be a lie.

So. My poor Tom. He has to be content with this: a hand stroking his neck. In the absence of a truth, it's all I can give him. Soon he takes himself away.

* * *

But it's in the night that it really comes home to me, what I have done to him.

He clings to me in his sleep. Harder than he has ever done before. A man at sea, afraid the sea will have him. His arm lies across my neck and clutches the pillow, so that I am locked under him. In a shipwreck he would sink us both, pressing my face beneath the waves so that neither of us can breathe. Makes me wonder if we are even safe to sleep, if in months from now people might not find us lying like castaways, far from the ocean, our lungs full of salt water. No one would understand how we came to drown.

Rain comes in the small hours. Falls hard then soft, reminds me of the watery echo I heard today. Everything is watery. There's a river inside me. When I sleep it runs through my dreams.

In the morning, I wake to find myself alone. Downstairs, Tom is on the phone, finishing off a call. He makes a show of looking guilty when he sees me. He wants to be caught in the act of something.

'That was Joaquin.'

'Oh?'

'He's desperate. It looks like a few days a month isn't going to be enough.' He watches my face. 'He wants me to spend more time up there. A lot more time.'

'How much more time?'

'Most of the week. Mondays till Thursdays. Some Fridays.'

'And what did you say?'

'I told him it was fine. I told him we'd welcome the money, seeing as you've decided to have a kid. I take it you have no objections?'

'Tom—'

'Good, then that's settled.'

He turns away from me, but it's not the end of it. We don't need the money. He wants me to argue with him. I can see it in the shape of his back. Every nerve, every muscle waiting for me to plead with him, beg him to stay. He wants me to stroke and coax and do all the things that I have always done. Letting him know he is still the centre, that the world turns tenderly, just for him.

If I could, I would.

He's waiting, but because he's turned his back, he hasn't seen that I've left the room. I couldn't stay. I couldn't coax. The centre has shifted, has come to settle inside me. Nothing I can do about it.

Now I've come here, to sit on our bed, and I suppose it's my turn to wait. Wondering if this might not be the day when Tom comes to me.

If he came, everything could be different. People change, don't they?

I wait and I wait, but he doesn't come.

Now he has gone, back to London, the place he was so anxious to escape.

He had more luggage this time. He's going to be away longer, of course. I drove as he sat scrolling through the menus of his iPod, choosing what he will listen to on the train, a way of blocking out everything else. Blocking out me.

Only as he was about to climb out of the car, did he turn.

'Sara...one last time. Is it really true you want this?'

And I shook my head. Because of course I don't want it. I

don't want any of it. I am as trapped as he is. Briefly his face lit up, only to darken again.

'I see. You don't want it, but you're going to have it anyway. Ruin everybody's lives – yours, mine. Turn everything upside down for something you don't even want.'

'I'm sorry,' I said. 'I'm so sorry. I had no choice.'

'Of course you had a choice. Every woman has a choice.' He got out and slammed the door.

And he's right, of course. I had a choice. It's just that somehow I let it swim away.

So here I am. Home. Except it doesn't feel like home.

A house that was too empty, it drove me straight outside again, back to the patch of soil with its roots and trailing things. I've been here for hours – digging, piling up weeds, wheeling a barrow back and forth to the bigger pile where Tom has his bonfires. Trying to make one moment disappear into the next. Trying and failing.

Yet time and again something has made me pause – the snap of a twig, or a twitch in the corner of my eye. And each time I stop, look behind me, thinking it must be Tom. Because I keep forgetting: there is no Tom. He has gone away, and I am alone.

It just doesn't feel like it. The woods are deceptive. Things move around me all the time. No wonder I forget.

Hours ago the sun rose to its highest point, stood above me as if expecting me to obey the signal. Stop. Go inside. Eat lunch. I ignored it.

What did the doctor say before I left? 'Just take a little care. Eat regularly and eat well. Rest when you have to. Your body will tell you what it wants. Be kind to yourself.'

But the sun slid off its high perch and began to sink towards the rim of the Valley. And I have kept digging. I am not going to be kind to myself or anyone. Least of all a stranger. I will be like those women the doctor mentioned, the ones who go to the hour, the minute of a birth not believing. I will act as if I don't believe.

But now it happens again. Movement in the corner of my eye. Perhaps even the faint snap of a twig. So close this time, it's impossible to think I am alone. I drop the trowel and stand up straight. Fast.

Which is when the day – bright until this very moment – turns black.

Although you wouldn't call it dark. Against the black, stars explode like fireworks and drop like petals. So pretty, I have to watch them, entranced, forgetting to be amazed.

Spellbound, until a weight pulls on my arms, drags me down.

And down again. The fireworks flash harder, brighter. Not so pretty. They come together as if to paint a signal in the sky. A warning. Then they go out.

And when I open my eyes a little girl is dancing on the path in front of me.

Dancing or spinning? She wears a dress of canary yellow, stitched with red. It stands out all around her, catching the air. I know that frock. It's mine. Marietta saw it in a bright Brazilian market and brought it home for me.

Now she's wearing it, the little girl. And I know her too. She's the child from the river, the child of my dream. Or do I

mean Mandy? Mandy who took the shape of my dream child so as to be real, so that I could be sad for her. When a child dies you need to be sad…

The confusion is too great. So I just watch. Watch her spin as the air lifts her frock like a tiny red and yellow sail, the way Marietta watched me.

But still I find myself frowning. It's not enough to be confused. She has to be one or the other. Which one, though? Mandy never wore my clothes. Then again, neither did my dream child.

I watch and wonder. If it is Mandy, what is she doing? I know all about her now; my mind made me see her, dressed her up as my dream child. But that was just to make me aware. Otherwise, I would have been like Tom, blind, deaf to the sadness of things. There's no need for her to appear now, dancing in front of me. Or spinning. She doesn't need to be here.

I shake my head at her, this girl. Show her I disapprove. But still she dances.

One thing I know – Tom wouldn't like it. He'd have something to say about a child coming to dance in his wood, amongst his trees – even if she is only a dream child, a mind child. He'd want to know what she was doing here. Angry as when the flies came to settle in our cherry tree, stealing our fruit, taking what's his.

She's nothing like the flies, though, he should realise that. She's lovely with the shape she makes and her skirt splayed out around her. Maybe I should warn her. Tell her not to stay, not with Tom the way he is now. Angry all the time, his shoulders hunched against me. Although for the life of me I can't remember what he is angry about.

I'll tell her not to dance, not here, with Tom so likely to appear. He'd shout at her. Scare her away.

In fact, it's beginning to alarm me, the thought that Tom might come now. All day I've heard the crack of twigs, caught movements out of the corner of my eye. Any minute he might come again. I don't want him to shout at her. Whoever she is, she's beautiful. Wears my dress in a way that would make even Marietta smile.

What if he does more than frighten her, though? Look at her, she's so fragile even the air seems more substantial. What if he hurts her? Tom is not in a mood to be kind. Tom is never kind when he's unhappy.

It's now a hand touches my neck. An arm moves across my body. It's Tom. He's here. And even though I expected him, I scream.

His arm heavy, like it always is. Pins me to the spot. I scream a second time. In fury now.

But his arm just grows heavier, harder. I hurl myself from side to side, yet it only makes him move with me, a shadow blocking out the world. I know what he's doing. He doesn't want me looking at her. Jealous, he wants all my attention. He'll stop me looking and he'll stop her dancing.

I hurl myself harder. And harder.

'Mrs Lewis.'

And harder still.

'Mrs Lewis. Sara.'

Who...?

The shadow arches, grows larger. Then dwindles. Not Tom. Everything about it is smaller than Tom. I stop moving, and let myself see.

It's Marsh. John Marsh. And Tom – Tom is a long way from here. He left on a train and didn't look back.

He watches me a moment, then gently loosens his grip on my shoulders. 'I'm sorry. I frightened you. You'd collapsed. I was going to turn you into the recovery position, but when I touched you...'

I stare into his face. I am flat out on the ground and he is bent over me, blocking out the sky.

He says, 'Are you back? Do you know who I am now?'

I nod.

'And do you know where you are?'

Again I nod. At the same time, trying to see past him. See her. Such a small movement of the eye, yet he catches it, looks behind him. And when he moves, I can see again.

It's a leaf.

It hangs in mid-air, yellow, shot through with red. The first coloured leaf of autumn, it spins, slowly this way and that. Hangs on a single thread of spider skein, all but invisible, attached to a branch above my head. This is what I see.

This is all I see.

It's all he sees – if he sees anything. I have a feeling he was staring further away, into the trees. Puzzled because there's nothing there. Only trees – and a single leaf suspended by a thread.

But he's looking at me again now. Trying to work out what to do next. At least he's not using the smile he used on Tom and me before, trying to seem like something he is not. He doesn't have to, of course. He's got what he wanted. Us here, instead of them.

He says, 'We need to get you into the house. Call a doctor.'

'I don't need a doctor. I'm pregnant, that's all. I stood up too quickly and...'

I stop. Without meaning to, I've told him about the Other Thing, something that was none of his business.

But all he does is nod. 'It took Carole like that when she was pregnant. She used to faint. She...' He stops. And like me, whatever he was going to say is left unsaid.

Abruptly he leaps to his feet and puts out his hand. 'Let's get you inside. He in? Your husband?'

'He's up in London.'

'Oh.' He frowns.

I take the hand he's offered. Smaller than Tom's hand, but harder, stronger, it pulls me to my feet, then keeps hold. He's waiting to see if I am steady.

So now we stand. I am the same height as him, a little taller even. Next to Tom, he would seem shorter still. But it means our eyes are directly level. He opens his mouth, about to speak again.

But then his eyes slide past me and his face changes. He's caught sight of something. The river. And suddenly he's forgotten what he was about to say. He's forgotten about me.

Of course. It was here, by the river. This is where they would have lost her. Mandy. This very place. And whatever he saw then, he sees it now, I can tell. His eyes give him away.

But only for a moment. Then it passes. He breathes once, twice, forces himself to relax. His eyes, which for a few brief seconds betrayed him, are shuttered once more.

And it's back, the switch, the smile. He even manages a note of impatience as he says, 'You want to take more care, all by yourself down here and Mr Lewis not around. Someone

in your condition – what if you do yourself an injury?'

He sounds normal, completely in control. Except for this: he has forgotten to let go of my hand. He is still holding it, clutching it hard. Hasn't even realised.

It's his hand I focus on. It's cold, much colder than mine. And it's the cold that tells me. John Marsh is talking as if nothing happened. But he saw something by the river. Now he's concentrating on not seeing it again.

Would he tell me if I asked him about her? Tell me I'm right?

I imagine the questions: How did you lose your child? Why did you take your eye off her? Did you find her after – or was it someone else...? Did you...? Was she...? Did your wife...?

Questions, and not one of them is it my place to ask. They're right, I see that now, Mary and Evie in the shop. Right not to talk of it. It's none of my business what happened to these people. It's their grief, precious and terrible and private.

Instead I can only watch, fascinated by what I see: a man calling on every bit of strength he has, knitting himself together just so he can keep breathing. So that he can smile at me. He uses the switch and the smile as a distraction, something to fool the eye, while the real, hard work is done in secret.

And it has an effect on me, watching him. So unexpected, I am utterly unprepared for the shock of it. Suddenly I am jealous. Jealous of his wife, his pale wife who lost what she loved best, but still has this man who is so determined to seem strong. A man who is not Tom.

Who is nothing like Tom, different from him in every

conceivable way. All at once, I feel myself beginning to give way again, tilting towards the ground.

'Steady.'

His hand tightens around mine, while his other catches me under my waist. And this is how he keeps me on my feet: by planting his body in the way, like a tree. And this is where I would stay, stopped from falling. For ever, for as long as he let me.

But then over his shoulder I see the leaf spinning slowly on its invisible thread. Imagine if she could see this. I imagine Mandy, watching me cling. I pull away, so fast it catches him off guard and he has to stagger to keep his balance.

'I'm all right,' I say. 'I'm all right.'

He stares, not knowing if he can believe me. Wondering how I can be limp one moment and rigid the next. Never guessing that a second ago I was someone else completely.

I have to stop him staring. If he stares long enough he'll see right through me. I force myself to stand up straight.

'Do you mind if I ask what you're doing here? Should I be helping you with something?'

I have sounded brusque to the point of rudeness. But I need him to take his eyes off me.

And it works. He blinks in surprise. Takes a step back.

'I came to speak to your husband – tried phoning a couple of times this morning, but there was no answer.'

'And...?'

He looks uncomfortable. 'And...well he's been talking to people. Up in the garage, down at the machinist's. He's telling folk he's not happy with the machinery he bought off me. Says it's not fit for the purpose. He's giving out I've robbed him in some way.'

‘Tell them he’s wrong.’

The words leave my tongue before I can stop them. I imagine Tom hearing them, imagine the look of horror in his face. But then it happens again. I say:

‘Those machines – he broke them himself. He was using them the wrong way. That’s why they broke.’

Treacherous words, taking me by surprise – and not just me. Marsh looks startled. ‘He tell you that?’

‘No. But it’s true. He has to blame someone so he’s blaming you.’

Again he looks confused. His wife would never do this, talk about him like this. Never. But after a hesitation, he shrugs. ‘All right, I’ll leave it there. If he wants to talk about it, get him to call me. I don’t want him thinking anyone has—’

‘He won’t. He has other things on his mind now.’

And there, that’s three truthful things I’ve said about Tom in a row, all in the space of a minute. Words that came rushing with a life of their own. Marsh throws one last bewildered look at me, then walks back towards the house.

Only when his car has disappeared do I allow myself to sag. In front of me the leaf spins slowly, then fast depending on the currents of air. Yellow and red, a carnival of colour in one tiny papery space.

Nothing but a leaf.

Why was she here? Why did I think she was here?

# Chapter Thirteen

Tom phones, says he can't stay on long. He tells me the journey has tired him out. He says he's shattered.

'I'm tired too,' I say. 'I've been working, clearing weeds. Digging up more roots. You could plant something when you come home.'

He doesn't answer. In not talking, he allows me to hear how very far away he is. Behind him, I can hear music and the buzz of conversation. People laughing the way they do over glasses of wine. He's a whole world away from me.

'I fainted this afternoon. I had a kind of dream. I thought I saw the little girl, dancing. The one I've seen in dreams all these years.'

He rattles the ice in his glass. Tom's not interested in dreams. Not even interested in hearing that I fainted.

'Then I thought it was Mandy, but I wasn't sure.'

Sullen, he says, 'Mandy? Who's she?' Already he's forgotten.

'The little girl who lived here. She died. We think she died. You thought so too, remember?'

He sighs. There's another silence, punctuated with a small sprinkling of piano notes. I know where he must be. He's at a cocktail bar, the one that he likes, just a step away from the magazine. He knows all the waitresses there, knows all their names. Doesn't forget them like he forgets Mandy.

'Well, you're talking to me now, so I guess it worked out all right.'

'John Marsh found me. I was outside—'

'Marsh?'

'He came to talk to you. About the machines.'

'I bet he did.' He sounds pleased.

'He helped me. I was all alone, Tom.'

'Good,' he says. 'He owes us. He screwed us over those machines.'

I feel a stab of anger. So much so, I am about to tell him the three truthful things. But in the pit of my stomach comes a twist. Sickness, nausea. Saliva floods my mouth. It's the Other Thing giving me a warning, a reminder of who rules us now.

I don't want to fight with Tom. Not now. I close my mouth, swallow the nausea and my own words, the three truthful things.

And in case I forget, it wakes me in the morning as it does every morning now. Nausea. Sickness. Long minutes of retching that is like a discipline, a punishment, until finally, finished with retching my body growls, ready to eat.

Eating soothes it. Only then can I begin to forget the Other Thing. Pretend to forget.

Outside, it's raining again – hard. Makes the letters arrive so wet I can't even open them. I have to hang them up around the kitchen on pegs to dry. Hours of rain, water that washes endlessly out of the sky, while our valley collects it, like a bucket.

It means I can't go outside.

But I've thought of a way to please Tom. Upstairs, in the baby's old room, he has already been at work. Ripped away the blue wallpaper, torn friezes of ducklings into strips for the bonfire. You can stand there now and never guess there was ever a baby here. I could carry on the job. Finish what he started.

I can do this because I know exactly what he wants. I've seen the blueprint he carries in his head. Bare, shiny floors and grainy walls; a fall of Egyptian cotton at the windows. Blonde wooden furniture and acres of smooth linen, just like in the organic hotel. And placed here and there, something that looks like art.

The only thing missing will be a mental asylum close by, with walls to swallow up the sun and stories of women who kill their own children.

Upstairs then, I prise lids off tins, and think of the people who will sleep here when it's done. Charlie and Jen, of course. Who will say they like it, admire the blonde sheen – while all the time thinking longingly of home, and walls covered with fingermarks, and ordinary curtains that won't carry a single jammy smear for ever, like the mark of Cain. Charlie, unbelievably clumsy outside the confines of an operating theatre, will spill tea on the sheets.

Babies won't be allowed in here.

Halfway through the morning I remember the mail. Nearly all of it is for Tom. Invitations to galleries and private openings, champagne launch parties for financial products in the City. That all stopped when he came down here. Now he's back at the head of the magazine and back on top of the mailing lists.

There's an invitation for me too, although mine is more by way of a summons. The clinic has sent dates for a whole battery of tests and, citing my age, recommends I take them all. This I put in a drawer. Out of sight, out of mind.

It's still raining.

I would rather be outside.

But the downpour doesn't stop. Not now it's started.

Two days on and it's raining still – harder than ever. Beats on the corrugated iron of the outhouse like twenty madmen sitting on the roof.

And now something is happening at the foot of the lane.

Overnight, a pool of liquid has appeared. It was there when I woke up, and ever since has crept steadily across the lawn. It's come down from the top of the lane – a growing lake of soil and fertilisers that's been rinsed off the fields above, to end up here, in our valley like in some vast run-off.

It's red and it stinks.

Is this something else no one told us? To expect an annual flood of chemicals, expensive detritus to foul up our land? It would explain the size of those great bulky leaves that continue to sprout beside the river: thick blotchy stalks bloated with nitrogen sap. Nothing organic about them.

Meanwhile I have run out of milk. And bread. And butter. I am going to have to drive through both run-off and rain to get them. It's different for Tom. Joaquin has ordered his cleaning woman to keep the fridge stocked just for him. Wine, French cheeses, breads. He doesn't have to lift a finger.

The lane is like a water chute, as I knew it would be. A stinking stream in full flood that makes the car bounce from bank to bank, crushing the ferns against the sides.

In the village, the car slews to a halt and I run into Tremaine's, bringing the weather with me – only to bump straight into Mary Coryn wearing a see-through plastic mac, all misted on the inside like a boil-in-the-bag meal. Despite being on her way out, she changes her mind when she sees me. Goes to stand by Evie simply so she can watch me wander between the shelves. Doesn't take her eyes off me.

Quickly I lever apples and oranges from cardboard trays. If I take too long in choosing, she'll say I'm picky, hold that against me too. But oh! she makes me long for Mr Georghiu, for a shop filled with aubergines and halva and Polish biscuits. Mr Georghiu also used to watch me as I shopped, but for different reasons. If he thought I'd made a bad choice of anything – an apple, a cauliflower – he would march me straight back to the pile and choose a better one for me himself.

But then a most surprising thing: the same happens here.

For when I arrive at the till, Mary Coryn leans across my basket and taps at the nearest piece of fruit. 'That one's gone soft, look. Evie, get her a nice one.'

And straight away Evie flips the orange out of the basket, goes off to find me another.

I take the new piece of fruit, almost too surprised to be

grateful. But Mary Coryn is watching me closer still, makes no bones about it. And it's not just her. Evie pretends to concentrate on the till, but the truth is, she's watching me too. Two women with nothing better to do than stare.

Heat rises in my cheeks. I need to bite my tongue, stop myself saying something rude. But then I look again. There's something different here. It's there in the way they both stand and look at me. For a moment I can't place it. And then I do.

They are smiling at me.

'So, how are you getting on down there? Suiting you is it, the quiet life?'

This is Mary Coryn. Her voice has become light, edged with...warmth. To claim surprise would be understating. I have to struggle to keep the wonder out of my own voice.

'Oh yes. Of course, it's hard work. These things always are, but I...that's to say, we...'

Something has gone wrong. I can't seem to finish the sentence. Everything that was meant to carry on from that *we* has vanished. Instead, my eyes drift towards the window where the rain beats down; and beyond the window to the churchyard where Coryns and Tremaines have gathered these last two hundred years, where everyone belongs except us.

Suddenly realising there is no *we*.

There was when we came here, Tom and I, but not anymore. Tom has gone, and I am alone. I'll pay for my bread, my milk, my fruit, then I will go home to a house where there is no one else but me. I will eat alone, sleep alone, with only the body I no longer own for company. This is what I have done. I had a choice, and I let it slip away.

Now there is no *we*.

To my horror, a tear slides down the side of my face. It happens before I've realised, before I can stop it or hide it. Now Mary Coryn has seen and no doubt it will make her smile. Something else she can scorn.

But I'm wrong.

'Oh no, pet.' Mary Coryn's voice is so soft, it takes my breath away. 'No, no, no. You mustn't be like that.' Beside her Evie clears her throat quietly, sympathetically.

But it's no good. I'm leaking even more. Mary's voice has disarmed me. *Pet*, she called me. Softness where I least expected it.

'It's like that with some folk,' Mary is saying. 'Sometimes I'd cry for no reason, no reason at all. Not that I ever carried to term, not once. Five times in all and I sobbed through all of them.'

Now I stare at her. Blankly, because it takes a moment to understand what she has just told me. She's letting me hear about babies that never got born, who made Mary cry all the time she carried them inside her. Five times of crying. And yet I never even wondered if she had children. I just assumed she did. Children, grandchildren. Maybe even great-grandchildren.

'Oh.' My voice is faint.

Softly, Evie pushes in the till, and here we are, the three of us. It occurs to me now: the reason Mary is always here. Mary would have known Evie since she was tiny, someone else's baby. It's Evie that Mary keeps coming to see, like a grown-up child who is still loved. Someone else's child. I always wondered why she was always here. Now I know.

'How did you know about me? How did you know I was pregnant?'

Mary says, 'Evie had John Marsh in here yesterday. He told her about finding you flat out in your vegetable patch. Worried about you, he was. Fretting that he ought to have stayed. Didn't like it, leaving you all by yourself.'

'It's because you were alone,' offers Evie. 'He was afraid anything could happen. But it was all right.' She sounds triumphant. 'I told him about you and your husband. How normally there's both of you down there, day in, day out. He was happy then, hearing that. He stopped worrying.'

Mary nods. 'Everything's different when you've got folk around, keeping an eye.'

'Completely different,' echoes Evie. And both of them smile at me. Because they think I have folk, and there will always be someone to keep an eye.

'Different from what?'

The two women look at me, as if astonished I have to ask.

'Well...from if you were by yourself,' says Evie at last. 'That's what got to Carole in the end, wasn't it Mary? Not having John around. If he'd been there more, who knows, she might never—'

But Mary has pressed her lips together and with a blush Evie snaps her mouth shut.

It's the same old story – keep the Outsider in the dark. Treat me like the foreigner I am. Or is it? I look from the one to the other, and suddenly I'm wondering if there might not be another reason. Mary called me *pet*. Evie is watching me with eyes as soft as wool. Maybe there's another reason they might want to keep a story to themselves.

What if it's not the Marshes they're protecting now? What if it's me? Because I'm pregnant, and pregnant women shouldn't hear about children who are lost, or about the river that takes them. There are things you don't want a woman who is about to be a mother to know. Never want her to know.

Maybe I should be grateful. I am grateful. For softness where I least expected it. Warmth when I needed it most.

At the door, though, I turn. 'You're wrong about Tom, I'm afraid. He's not going to be around actually. Not for the next few months. He's having to be in London most of the week.

Not so different for me after all. Something I share with Carole Marsh.

And look at the effect. Evie's mouth drops open in dismay as she turns to Mary.

Outside the shop, I'm fumbling for the car key when there's a touch on my arm. It's Mary Coryn, rain pattering noisily on her plastic coating. She has hurried out of the shop after me, doesn't even have her shopping with her.

She comes to stand between me and the car, small and severe in her rain gear.

'You got parents, Sara? Brothers? Sisters?'

'No.'

'No one to come and stay with you, down there? Give you a bit of company while your husband's away?'

I shake my head. Remembering Jen who wanted just this from me. A bit of company.

'Well then, you listen to me,' she says. 'Listen to me hard. Starting from today, if you need anything, anything at all, you come to me. Or Evie. Or…or…' She stops, looks around us for inspiration – and finds it.

shouldn't hear about children who are lost, or about the river that takes them. There are things you don't want a woman who is about to be a mother to know. Never want her to know.

Maybe I should be grateful. I am grateful. For softness where I least expected it. Warmth when I needed it most.

At the door, though, I turn. 'You're wrong about Tom, I'm afraid. He's not going to be around actually. Not for the next few months. He's having to be in London most of the week.

Not so different for me after all. Something I share with Carole Marsh.

And look at the effect. Evie's mouth drops open in dismay as she turns to Mary.

Outside the shop, I'm fumbling for the car key when there's a touch on my arm. It's Mary Coryn, rain pattering noisily on her plastic coating. She has hurried out of the shop after me, doesn't even have her shopping with her.

She comes to stand between me and the car, small and severe in her rain gear.

'You got parents, Sara? Brothers? Sisters?'

'No.'

'No one to come and stay with you, down there? Give you a bit of company while your husband's away?'

I shake my head. Remembering Jen who wanted just this from me. A bit of company.

'Well then, you listen to me,' she says. 'Listen to me hard. tarting from today, if you need anything, anything at all, you ome to me. Or Evie. Or...or...' She stops, looks around us or inspiration – and finds it.



grateful. But Mary Coryn is watching me closer still, makes no bones about it. And it's not just her. Evie pretends to concentrate on the till, but the truth is, she's watching me too. Two women with nothing better to do than stare.

Heat rises in my cheeks. I need to bite my tongue, stop myself saying something rude. But then I look again. There's something different here. It's there in the way they both stand and look at me. For a moment I can't place it. And then I do.

They are smiling at me.

'So, how are you getting on down there? Suiting you is it, the quiet life?'

This is Mary Coryn. Her voice has become light, edged with...warmth. To claim surprise would be understating. I have to struggle to keep the wonder out of my own voice.

'Oh yes. Of course, it's hard work. These things always are, but I...that's to say, we...'

Something has gone wrong. I can't seem to finish the sentence. Everything that was meant to carry on from that *we* has vanished. Instead, my eyes drift towards the window where the rain beats down; and beyond the window to the churchyard where Coryns and Tremaines have gathered these last two hundred years, where everyone belongs except us.

Suddenly realising there is no *we*.

There was when we came here, Tom and I, but not anymore. Tom has gone, and I am alone. I'll pay for my bread, my milk, my fruit, then I will go home to a house where there is no one else but me. I will eat alone, sleep alone, with only the body I no longer own for company. This is what I have done. I had a choice, and I let it slip away.

Now there is no *we*.

To my horror, a tear slides down the side of my face. It happens before I've realised, before I can stop it or hide it. Now Mary Coryn has seen and no doubt it will make her smile. Something else she can scorn.

But I'm wrong.

'Oh no, pet.' Mary Coryn's voice is so soft, it takes my breath away. 'No, no, no. You mustn't be like that.' Beside her Evie clears her throat quietly, sympathetically.

But it's no good. I'm leaking even more. Mary's voice has disarmed me. *Pet*, she called me. Softness where I least expected it.

'It's like that with some folk,' Mary is saying. 'Sometimes I'd cry for no reason, no reason at all. Not that I ever carried to term, not once. Five times in all and I sobbed through all of them.'

Now I stare at her. Blankly, because it takes a moment to understand what she has just told me. She's letting me hear about babies that never got born, who made Mary cry all the time she carried them inside her. Five times of crying. And yet I never even wondered if she had children. I just assumed she did. Children, grandchildren. Maybe even great-grandchildren.

'Oh.' My voice is faint.

Softly, Evie pushes in the till, and here we are, the three of us. It occurs to me now: the reason Mary is always here. Mary would have known Evie since she was tiny, someone else's baby. It's Evie that Mary keeps coming to see, like a grown-up child who is still loved. Someone else's child. I always wondered why she was always here. Now I know.

'How did you know about me? How did you know I was pregnant?'



Mary says, 'Evie had John Marsh in here yesterd told her about finding you flat out in your vegetable Worried about you, he was. Fretting that he ought tc stayed. Didn't like it, leaving you all by yourself.'

'It's because you were alone,' offers Evie. 'He was a anything could happen. But it was all right.' She so triumphant. 'I told him about you and your husband. normally there's both of you down there, day in, day out was happy then, hearing that. He stopped worrying.'

Mary nods. 'Everything's different when you've got around, keeping an eye.'

'Completely different,' echoes Evie. And both of th smile at me. Because they think I have folk, and there w always be someone to keep an eye.

'Different from what?'

The two women look at me, as if astonished I have to as

'Well...from if you were by yourself,' says Evie at l 'That's what got to Carole in the end, wasn't it Mary? having John around. If he'd been there more, who knows, might never—'

But Mary has pressed her lips together and with a Evie snaps her mouth shut.

It's the same old story – keep the Outsider in the Treat me like the foreigner I am. Or is it? I look from t to the other, and suddenly I'm wondering if there mi be another reason. Mary called me *pet*. Evie is watcl with eyes as soft as wool. Maybe there's another rea might want to keep a story to themselves.

What if it's not the Marshes they're protecti What if it's me? Because I'm pregnant, and pregnar

'Reg!' Her voice rings out above the rain with the high-pitched, chippy sound of the elderly when they need to raise their voices.

I turn round. Across the road an old man is walking beside an equally old dog. It's the man I have seen sitting next to Mary, manoeuvring his car in and out of his drive.

Mary beckons and, unhurried, he comes. Crossing the road, not so much obedient, as obliging.

Mary is brisk in her introductions. 'This is Sara, Reg. You've heard Evie and me talking about her. She's living down the Old Lane, in the Marshes' house.'

Reg nods. For a moment I am more fascinated by his clothes than him. He's wearing a tweed jacket, so old and so weathered it has a patina of its own. Raindrops bounce and slide off, unable to keep a purchase. A tweed cap does the same job. Not all of Tom's expensive wet-weather gear could do the work of this old jacket.

Beneath the cap Reg is smiling, although not much. Old brown eyes cool as they take me in. Polite but restrained, the way I'm used to round here.

Mary says, 'We've got to keep an eye on her, Reg. She's in the family way, and she's all by herself down there.'

It's as if a light has been switched on. Reg's face creases into a proper smile reminiscent of Mr Georghiu's. 'Expecting are you? Glad to hear it. Always glad to hear it.'

Almost imperceptibly, his hand touches his wife's arm. And I remember: five times of crying and never a baby. I am learning about this place and the people in it.

Mary's eyes have turned to mine. Deep blue I see they

are now. Sharp eyes that measure the world, reminding me suddenly of Marietta's.

Her hand is gripping my arm. 'You know where to come, then? When you need anything, you know where we are?'

She is almost fierce. I nod. Only then does she let go of my arm and release me from that blue stare.

Now when I drive, I hardly notice the rain. Too busy thinking about Mary and the sudden softness. About change.

It's happened because of the Other Thing. Because I'm alone.

~

# Chapter Fourteen

'Well it's not as if we didn't expect it, Sara. It's a wet part of the world. Rain falls and this happens. Après moi le déluge. It'll pass.'

'If you could only see it, Tom...'

But Tom barely has the patience for this. I have done all I can. I have told him about the septic froth that has spread, the stink which seems to have developed a life of its own. Last night it peeled away from the surface to drift over the Valley. Now, a creature in its own right, it hovers permanently outside the door, like a dog eager to come in.

But he is talking to me from within the clean white walls of his office, the scent of fresh coffee drifting up from the Italian cafe downstairs. He can't imagine any of this. And doesn't see why he should. He asks:

'Does the river look like it's about to break its banks?'

'No – I told you. The river has scarcely risen. We're being flooded from the land. It's coming from above, not below. It makes it worse somehow. There's so much coming down that lane. Chemicals and muck and—'

'Oh Sara, how can it be worse? If it had been the river, then we'd have a problem. Imagine the damage that would do. You're letting a bit of weather get to you. A bit of mud.'

There's a silence, the sort that happens all the time now, when the distance between us seems to yawn and deepen. A gulf into which I throw an offering.

'I'm working on that room upstairs. The blue one. I've got rid of the rest of the wallpaper, and sanded the skirting boards and—'

'No,' he says curtly. 'Stop. Just leave it.'

'Leave it? But I thought—'

'I've got plans for that room.'

'I know. That's why—'

'Listen to me.' His voice is stony. 'I want something, Sara – just one thing that's mine. I want that room to be mine. Everything in it. I want it...I want it the way I want it.'

'Tom—'

'Is that too much to ask? You're getting everything you want. Is this too much, Sara?'

'No.' My own voice is faint.

'If you want to do me a favour, finish off the kitchen. There's more paint in the outhouse. Get rid of those damned marks once and for all.'

There's another silence, which neither of us tries to fill.

So now, in front of me, a little girl grows taller.

Two-year-old Mandy. Three, then four-year-old Mandy. But after that, she stops. Doesn't grow another inch. Soon she won't be there at all. One sweep of the brush and she will be gone. A child who grew, until all growing stopped.

It's time to lift the brush, make her disappear for good.

At the same time, I am listening. Trying to detect a shift in the rain, a pause – anything that might hint of letting up. If it would only stop raining, I would go outside. Leave the marks as they are. Let her grow another day.

But the rain has no intention of stopping. And anyway, I was forgetting. If I went outside now, the stink of the run-off would be at my throat, making my eyes and mouth sting. It would make me sick. As if I were not sick enough already. Nothing for me to do but paint.

But then, against all expectation, comes a change, a shift. Still the beating of rain, still the sound of water, but with something added, something bigger. Loud, and getting louder by the second. A sluicing, momentous clatter of things on the move. For a moment I cannot think what it can possibly be.

I drop the brush and run outside.

It's a small tidal wave. Channelled by the drive, it rolls over gravel, headed for the house; a frothing, foul-smelling red river, coming towards me. I need to jump out of its way before it arrives and soaks me with its filth. But before I can move, it plunges on and down, without so much as touching my feet. Past the porch, past the front of the house, it's making for the real river. Our river.

This is what has happened. The lake has burst. Tipped over the rim of the lawn and gathered into a fast-flowing stream. Now it has nowhere to go but down.

The clattering is the noise of things it's taking with it – planters, watering cans, old paint pots. One of Tom's wellington boots bobs past me, like a small green boat along with the rest, carried away with the flood.

I follow it all to the riverbank, where the path I cut through the undergrowth makes a final channel for the stream of frothing bilge water. And here it drains into the river, churning the waters where it enters, tainting them with red. But only briefly. The river rushes on and washes it all away, washes the Valley clean, while the rain, still falling, rinses away the traces.

As for those paint pots and bottles, the watering can and the planters, they are floating off in a wobbly line downstream. Gone for ever. I scramble down the bank to the river's edge to see them off, wave them a goodbye. A small price to pay.

After that I stand by the water. I'm soaked through, as wet as the trees. It doesn't matter. I need to go inside, phone Tom and tell him it's gone, the filthy lake spreading over his land. I'll be laughing as I tell him and maybe, just for a minute, we'll forget we have problems.

Then I remember. He won't care. He never saw the lake, wasn't willing to listen when I told him, so he couldn't even imagine what it was like. He'll just say he was right all along. The rain fell, things got washed away. Nothing to get excited about. No reason to smile.

The laughter dies in my throat. Nothing to do but to go back inside, and carry on painting. Cover up those marks. I turn my back on the river, prepare to climb back up the bank.

Yet it's not that easy. The place seems determined to make me stay. Halfway up, the ground slides under my feet, sends me skating backwards. I grab at bits of grass but they come away in my hands, so that I carry on slipping. By the time I stop sliding I'm further back than where I started. There's water lapping round my heels, and my hands are in the mud.

Which is how I come to see it...

There, in the mud, pale against the mud – it almost seems to shine. The way flesh would shine.

Too much the way of flesh. Already my teeth have begun to chatter. For here, in the soft mud of a river, is an arm. Dimpled at the elbow, narrowing to a wrist still hidden by weeds. More than just an arm. In a tangle of weeds and water and mud, there's a dress here. Hair. The faint sheen of more flesh.

How long do I stare? If it was only the normal space between heartbeats, then not long. But I do believe that in that instant my heart stopped dead. Inside me, only silence. Empties and fills and empties again.

Then my heart thumps. And Time begins again.

It's a doll. Caught up in weeds and washed by the river, only a doll. Yet even now it's an act of will to pick her up. Not quite ready to believe, I have to touch her to know. The hardness of plastic, the rigidity of not-flesh. Only then am I convinced.

She is half the length of my arm with a calm, lifelike face, and long brown hair draggled by mud. A sodden tartan dress that clings. The flood must have found her and carried her here with everything else – the boot and the pots and planters. Except that, unlike them, the river made an exception. It let her stay.

Unless she didn't come with the flood. Unless she was here all the time, close to the river's edge, as close as it's possible to be. The moment the thought occurs, I am sure. She was here. This is where she belongs.

And now I have her. There is mud on her scalp, mud in the rims of her eyes. She smells of water, of the river. Her fingers curl like a baby's, her mouth is pursed and wet, a reminder of those other dolls, all those weeks ago, lined up in a tidy row on a shelf in a pink room but untouched by water, undamaged.

What do I do with her? I never played with dolls when I was young. Creature of Marietta, I was more familiar with Balinese puppets or voodoo fetishes. They never made me think they were anything other than what they were, never made my flesh crawl with the suggestion of more flesh.

Doll in hand I scramble up the bank, and this time I take the greatest care not to slip.

Up on the path, though, I'm at a loss. I stand with my back to the river, turning her over in my hands. What am I to do with her?

*Give her back.*

Words like a whisper in my ear. And of course, that's the answer. Give her back. It's all I need to do. It's simple. Turn and smile as I hand her over, because who wouldn't smile as they gave a doll back to the child who'd lost her?

Turning, already smiling – only when I have turned full circle, do I remember. And still I turn, and turn again, even though I know:

There is no child. There is no one here but me.

Except there is. I stop turning and listen.

It's the river that tells you. Tells me. And what it says makes the nerves fail in my fingers and the doll drop to the ground, sends it rolling back down the slope to the river's edge – where it belongs.

*Listen.*

No. I've clapped my hands over my ears, blocking out

the river's noise. But it's too late. My body, that stranger, has already heard. And understood. It sends its messages to my brain, pricking out the words on the backs of my hands. Triumphant and treacherous because it knows something I don't.

*Stupid. Haven't you understood even now?*

River clatters by my feet, makes words of its own. Syllables knocked out of stones. Everything is telling me.

*Not a mind child. Not even a dream child.*

But I don't want to understand.

*Did you really think you were alone?*

Down by the river, the doll stares up at me through half-shut eyes, a glimmer of water under the lashes. It knows. Everything knows. Mandy's doll gives me a look that makes me whimper with terror.

I've been wrong. Thinking I created her, thinking I put her here, beside the river – Mandy, my mind child. Padded out and given shape by the image of an old dream. Something to be sad about, but never more than that. And all the time I was wrong. I didn't put her here. She belongs here. A real child. No living child. Something the river took.

Only then she came back. That's what she wanted me to know.

Mandy's still here.

# Chapter Fifteen

Tom's train pulls in, and I am on the platform waiting. When I see him I run, pitching towards him. I want him to catch me, hold me…

And it's as if he counts to three. Tom goes very still, then carefully steps out of my arms. We drive home in silence.

At the bottom of the lane, he says, 'So, where was the flood?'

I point. 'Right there. It stank.'

'I can't smell anything.' He gets out of the car and slams the door.

When I join him, he is standing in the kitchen studying the wall. He nods. 'You got it done then. You finally painted over the damn marks.'

But I can't look at the empty patch beside the door. Instead I go to pour him some wine, hand him a glass. He takes it, and this time lets his eye play briefly over me. Unsmiling, he says, 'It doesn't suit you, you know.'

'What?'

'This thing, what you're doing. You look tired. Older.' He sips, swallows. 'I'm only telling you what I see. If you're going ahead with the…the Other Thing, you should at least try and look after yourself.'

'I didn't sleep last night, that's probably why I look like this.'

'Well if it's a question of not sleeping…' He shakes his head and drinks the rest of his wine in one. He's letting me know that sleep hasn't come easy to him either.

Yet neither of us asks the other what has been keeping us awake. Probably Tom thinks he knows. Certain that what plagues him, drives away sleep, is the same as what plagues me.

'Done any more work outside?' he says.

'No. It's been raining so much.'

'I thought you said it stopped a couple of days ago.'

This time I don't answer. The rain did stop, but I have stayed inside. Outside is where *she* is. Where the river is. And I…

It doesn't matter, though. He's not interested. He goes upstairs to change and doesn't see that my hands are shaking. It's what they do now, all the time: shake.

But when he comes back down, he's in a better mood, wearing the mock shabby clothes of a man returned to the land, stepping into the part. I remember how he eyed Charlie's old panama, wishing he had one of his own. Something battered in the right way, looking as if it belonged to him.

I was going to wait until after his second, perhaps his third glass of wine. But the words come in spite of me, before he's even poured himself another. 'I want to come back with you next week. To London, just for a few days.'

He frowns and puts the bottle down.

'I told you about not sleeping. Well, I would sleep – if I wasn't by myself, if I was with you. Let me be with you next week.'

And it's absurd. I am blushing. Telling Tom I want to sleep with him, be with him – it makes me blush.

But maybe I have a reason. Because here is Tom, frowning again, as if somehow the question is an embarrassment to us both. 'Sorry. You can't do that.'

'Why not?'

'Joaquin's come over from Portugal for one thing. I've just spent the last few days with him, and it's been fine. We get on. He's told me to stay on in the flat even while he's here.'

'But I could—'

'No, you couldn't, not just now. He'd think we were taking advantage. Like I said – sorry.'

He's not sorry. Tom reaches across me to retrieve the bottle. Avoids my eye.

Later, though, he softens. Maybe it's because I haven't argued with him. He smiles and leans into me, begins to tell me about his week, about Joaquin's relief to have him back running his magazine, his big expensive clock.

'Sometimes you have to walk away just so people can know what they're losing. So they can appreciate you. God, I should have done it years ago.'

Do what? Walk away, just so he could walk back? I say nothing. I want him to stay like this, softened by wine, by homecoming. I even get my wish: for the next hour, the Other Thing seems to hold no sway. Tom is perfectly happy.

It confuses me, at the same time as it feeds a hope. Perhaps all it takes is time...

We settle down in front of the television, linked on the sofa like in our old days, watching anything that passes on the box. But halfway through the evening something happens to the TV. The picture continues but the sound dies away to mute, leaving the actors to mouth their words in a vacuum. Tom twiddles the knobs, then gives up.

'Never mind,' he says. 'We'll go to bed.' He smiles at me.

He's still smiling as he pulls back the covers, his eyes expectant. I climb in, turn off the light and immediately the dark grows warm around us.

Different from last night, when I lay, staring into this same dark until my eyes ached. All night long the river flowed, tried to call me to the window, offering to share all kinds of secrets. I pulled the covers over my head, and still I didn't sleep.

Now I turn and reach for Tom. Tonight I am not alone...

And he freezes.

'Tom?'

He shakes his head. He is moving away from me in the bed.

'Tom, what is it?'

'Do I really have to spell it out, Sara?'

'But all this evening you've been happy—'

'Yeah well, I forgot, didn't I? Blame the wine. Now I've remembered and you...you don't look the same.' He hesitates, then says, 'Look at it my way. I didn't choose this, Sara. None of this is down to me.'

After that we lie in the dark, until he falls asleep, snoring faintly because of the wine. Yet even this is better, safer, than being alone. And when I wake again, Tom's arm is thrown across my neck. In his sleep, he has forgotten once more. He is clinging to me, almost throttling me. It's the old grip, hard and fast, as he fights to stay afloat.

A case of sink or swim.

* * *

After breakfast, I wait for him to put on his boots and go outside, start up the rotovator, the electric saws, and fill the air with noise, leaving no room for anything else. I'm ready to love the sound of machines again.

Yet Tom doesn't move. He stays in his dressing gown, puts on another pot of coffee.

'Aren't you going to work outside?' I ask him at last.

The question astonishes him. 'Sara, I've been working all week. That is when I've not been sitting on a fucking train for hours. Most people would say that was enough.'

'I just thought—'

'Yeah. You thought.'

Now he sits with his laptop, scrolling through bathroom sites. He's looking for a bathroom identical to Joaquin's with granite tiles and chrome pipes. Frowns as he peers into the screen, makes lists. Ignores me.

But at least he is flesh and blood. Resentment seeps from him, makes him real, all too solid. Makes me dare to think nothing else could exist alongside. Least of all ghosts.

Makes me almost brave. I will go outside, where she is.

Leaves are dying on the trees.

Changing colour, turning red and yellow. When they fall, they will dance and spin like so many bright Brazilian frocks. They will fill the air, touch my face like the skirts of small dresses. I know now: this is how a child – no living child – is able to be everywhere.

This is her place. She was here before we came. This is where she belongs. I have to force myself not to run back to the house, to Tom.

Instead I wait. This is where she should be now, the thing that moves and flickers in the corner of my eye. Any moment she will come. I'll feel her. Already my skin has become thin, ready for her touch; for breath that lights on my neck.

Leaves twist. Sun darts between clouds. Birds fly and crows caw. But where is it – the touch that signals her arrival, the extra beat of my heart? It doesn't happen. Nothing happens.

She's not here.

Is it because of Tom? He is inside the house frowning over bathrooms, over pipes and shower trays. If I went and mentioned ghosts to him now, he would look at me as if I had gone mad. And he'd be right. Plumbers and adults – they do not believe in ghosts.

Relief. Washes over me like a warm rain.

This is what Tom's done with his websites and his tiles. By a feat of the banal, he has made her utterly impossible. And not just her, but every ghost and ghoul and undead thing that ever walked. There is nothing to be afraid of.

I should run inside now and hug him even though he'll frown. Surprise him with warmth. Softness where he least expects it.

But then...

Then I hear it. The river. Quiet at first, it grows. Louder, then louder still, making sure I hear. Different voices rising and falling, but all in agreement. All saying the same thing.

She's here.

Cold flares along my arms. A leaf spirals past my face, yellow shot through with red. What drove me from the river, drives me now. Terror. And in terror, I run.

Inside the house, I drive the bolt home and lean against

the door. Upstairs I can hear noises. Tom has moved to the bathroom, is busy with his measuring tape. There's the sound of water running in the pipes. Tom, the would-be plumber, has a head full of plans. His next project.

'What are you doing?'

It's Monday and Tom – washed, dressed and ready for the train – is frowning at the bag on the bed and the clothes I am stuffing into it.

'Coming with you.'

I pull the zip on the bag. It catches.

Tom watches me struggle a moment. He says, 'We talked about that. Not this week.'

But he's wrong. Apart from the evening he arrived, we haven't talked at all. We have worked, painted, eaten, slept in silence. Strangers would have more to say to each other.

And yet there have been moments when I have caught him looking bewildered, utterly confused. Saturday, he walked into the bathroom while I was taking a bath, and stopped dead, seeing a woman grown so thin as to be nearly skeletal. A hollowed-out space cradled between her hips.

And he couldn't help himself. 'Sara, are you sure that you are actually...?' He'd expected a slow fattening up, a blossoming at his expense, and that's not happening. The Other Thing grows by feeding off me like a worm, takes what little fat I had. And now there's something else to gnaw me away: fear.

'I have to come with you, Tom.'

'I told you. Joaquin's there. It's his place. You can't just come waltzing in.'

The zip frees and the bag closes. 'I can't stay here, Tom. Not by myself.'

He sighs, checks his watch. Moves the bag to the floor and sits beside me on the bed.

'What's this all about, Sara? I told you the problem. I'm not by myself there. Come with me, sure – but another time, when Joaquin's not around.'

'I'm frightened.' The words wrench themselves out of me. For the first time in days, our eyes meet.

'Frightened? What the hell is there to be frightened of?' Then he stops. A thought has entered his head. Makes him brighter, suddenly altogether gentler. 'Is it the Other Thing? Are you having second thoughts? Is that what's frightening you?'

He watches me, hopeful, willing the answer to be yes.

'No.'

His face falls. There's a silence, then he jumps off the bed again. 'Well it doesn't make any sense. I tell you something's impossible and you ignore me. Like...like you ignore everything else.'

'But it's true. I'm frightened, Tom.'

'Oh yes?' He aims a kick at the bag. 'And what exactly are you frightened of? It's not having a kid that scares you, that's for sure. And it's not the fact that you're killing every good thing we ever had – that doesn't worry you at all. And it's definitely not the terror of going ahead with something that neither, neither of us have ever wanted. So what is it you're frightened of, Sara?'

What am I frightened of? A child. No living child.

'A child?' barks Tom. '*What child?*'

Hearing him, I blink. I hadn't even realised I had said the words aloud.

Then I see the look in his face. He is bewildered, as confused as it's possible to be. And who can blame him? This is Tom. Who for ten years has told me every thought that has passed through his skull. Rehearsed every problem, every hope and fear. For ten years I have listened to him. And in return, what have I told him?

Almost nothing. Child of Marietta, there was nothing I needed him to know, not after that first confession: that both of us were orphans. Now look at the result: he hardly knows me. It's not even his fault.

Perhaps I should tell him now, exactly what I am frightened of. How else could he possibly understand? How else can he help me?

I need him to help me.

'Tom?'

'What?'

And keeping my voice steady, I begin to speak. I tell him the story I told myself. About the child taken by a river and the people who lost her. About how first I thought I imagined her, and only now do I understand. I tell him what it means, knowing she is here – *here* – the child the river took. No living child. I tell him everything, but most important of all, I tell him what she has done to me, waking something that will not leave me. Always there now.

It's fear. Fear of a...

'A *ghost*,' says Tom. There's wonder in his voice. 'You're telling me you're frightened of a ghost.'

I look away, afraid to meet his eyes. I have explained, kept nothing back. Now all I can do is wait. Is Tom about to step toward me, tell me to pick up my bag and come with him? Hold out his hand to me, not because he believes in ghosts, but because I believe. Insisting that I leave with him, stay with him until I stop believing and the fear, the lizard fear, goes away.

This is what I would do, if he were in my place. If all he wanted was to be with me, I would tell him to come with me. If all he wanted was my help, I would help him.

Then it comes, his answer.

'Oh for God's sake, Sara. It's not ghosts you should be afraid of. It's losing your entire fucking mind.'

And even though I expected it, I am not prepared for this – the sheer depth of contempt in his voice. Because not even Tom, who feels, expresses scorn for so many things – people, objects, styles – not even he has ever expressed a scorn as deep as this.

Blood wells up in my cheeks, spreads over my face and neck.

Tom sees it, thinks he knows the reason for it. Triumphant, he says, 'It's stupid, mad. You see, don't you? A ghost. You can't have expected me to believe that.'

And he's right – I never did expect him to believe. Not for a moment. What's making me blush is how little I expected of him – and how even then it was too much. I am blushing for him, for how little he has to give.

Only now look at him. Something has clicked, something is understood. Tom has stopped smiling. Already the contempt of a moment ago has gone, to be replaced by something else. Grows by the second as he begins to understand what it means for him to be right.

It means a Sara who's afraid, foolish. Nothing like the Sara he knows, relies upon. Constant as a mother who never lets him down, who has always known what to do. That Sara is gone. And it makes him reel. He's like a child who, after the first triumph of discovering his parents are no stronger or cleverer than he is, then realises the logic of what follows. There is no one bigger than him. No one he can rely on, no one to make everything right. Suddenly the world is infinitely more dangerous, and he is infinitely more alone.

I understand. I have always understood. He needs the Sara who tells him nothing more than he wants to know. Who he clings to in the night like a drowning man. It's the only way Tom can be Tom.

Now she's gone. Fear has driven her away – or is it madness? I watch him trying to work out which it is, and realising it doesn't matter. She's gone.

But look at the result. Already he is growing smaller, shrinking inside the expensive lines of his suit. His cuffs are too wide for him, his collar too expansive. Even the designer watch – another present from Joaquin – is too heavy for his wrist. And it doesn't stop. Every moment I am like this, he loses the thing that made him what he is, everything he has wanted to be true.

And in his eyes, panic. Pleading for me to come back, the woman he prefers not to know.

And what can I do? I've made him this way. I made him trust me when I coaxed. I made him believe he was the man he wanted to be. For ten years he has relied on what he needs to be true, and I have made it true. Now I have to do it again, or Tom will continue to shrink inside his clothes until there is nothing left.

I know what I have to do. I have to call on the switch. The smile. I am like John Marsh, knitting myself together so that the world can carry on as normal. It's what I do now. I switch. I smile. And force the words to come:

'Oh Tom, you're right! It's ridiculous – all of it. Forget what I said. Just forget everything. Of course I'm not afraid. What on earth is there to be afraid of?'

He glances at me, suspicious, still fearful. Not quite so foolish as to believe, not yet. He sits rigid on the bed, continues to shrink.

But the switch, the smile – they become easier by the moment. I look at my watch. 'Oh lord, look at the time. We need to get you to the train.'

And still he stares at me. I stand up and laugh at him.

'Tom! I'm all right. I told you, it was a stupid thing. Hormones, making me weird.'

'Hormones?' He repeats the word. And hope dawns in his eyes. 'You mean...?'

'I mean it's nothing. It's not going to happen again. I promise.'

I catch sight of myself in the mirror. My smile is cool, relaxed. The smile of a woman in charge of herself.

And it works. Relief washes over him. So intense, so heartfelt, he can barely contain himself. He pulls me to my feet and kisses me. 'That's my Sara. That's my girl.'

In the car, he glances at me now and then, checking that I'm still there, the Sara he thinks he knows. And finding her, gradually he relaxes, eases back into his seat.

At the station, he holds me, kisses me again. 'Listen – I want you to take it easy this week. Look after yourself a bit. I want you to be all right, Sara, I really do.'

His eyes are sincere. He means what he says. Of course he wants me to be all right. His entire life depends on it.

~

# Chapter Sixteen

In the village, I search for people: Mary or Evie, a familiar face, but there's no sign of anyone. The shop is closed. Evie is visiting the dentist.

But then I catch sight of Reg walking the short distance between his house and the churchyard. He's carrying a scythe and a can of weedkiller. He waves and I wave back.

'Proper autumn weather this is,' he calls out. 'Cold one minute, warm the next. You want to get outside, girl. It's perfect for working that vegetable patch of yours.'

And he's right. At the bottom of the lane, the sun ducks and darts behind clouds. A breeze ruffles the surface of the river, makes light dance on the water. But when I get out of the car, the breeze touches my neck, light-fingered and knowing.

She's here.

I scurry inside. Stand behind the door I have just locked and bolted. On impulse I reach for the phone, and far away Jen answers.

'Yes?'

The words come in a rush. 'Jen, it's Sara. You were right. I'm pregnant. It's why I couldn't come to you when you asked. I thought I was going to get rid of it, but I didn't. I kept it. Do you forgive me?'

A silence, then a shout rips from her.

It's the end of being alone. Jen picks up the folds of the map that separates us, pinches them together between finger and thumb. London pressed hard against Cornwall. Warmth floods along the wires. My ears are full of it. The warmth of Jen.

'So you did want a child, Sara. After everything you've said.'

'No – I'm like you, Jen. Just like you. I don't want it. But it doesn't seem to matter what I want. I had a choice, and I lost it.'

And I tell her how it was that day, taken to that underwater place, knowing she will understand. How one's body becomes a stranger, makes its own decisions and all one can do is watch, appalled, Jen will understand all this.

Or will she? Her reply is another silence, longer than the first. Then: 'But I do want it. I want it now. Oh God, Sara, I can't believe it. Suddenly I want it.'

She's talking about herself. Only herself. A hit of disappointment, so intense I am weak with it, makes the distance between us greater than it ever was. As if from another planet I hear her say:

'I knew this would happen. I knew I'd feel like this, if only you were pregnant too. Everything would seem like a miracle again, life starting over. I wanted you to be pregnant so much, Sara. I told you, remember?'

'I remember.' A pause. 'Jen, I have to go.'

But she's alert to me. 'No! Sara, don't. I know this isn't

what you wanted to hear from me. But it's the truth. You've made me so happy. No one else could have done this, no one.' She stops. 'You're not happy, though. I know that. But one day soon you will be. Things change, Sara. I promise you. I promise you they change.'

'Jen.' My voice is biting. 'How can you say that?'

'Because you're pregnant. If I was wrong, you wouldn't be.'

'What does that mean?'

'You say you'd decided on a termination, but your body decided on a child. Well, I think the body knows, Sara. If you truly hadn't wanted a child, you wouldn't still be pregnant now. You wouldn't have been able to stop yourself from ending it. You'd have gone ahead and had that abortion as you had every right to do. Your own legs, your own body, would have taken you where you had to be, made sure it happened.'

'Jen,' I say wearily. 'I don't know what you're talking about.'

'I'm trying to say that I don't think the body lies, Sara. It's the one part of our selves that can't hide the truth. Hungry, happy, thirsty, sad, the body knows what you need and lets you know. Sometimes it knows things before we do. And once you realise it knows what you want, then you stop feeling like a prisoner. You start realising the choice was yours all along. I'm trying to say you want this child, and you don't even know it.'

'And if you're wrong?'

'If I'm wrong, then it's the worst mistake I've ever made.'

For a moment neither of us speaks.

'Jen?'

'Yes?'

'Do you believe in ghosts?'

She laughs, taken by surprise. But she doesn't hesitate. 'No, of course not. Why on earth do you ask?'

And I can't tell her. If Jen had paused, if she had needed to think about the question –even for a second – I could have told her about ghosts. My ghost. But she didn't and so I can't tell her.

Why not? I'm not afraid of her laughing at me. Jen, when she is tickled, has a laugh that makes her sound like a friendly horse. But I am afraid of what would happen when the laughing stops and she looks at me more closely. Realises that I am not joking. That I truly believe that there is a ghost here. No living child.

She'd think I was mad. And mad people have no friends. It's because no one believes a word they say, even the folk who love them. And if no one believes you, then truly you are alone. Look at Tom and me.

I need her to be my friend, to believe the things I say. I am so close to losing Tom. I can't lose Jen.

So Mandy stays a secret.

Eventually we say goodbye, but after her voice the silence is appalling. Even the radio in the kitchen is dying. I turn up the volume, but it's no good, it needs more batteries; gradually the voices in the wireless vanish into nothing.

Which is how I hear it.

At first it's nothing. I have come to the kitchen, picked up a pencil and a measuring tape, pretending I can keep myself busy measuring for cupboards. It begins in the smallest way imaginable. A sound. Comes from inside the house. Comes from above.

It doesn't bother me; I'm so busy pretending to be busy and the sound is so small. Minutes pass and still I pay no heed. Finally, though, I put my pencil down and there it is again. Finally I listen.

It comes from the ceiling. Familiar. A noise I've heard in Jen's house. A noise Marietta would have heard, years ago. Pattering, scraping, scuffling. So faint you wonder what could be so small or so far away. It's the sound I hear now. Comes from the pink room.

Mandy's room.

The body knows things before we do. I look down at my hands. They have started to shake again.

I know this noise. I used to make it myself, playing tricks on Marietta. Knowing full well she was busy, teasing her, letting my footsteps patter and scrape until finally she noticed.

*Come and find me, Marietta.*

Come and find me. I try to steady my hands against the table.

I thought she belonged outside, to the river, the child the river took. I thought inside I was safe. But the body knows things…my hands fall away as my knees buckle, and I slide to the floor. Sink beneath another small flurry of sound.

*Come NOW.*

No.

*Find me.*

Folded against the ground now, head butted into the

kitchen wall, I clench my fists and cover my ears.

And the noises stop. The house is quiet.

Cautious, I let my fists fall away, and listen to the silence. A long, long minute of silence – then it comes again.

*Come and find me.*

A summons that arrives with a stab of pain, sharp. It pierces the centre of my right hand. I look down to find I have driven my pencil clean into the palm. Blood drips to the floor as slowly I get to my feet.

She cannot come inside. She belongs to the river. This is not her place.

It's what I tell myself: this is not her place. But how do I know that? Here on the landing, I don't know anything. A shaft of sunlight slants onto her bedroom door and this is where I put my hand, where the sun pales the wood. Blood runs down my wrist as I push open the door.

And the room is empty. As pink and achingly empty as the first day we saw it. The only things in here are Marietta's boxes. Side by side they stand, the lids battened down.

But the noises – the noises are still there. I can hear them better now. Scratching, gnawing, tapping, they come from inside the boxes still bearing their tags: *from the Ravenscroft Collection.*

I look at the boxes, and I'm not frightened anymore.

It takes a while to get them open, to lever out every last nail, but finally I lift the lid away from the first box.

And breathe. Dried blood, matted hair and earth dyes. Pungent and sweet.

Breathe again. The underlying rot of things that have been

preserved. Tanned hides, mummified skin. Acrid, catching in your throat.

Bones. Teeth. Claws.

These are Marietta's things. And this is the smell of my childhood. And that scratching, gnawing, tapping – is the sound of my childhood. Things that rattled and rolled even when there was no one in the room.

I just forgot, that's all. I have been grown-up for so long.

One by one I take them out of the boxes – masks from Kenya, heads from China. Fly switches from the Ivory Coast, voodoo dolls, fetishes and monkeys' claws.

And I remember them, each and every object. I roll the gourds along the floor, just like when I was a little girl. Toss knuckle bones into the air to see which way they land. Flick the drums, knowing they will vibrate long after I leave the room.

And all the while, motes of dust rise out of the boxes, coat the back of my tongue. I breathe and swallow at the same time – particles of skin and bone, human hair and blood.

And I feel safe. Safer than I ever felt when Tom was here.

At the bottom of the second box, I find what I've been looking for: a nest of baby mice. Newborn, they are curled around each other, hairless and blind. Their parents are nowhere to be seen. They'll be hiding, waiting for me to disappear. When I go, they will start running again under the floorboards, making the noises I heard before. Not children, but mice – always mice in Marietta's house. I take the greatest care putting everything back, sorry for these babies. Probably they will die. There is nothing to eat here. Only skin and bone.

So why do I feel safe, not frightened anymore? How can blood and matted hair – old magic – make fear go away? It's because at long last I've remembered: everything I let myself forget in all the years I've been with Tom.

Marietta explained – long, long ago when I was still young enough to understand. Making sure I never had to be afraid. As usual, Marietta explained everything.

Everything has power. Every thing. The masks, the skulls, the statues, the heads. Even the netsuke in my bedroom, my family of tiny Japanese demons, carved and set out like a chess set. Even the porcelain cat that sat on her desk, next to her papers and the picture of my mother.

Especially the cat, with its painted eyes and oriental smile. Of all her objects, this was Marietta's favourite. She'd touch it as she worked, her hands long and sinewy, forever ink stained.

This is what she told me: if something has eyes, it can see. If it has ears it will listen. It's where the Dead are to be found. They slip behind the masks, gather in the crevices of bony skulls and there they look and listen. The people who made the masks and kept the skulls, they knew that, they knew what they were doing. They were keeping the Dead close, keeping them friendly. Letting them keep watch.

Everything has power, Marietta said, if it is made with the Dead in mind. And now I remember what I had almost forgotten: I grew up with the Dead, and I never was afraid.

It's Marietta's hands I remember best, flitting across the objects on her desk. Touching her porcelain cat. Marietta taught me how to live with the Dead. Now, thirty years on, I glance at my own hands. They are the same shape as Marietta's, and they have stopped shaking.

What will happen now, if I go outside?

This.

Sun shines, river flows. Trees nod and send the leaves spinning. Yellow, shot through with red, they touch my face as they fall. And I am not alone. She is everywhere. I can feel her: Mandy. Trees, river – this is her place.

Just for a moment, it's back: the fear, urging me to run inside and bolt the door, put myself where she cannot follow me. Safe between four walls. Safe and trapped and frightened.

Then I think of Marietta, and Marietta's things. Masks that watched and listened while I never gave them a thought, because this was how you live with the Dead.

I think of the child I was, and slowly the fear crawls back into its hiding place. Settles in the base of my spine and goes to sleep. Leaves spin, breeze touches my neck – but we can share this place, she and I. We have no choice.

I've got my tools with me, my trowel and my fork. The earth is heavy, almost impossibly clogged after all the rain. But it smells the way earth should, and catches my fork with the old tug, pulls me closer.

I am Marietta's girl. I can do this. I can stop being afraid.

~

# Chapter Seventeen

And now Tom is coming home again. It's Thursday already.

How did that happen? I knew about the hours, the way they could disappear, one minute flowing into the next. But days? Who would have thought that days could vanish in the same way?

Now he's stepping off the train.

He puts down his bag and stands, watching me walk towards him. Perhaps he'd been dozing when the train stopped, because he looks flustered, as if the journey has ended sooner than he'd expected. Now, caught off guard, he has to think whether to be warm or cold. Hostile or friendly. Can't remember which impression he had decided to make.

So I make the decision for him. I stop, turn on my heels and march back to the car. I'm already there, sitting behind the wheel when he arrives.

He throws in his bag and gets in beside me.

'What's the matter with you?'

'Nothing.' I start up the car.

'You saw me coming and you just walked away.'

'You didn't look ready. I thought I'd give you time to decide.'

'Decide about what?'

'Whether you were going to be friendly or not.'

He bristles. But then, having looked at me, he looks again. And for some reason, he closes his mouth. A minute later he touches my hand on the wheel. Apparently he wants to be friendly.

While he opens a bottle of wine, I go upstairs, to our bedroom. I need to know what Tom saw that made him change his mind, so that he turned from cold to conciliatory. And closed his mouth.

It's my face. For years, people have said we looked alike, Tom and I. Both of us tall and slim, both appearing to be younger than we really are. The well-rested look of people who have no children, Jen used to say. They wouldn't say that now. I see another resemblance. Something about the cheekbones and jaw. Sharper. Eyes turned inward – even now, when staring at myself. This is what Tom saw in the car. A face that somehow looks as if it should be seen in profile, intent on something else.

I look like Marietta. That's the resemblance. It's the difference less than a week makes, the difference of living with the Dead. It has changed the lines of my face. Now, inside and out, I match, just a little better.

Supper, and Tom helps me before helping himself. He's making an effort. He tells me about his week, about Joaquin and the strange club he took Tom to on Tuesday, where the women sit primly dressed, their ankles neatly crossed. Very beautiful women who talk about history and art and books, and sip from tiny glasses of clear liqueur not available for sale. No one gets drunk, huge tips are bestowed and no one leaves together. Tom's not sure, but he thinks Joaquin might own this club, and every woman there reflects what Joaquin would want in a woman, a lover.

I listen and for the first time in weeks my mind is snagged not by Mandy or the Other Thing, but Joaquin. Joaquin, whose mouth curved as in all seriousness he mocked me. Traces of heat where his skin touched mine.

What would Joaquin say if I asked if he believed in ghosts?

Tom has stopped talking. He's asked me a question and, distracted, I've said nothing in reply. He sighs and reaches to turn on the television instead. Looks aggrieved when all that comes is the picture.

'There's still no sound. Have you not got this fixed?'

I glance at it, vaguely surprised. I had forgotten it was broken. 'No.'

Impatient, he reaches for the radio and it too is silent. 'Sara, didn't it occur to you to get batteries even?'

'Yes,' I say. 'But then I...forgot.'

Tom is astonished. 'Good God, what did you do all week? No radio, no TV. Didn't you want to know what's going on in the world?'

I ponder this. 'No,' I say eventually. 'I suppose I didn't.'

He shakes his head in wonder, then turns back to the TV, tries to watch it without the sound, by reading people's lips. But even that has to stop. While he is trying to decipher the news, the picture disappears and he's left staring at an empty screen.

Monday morning, and once again we are standing by the train. A wind has blown up and here on the platform, as far from the coast as one can be in this county, it smells of the sea. Tom shivers and pulls at the collar of his coat.

'Listen,' he says. 'About last week, not being able to let you come – I'll try and fix something. See if I can't get you up to stay. You'd like that, wouldn't you?'

'Oh...yes. Thanks.'

But the truth is, I was thinking about something completely different. About being outside. At home the patch of soil is waiting and I'm wondering if this watery wind will bring more rain. Tom looks at me, then sighs and gets on the train, but inside the door, he turns. Reaches out to catch me by the arm.

'You've been like this all weekend. How long are you going to keep it up, Sara?'

'Keep what up?' Torn out of reverie, I am bewildered.

'Pretending you're not listening to a word I say. Acting like you don't care if I'm there or not.'

I open my mouth to protest, but he lets go of my arm and pulls the door towards him. It closes with a slam, so fast and so violent I only just manage to snatch my hand away in time. He stares through the glass, aghast at what he nearly did. At the same time, satisfied.

Now he's gone, and it's like having the day begin all over again. The car starts with a hiccup, as if eager to be moving. In Tremaine's, Evie tots up my bill. Naturally Mary is there.

'We've not seen you this week,' she says. 'Why's that?'

'Probably doing all her shopping up in the big Asda,' offers Evie. 'It's where everyone else goes.'

'This is where I do my shopping,' I tell them. 'I wouldn't dream of going to Asda.'

Evie giggles. 'My mum does, and this is her shop.'

'Well more fool her,' sniffs Mary, then looks me up and down. Decides she doesn't like what she sees. 'You know, you want to start putting on a bit of weight, my girl. Too thin, by half. There'll be nothing to this baby if you stay like this. The wind will blow you away if you're not careful.'

I smile, but she's right about the wind; it's getting stronger, probably is buffeting the sides of Tom's train by now. Not that he'll notice, cocooned by his iPhone and his magazines. Tom has spent these last weeks carefully building walls that nothing can penetrate.

Down here, though, it's a wind to blow the leaves off the trees.

And sure enough, in the Valley, the wind does just that. I get out of the car and they fly – *she* flies – towards me. I have to close my eyes, hardly daring to breathe as she makes the air spin – this child who is everywhere.

It would be so easy to be frightened now. And sure enough, in my spine something stirs. Goosebumps flare along my arms.

But I remember who I am – Marietta's girl. I push the fear away. I cannot be alone here and be afraid. I would go mad.

Late in the day, Tom phones. 'Sara, I've sorted it.'

'Sorted what?'

'You coming to stay. Jump in the car and drive up here tomorrow. We'll travel back down together on Friday.'

'But Joaquin...'

'We won't be staying with Joaquin. We'll be at Jen and Charlie's. I've just worked it all out with them.'

'But...'

'But...what?'

I'm thinking. Imagining the comfort of Jen. At the same time, torn: the world is full of Mandy. If I saw Jen now, how could I not tell her everything?

In hesitating, however, I have offended Tom. 'Look,' he says coldly. 'Decide what you want to do. I've got to go. Ring me in the morning. Only watch out, we might both have changed our minds by then.'

'Tom—'

But he has rung off.

Then I forget about Tom. The sun fell beneath the cliff hours ago. The days are growing shorter. Soon it will be night. I need to pull the curtains, bolt all the doors. Make sure not even a crack remains open to the outside.

Marietta has reminded me not to be afraid, but when night comes, I have to be wary. I have to be wise. I need to keep out the dark, seal up the cracks; make sure that what belongs outside, stays outside.

But it's not enough. Even Marietta is not enough.

In the small hours comes a noise to tear the house apart.

*What?*

Bolt upright even before I am awake. I hear myself shout the word. 'What?'

Downstairs in the house – in the house – a woman is screaming. Her voice splitting the dark. No words, only screams.

My hands fly to my mouth, stopping it, trying not to scream too, my voice mingling with her voice, the woman in my house. But I scream anyway, my scream drowning out hers. In terror we are the same.

Where has she come from? There is no woman in the tale I've told myself. Only a child, taken by the river, who belongs outside. Where is the woman in the story? And why is she screaming, here, in the house?

Disembodied by terror, I scream, louder still. Scream until I realise the other screams have stopped. There's quiet from downstairs – but in a moment this too is broken. Pushing my fist harder against my mouth, I listen to a new sound. She's crying. A terrible sobbing that takes my breath away.

She's more frightened than I am.

Suddenly I'm almost sorry for her, this woman who has come from nowhere. Slipped through the walls like water and made hideous the dark. But all that pity does is add another note to the horror. Another unknown.

Yet slowly, this noise also dies away. The crying stops and the darkness becomes formless. There's nothing but silence as now we wait.

Then it comes, something else to violate the stillness. Not screaming this time, not crying – but music. Music? The stabbing of violins – so unexpected that even terror has to falter, give way to an instant of wonder. Music, playing like a soundtrack to fear, punctuating terror. Music to die to.

Something dawns in the surrounding dark. I'm beginning to understand who she is, this woman in my house, why it is she's here. But I can't know for sure, not until I've found her. It means I have to force myself to get out of bed, follow the killing sound of the music. And that, somehow, is what I do. Downstairs a light flickers under the sitting room door and, like a moth, I am drawn to it.

And there. She stands where I knew she would be. A woman. Broken by fear, she's trying to shrink into the fabric of the wall, hands groping behind her for a door that is not there. At the same time the music swells as if to greet me, louder, terrible in its welcome. But then it falls away, grows softer, and in softness becomes infinitely more menacing. She watches me walk towards her and in her eyes all hope of mercy dies.

*Where is she?* She mouths the question. Pleads with me. Where is she?

*Not here,* I tell her. Knowing she cannot hear me. But I can do this for her. I can put her out of her misery.

I reach across and switch off the television, which is working again, the volume at full blast where we left it, forgetting to turn it off after giving up.

The woman disappears, swallowed up in a small white dot on the screen. Silence now. Silence and dark.

And slowly I come back into myself. I become Sara, and there is no one in this house but me. Gradually I become aware of my hands which are numb, and my legs, damp underneath my nightdress. And last of all, rising up around me, the sharp, astringent scent of pee. Terror made my body not mine to control anymore. Now it has leaked, and shamed itself.

Shamed me.

In the morning I phone Tom. It's early, barely light. His voice is croaky as he answers.

'Yes?'

'I want to come, Tom. So badly.'

He grunts a reply that could be anything. And so it's arranged. Although later, when the sun is riding high in the sky and I am ready to leave, I almost regret it. The journey is so long, and at the end of it will be Tom...Tom as he always is now.

Weary at the thought of it, I switch on the television.

And it's silent. Blank, just like before. Only in the night, in the dead time, does it come alive. Shuddering, I seize my bags and run out of the house.

~

# Chapter Eighteen

Jen hugs me, then steps back to look me over, from head to foot.

'Skinny,' she pronounces. 'Skinnier than the proverbial rake. Are you keeping an eye on her, Tom? She needs feeding up.'

Tom stiffens. 'She's an adult, Jen. She can feed herself.'

'Quite right,' says Charlie, and hugs me too. Then we stand, the four of us, slightly awkward, our smiles already becoming fixed, conscious that something has changed – and for the worse. It's not Charlie or Jen – they are the same as ever. It's Tom and me. We are no longer *we*.

For a moment I wonder how it can be so obvious. Then I glance at Tom and see him with their eyes. He wears his disappointment in me like a suit of clothes, ill fitting, weighing down his arms and legs. Carries it like a man cursed in his luck, not caring who knows.

Up in the spare room, Tom sinks down on to the bed. 'They're going to go on about it, aren't they? They're going to just eat us up. It's going to be baby talk from now till Friday.'

I shrug, and sit beside him. For once we are agreed about what grieves us. Surprisingly, instead of moving, he relaxes, leans into me, so that we sit, propping each other up. And there we might have stayed, for hours, until Charlie and Jen had wondered what had happened to us. But then the door to the bedroom, which like every door in this house fails to shut properly, slowly opens.

It's Pig, framed in the doorway, wearing her pyjamas ready for bed. While the Duke has grown yet more solid, she seems even smaller, wirier than before. But she has a monumental stare, which she uses on us now. Unsmiling, stony. We find ourselves moving apart, setting our faces into the smile expected from adults.

But it cuts no ice. She continues to stare until finally Tom says, 'So what do you want? Exactly?' With no Jen and Charlie present, he can sound as impatient as he feels.

With that, she turns the stare exclusively upon him, more expressionless than ever. Unblinking, until at long last she steps away from the door, leaving us sitting in the aftermath.

I have an urge to laugh. But Tom looks shaken.

'You see,' he says, as if it proves everything. 'You see?'

And somehow I do see.

Supper, and things improve. Jen chops vegetables, and Tom and Charlie settle into the wine. And no one says a word about children. I have misjudged Jen, misjudged my best friend. I help with the food and, as if from the outside, watch the effect we have on each other – the effect we have on Tom.

Even though it's only Charlie and Tom drinking, it's the wine that does it, making everything seem close to the way it used to be, making us eat and talk and laugh as if nothing has changed. When the wine runs out, Charlie finds a bottle of ouzo and Tom shakes his head in disbelief at such a lapse in taste, but drinks it anyway. Smiles at me, at Jen, at the ceiling.

It's the smile that gives him away. I know what's happened.

Tom has forgotten we are here for anything but dinner. Believing that after this, he and I will walk back through the streets of Belsize Park, up the hill to our Highgate home. Taking my hand as we go, making sure I don't slow him down on the steep pavements. Thinking we will unlock our front door, and go to bed in the room with the lime tree outside the window, filtering streetlight now, orange on our bedroom wall...

And parentless, childless, lie until one, then the other, falls asleep, side by side. The only family we could ever need. He has forgotten every moment of the last few months.

Meanwhile, I watch him talk about the magazine, about the things that mean everything to him, and nothing to Jen and Charlie – the importance of having the right shoes, the right barber; the poor quality of the cappuccinos in the place where he eats his lunch. They are laughing at him, and he doesn't mind, because he knows he is right, and he's sure that deep down they know it too.

I listen to him and discover I am holding my breath, so certain am I that I know what he is going to say next. Everything so familiar, so close to how it was, that for Tom, the forgetting is all but complete. Now he's complaining about the traffic, the crowds, the dissatisfactions that simply mount, day after day, and I watch him, thinking I should say something, make it so it doesn't happen. Save him. Instead I say nothing.

Then it does happen.

There's a pause. Tom shakes his head. 'You may laugh,' he says quietly. 'You may laugh, but I'm telling you, there's only so much more I can take. One day I'm going to jack it all in. I'm going to find a place right out of the Smoke, away from anywhere, and I'm going to grow things. And it's got to be soon, because I'm telling you, there has to be more to life than this.'

Now there's a real silence, prolonged. Jen and Charlie are blinking at him, wondering if they've heard him right.

Charlie coughs, then says, almost nervously. 'Silly bastard! You've already done it. You've got the place. And the vegetable plot. We've been down there and everything. Got the miles on the clock to prove it.'

Tom stares at him blankly before his eyes swerve away from Charlie to me.

Then the colour sweeps up through his face and I understand. He has made himself look a fool, right here in front of Charlie and Jen, forgetting what everyone else remembers. And it makes no difference that they are his closest friends, the people least likely to care. No difference at all. This is Tom's worst dream, come true.

And it's my fault. Because I knew he had forgotten. I knew it was going to happen. I could have stopped it and I never did. Something malicious, deep down inside me, must have wanted it.

Now, somehow, I have to make it right. Before Charlie's nervous giggle turns into helpless laughter; before Jen, clapping her sides with mirth, proclaims that this is one for the annals, never to be forgotten.

So I act – banging the table and bouncing in my chair. Laughing. 'Oh look at them, Tom! You fooled them. Look at their faces! They think you're serious.'

I turn to Charlie. 'Idiot, how can you be so easy? He's got you believing he's for real!'

Then it's back to Tom. 'And you, you are just a menace, getting one over like that. They're giving us a bed, remember. They're our hosts, we're supposed to be nice to them.'

It's all it takes. Straight away, Charlie begins to chuckle. 'Bastard,' he says. 'Bastard! You nearly had me there. Ha bloody ha. Have some more fucking ouzo, seeing as we've drunk all the so-called wine you've brought. Don't they sell anything but antifreeze where you come from?'

Across the table, Tom's face creases into the broadest of smiles. The flush has vanished, gone as quickly as it arrived. Charlie probably never even noticed it. In any case, he's an anaesthetist, and doesn't mind what colour people go so long as it's not blue.

Charlie starts a rant of his own, about country folk always complaining and Tom answers in kind, trades insult for insult. Meanwhile I watch Jen spooning the remains of the trifle straight from the serving bowl into her mouth. She is watching Tom.

Pregnant and sober, her eyes are cynical, completely knowing.

Because this is Jen, who knows us. Knows Tom. She wasn't taken in by any of it. Not by me, and definitely not by Tom. Now would be a good time for the Duke to wake and summon her with one of his cries, take her away. But the Duke sleeps soundly, and Jen licks her spoon, saying nothing. Sparing me the look that would tell me she knows everything I've just done.

* * *

Getting ready for bed, Tom says, 'I suppose that wasn't so bad.' He's forgotten his lapse. Already convinced himself that it was only a joke.

I don't answer. I'm stretching, plumping up pillows. Tonight sleep will be easy. Outside the window, all I can see are the roofs of other houses, and in those houses are other people just like us – lots of them. No trees, no river. No ghosts. Just layer upon layer of flesh and blood. Marietta's masks are not needed here.

'Leave the curtains open.'

Tom looks surprised, but he does as I ask.

It means I can see the landing lights of planes, and stars twinkling in the subdued way they have in the city. While in the streets, trees stand solid and safe as policemen, and rivers run secretly underground. They don't talk with a language all their own. In this house no one believes in ghosts.

So why do I not sleep?

I lie in bed, looking at these same stars struggling to pierce the city haze. Stars that hardly seem worthy of the name. And little by little every memory of this evening disappears: Charlie with his ouzo, Tom with his terror, Jen with her spoon. I try to remember sitting in the kitchen, surrounded by noise and people. People who don't believe in ghosts. But somehow none of it seems real.

The only thing that keeps the hard shine of something true is Pig. Standing in the door with that long expressionless stare. She was real.

I try to close my eyes, but I can't. My eyelids drift upwards, weightless as wings on an insect. I was so sure I would be able to sleep here. I thought everything would be different. And it's not. I am missing something and it will not let me sleep.

It's the river.

There is no river. For weeks and months it has been there, the keynote running beneath every other thing. Now it's absent and it changes everything. Outside, in the street, noises rise and drift, meaningless as smoke. There is no foundation, no anchor. Nothing to thread them together. No wonder the evening has faded. It was like a picture painted on a cloud.

This isn't how it used to be. I used to lie in this city, happy to be awake, listening to everything, feeling I belonged. Now I lie in Jen and Charlie's house and it's not where I belong.

And when I do sleep, I wake shrieking.

'Sara. What's the matter? Don't scream, don't scream like that.'

The shrieking stops. But Tom I don't recognise, not straight away. It's as if I have been drowning and he has found me on the shore, washed up and with no memory of how I got there.

What I remember is this. She stands on the riverbank, one small foot poised, ready for the final step. But this time is different – I am not there. I'm here, in this house far away from where she is, and what happens is happening without me. When I scream, she cannot hear me.

She has looked for me, I was all that could have saved her. But I'm not there.

Now here's Tom, woken by the wild thing in his bed.

I am crying now. There is nothing to do but cry. After a

minute, Tom takes me in his arms, awkwardly, pats me on the back, wishing I would stop. But I don't stop. I'm still crying when finally I fall asleep.

In the morning, he says nothing about it, even though I'm awake as he moves about the room, getting ready to go to work. Pretends he's in too much of a hurry to linger.

Jen takes one look at me and says, 'Go back to bed.'

She doesn't take no for an answer, pushes me back upstairs.

'I'll get you some tea.'

When she comes to the bedroom, I'm pretending to be asleep, but she's not fooled. She sits on the bed and waits. Eventually I open one eye, and find her watching me. She puts the mug of tea into my hand, wraps my fingers around it, and around them, hers.

'I heard you crying in the night...'

'A nightmare, that's all. It was nothing.'

But all she does is frown. 'Tom,' she says finally. 'Tom really, really doesn't want this child, does he?'

I look down at my tea. She shakes her head.

'Watching him last night, acting like such an arse. All that stuff about leaving the city – how can you bear it? How can you bear him? Why don't you get angry, Sara? I'd get so angry I'd...I'd kill him.'

In answer I point to my stomach. She snorts.

'Oh I see. You're feeling guilty because you're going ahead and having his child. *His* child. And that gives him the right to be an arse.'

'I had a choice about it, Jen. He never did. All he can do is watch.'

Again she shakes her head. 'But Sara – he does have a choice. He's got all the choice he needs. Too much choice. It hit me last night, just how much choice he has. I know what will happen. You'll have this baby and he'll leave you, I know he will. Oh God, Sara! How will you forgive me for saying this?'

She touches my cheek. Jen's hands are big, clumsy, always dropping things. But they feel soft now – soft as a child's. She says sadly:

'But who am I to tell you about Tom? There's nothing you don't know.' Then her mouth drops. A thought has occurred to her, made her catch her breath. But a moment later she seizes my face in her hands, grips it as she frowns into my eyes.

'Is that why you're doing this, Sara? Are you trying to drive Tom away? Are you using one child to get rid of another?'

I pull away. 'Jen! How can you say that? Of course I'm not. I hate what I'm doing to him, I hate it.'

'Sara—'

'No! Listen to me. Tom doesn't want a child. Neither of us did. Some people marry so they can have children. Not us, Jen. Never us. But look what I'm doing. I'm breaking a promise, forcing him to be a…a…'

'A father.'

'Yes! A father. And he can't stop me. Remember what you said about destroying an entire perfect world? That's what I'm doing. Tom's world was perfect. Now I'm going to destroy it, for something I don't even want. So you tell me. What right have I to be angry with him? I know how he feels. How can I blame him for anything?'

Jen looks embarrassed suddenly. 'But he wasn't happy, Sara. He was never happy.'

I stare at her.

'He wasn't happy,' she says again. 'Not even with the land and the house thing. We saw him there and he was already twitchy. You could see he was getting fed up. He'd got what he wanted and it still wasn't enough. Just like I said would happen,' she adds flatly. Her voice is devoid of triumph.

'He was happy with me.' My own voice is defiant. Wondering if she will argue with this.

For a moment it's enough to silence her. But then Jen shakes her head.

'You know, when the Duke was born, Pig's whole life collapsed. For three years she'd had everything – Charlie, me, dancing round her like a pair of fools. She thought that's how the world whirled. Then the Duke came along and her world ended. When she's not seething with resentment, I think she's in deep, inconsolable grief. But what should we have done, Sara? Never have had another child? Let her keep thinking this was a universe made only for her? What sort of human would we be inflicting on everyone else?'

'What are you saying?'

'I'm saying Tom's lucky compared to Pig. She only had three years believing the sun shone out of her backside. Tom's had ten.' She stands up. 'Blame yourself if you must, Sara. Hit yourself over the head every day if you want to. But it doesn't make you right, and it doesn't make Tom any different from what he is. A man who wants the world to keep turning only and entirely for him.'

At the door, she stops. 'And you know? You still haven't told me why you were crying last night.'

'Tom…' I begin.

She waits, this friend of mine, ready to hear anything. And it sweeps over me then, a desire so strong I am almost faint with it. Tell Jen. Tell her about the child and the river that took her. Describe how the air is filled with her, spins itself around me. Tell her.

It's a desire so strong, the words are already forming on my lips. 'Jen…' I move towards her.

But I have woken the nausea inside me. The movement becomes a desperate lunge past her, pushing her aside to get to the bathroom.

Yet as I stand, emptying myself of hot, barely swallowed tea, a hand comes and holds my head. Cool, soft-palmed as a child's, it shelters me from the force of my own heaving. Stays till I'm all done.

I don't need to tell Jen a thing. Gentleness – it's enough to have this. Just this.

In the evening, we wait for Tom to come home. And wait. It's after ten, finally, when he arrives. When I mention it, he looks impatient. 'It's the job. What do you expect?'

Didn't he realise I could smell the wine when he came in? White wine, there on his breath. Chablis probably. It's the same the next night, and the night after. Charlie and Jen look resigned and make no comment.

But Jen's eyes say it all.

As for Tom, she allows herself one small observation. Two observations. Sharp. It happens on the last night, as we are eating, as she hands him a bowl of potatoes.

'How come, Tom,' her voice is pleasant, conversational, 'how come in all those years of talking about having land you never tried to grow anything? When you were still in Highgate, I mean.'

'Are you serious? We had about twelve square feet of yard. What did you expect? Fields of cabbages? Harvests of oilseed rape?'

'No, no,' says Jen sweetly. 'But even in twelve square feet, surely you could have planted something, just to watch it grow.'

Tom is frowning now. 'Like what exactly?'

'Oh I don't know – mustard and cress, parsley. It's what children do. You know, when they've really got the bug for growing, but they don't have the space. They'll push seeds into yoghurt pots if that's all there is – if that's what they really, really want to do.'

She smiles at him again.

'And how come,' she says, 'you don't mind about the terrorists anymore? I thought you were never going to ride on the Tube again.'

Sullen, he answers her. 'I take taxis. And anyway, things are better now. Everything is. The government has finally woken up. They'd let everything slide before, not keeping proper surveillance, allowing people to say and do what they like. They've taken a grip, got things under control. Thank God.'

Jen raises her eyebrows. 'I see. So I take it you've stopped your subscription to Amnesty International.'

There's a silence. Tom pushes back his chair. 'You know,

it's been a long day. I think I might hit the sack. Coming, Sara?'

Our eyes meet.

'I'll stay down here for a bit. Help with the washing up.'

His glance flicks away from mine, and off he goes. He's asleep when I come to bed – or pretends to be.

And the next day, when we're meant to be going home, he announces he's not coming.

He says he's had a message from Joaquin. He needs Tom to be with him to meet some advertisers over the weekend. International property developers who want to insert a spread into the magazine about a purpose-built ski village in the French Alps. Very important people with very important money.

'You can see why I need to be here, Sara,' he says. Doesn't wait for an answer.

It means driving down by myself. Jen comes to the pavement to wave me off, carrying the Duke on her hip. All through breakfast she's been fussing about the length of the journey, about remembering to take breaks. There's more she would like to say, much more, but somehow we have agreed. Say nothing.

All the same, as I'm about to turn on the engine, it blurts out of her:

'I wasn't nice enough to Tom last night. Now he's cross with you. That's why he's not coming home with you, isn't it?'

'He's cross with me all the time.'

She presses her lips together, shifts the weight of the Duke on her hip, and concentrates on holding her tongue. I am ready to leave now, but as I'm putting the car in gear, a black cab draws up alongside, stops me going anywhere.

Joaquin gets out, carrying something in his arms. Large and lithe, he walks around the front of my car, comes to stand beside Jen. He smiles at her, making her blush in a way I've only seen Charlie manage. Smiles, too, at the Duke who beams back and offers him the rusk that is already half smeared over his face. But most of all he smiles at me.

'Ah, I am just in the nickel of time. I was afraid I would miss you.'

*Nickel.* Jen's eyes grow bright and amused.

But I say nothing. Through the open window, his eyes meet mine. And there it is again. The unexpected closeness; heat that pours out of him and into me.

Heat? I am sitting in a car, surrounded by metal, while he stands on the pavement. Yet heat is what I feel, blood rushing to my face, my hands.

He looks around then, as if someone is missing. 'You're waiting for Tom? You are late, no? You have a long journey, the two of you. It's why I feared I would miss you both. I have a gift, you see. Something to take home with you.'

Beside him, Jen hears him and stops smiling. Tom? She mouths the name.

'But I'm not waiting for Tom! Tom's with you.' Confused, I have replied with an obvious nonsense. 'He's meeting clients with you today. This morning. Now.'

Then I understand – we both understand – and the confusion dies. After the shortest pauses Joaquin says, 'Of course. We do this a little later, Tom and I. And he will be his usual, invaluable self.'

Our eyes meet again and stay met. He is measuring the effect of Tom's lie – Tom who is not with him – watching me for damage.

Yet something must have reassured him, because then he smiles – his mouth easing into that familiar curve. His teeth are not the bright dentine white of Tom's, who pays to keep them that way. Joaquin's are the colour of ivory, stained by the tannins of the wines, and the strong, dark coffee I've seen him drink.

'I have something for you.' He means me. Something for me. His eyes say so.

Joaquin holds up to the window what looks like a bare stick in a pot. A slender growth of wood, nubbly and worn.

'A fig tree,' he says. 'If you keep it warm, keep it safe, then in the spring you can plant it. And if you can spare it, pour a little blood into the soil as a libation. With a little care it will grow for you, Sara – bear fruit if you want it to, even in this cold country.'

I stare at what he is offering me; until, as if from a distance, I hear Jen's voice. 'Aren't you going to get out of the car, Sara? It would be easier to get the pot inside...'

'No,' I say quickly. I put my arms out of the window, let him place the pot in my hands. Briefly our fingers touch. 'I don't need to get out of the car.'

At which Joaquin nods almost imperceptibly.

When I move off, I see them in the rear-view mirror – Joaquin, Jen and the Duke. I see Joaquin leaning to take the Duke into his arms, as if nothing could be more natural or required, and never mind that dribbled rusk will cake his expensive clothes. I see Jen beaming as she hands him over. I drive and the fig tree stays in the seat beside me, where Tom was meant to be. All the way down to Cornwall it's there. A gift, an offering. Something I can choose to let grow, or not. Bear fruit.

Where might I find blood?

Five hours later, the car nudges its way down the lane to the bottom of our valley. I have left the lights of the village behind. Here it's nothing but dark, clouds covering the sky, hiding what little moon there was. There aren't even any stars.

Stupid, stupid of me. I should have thought ahead about arriving, left a light burning to guide me inside. But it didn't occur to me. I'd thought we'd be coming home together, Tom and I. Imagined we'd be striding through the house, switching on radiators, bringing it back to life. Instead I am alone in the pitch black. I turn off the engine and listen to the silence.

Only there is no such thing as silence, here in the Valley.

First there are the trees; then all the nameless things moving in the undergrowth, each with its own sound. Then the river. And finally a noise to drown them all out: the sound of my own heart beginning to pound.

I should have left earlier. I should have made sure of light. Now it's dark and thoughts of Marietta are not enough. I have to get out of the car and find my way to the house, fumble with the locks to open the door – all outside and in the dark. And I am afraid.

It's because I've been away. Four nights surrounded by houses, pavements, roads and bridges – I have let myself become weak. Soothed by all those layers of people who do not believe in ghosts. Now I'm alone, in the dark – and I don't know that I can get out of this car. Minutes pass, small green numbers changing on the dashboard clock, and fear keeps me in my seat. Fear of the dark, fear of *her*. And all the time, night seems to thicken, threatens to become a Thing in itself. It presses against the window, settles like a growing weight on the roof.

Yet gradually, it dawns on me: I have to get out of the car. Have to, for all kinds of reasons and one pressing reason in particular. So mundane, so ordinary it seems to have no place alongside fear.

I need to pee.

It happens all the time now, something not to be mentioned to Tom. For four days I have excused myself while Jen smiles, because she's having to do the same herself. A need as undeniable as the urge to retch every morning, as if my body were determined to empty itself of everything except the one thing that clings inside me, will not let go. I grip my seat, try to ignore it, but I can't. Soon, despite the dark, despite the river, despite the trees gathered like people waiting for something to happen, I am going to have to get out of the car.

I would laugh, if I were not so frightened.

Then suddenly I am laughing. Or maybe I'm crying. Incontinence is going to drive me out of the car and into the dark. It couldn't happen in a film or a book. It would have to be something else that drove the victim into the night, the unknown.

But this is what drives me – the need to pee – and there is nothing I can do. I have to seize my bag, seize my key. Throw open the car door and run.

And that's what I do. Falling out of the car to canter, knock-kneed through the dark. Running like a child caught short. Like Pig at the bottom of her garden, racing indoors, fit to burst.

But as I run, a cry bubbles in my throat. Under my feet the ground has begun to move, is rising in a feathery cloud that folds itself around me. It's leaves. Leaves that have fallen, coming back to life. I feel them touching my face, soft against my hands. Flying faster, higher than my head – dead leaves flying with me as if they were alive...

In my throat, the cry turns to a sob.

But then, like a distant lantern, a slivered moon slides from behind a cloud and as I run, I see. Not leaves. These are moths. Moths that had lain, blanketing the ground, laying out their wings in the dark. Now as I run, they have taken flight alongside, their wings grazing my cheeks, fluttering against my arms.

And having shown me, the moon disappears again; and I run faster, expecting the dark to be an obstacle, something solid standing in front of me. But it's not like that. I run, and the winged darkness lets me. It streams past me like water, speeds me on my way.

I've reached the front door. Pressing the key into the lock, I hear the workings glide and tick. A moment later, I slip inside my house as easily as if I was a ghost walking through a wall. Home.

And safe. Fingers already reaching for the switch to flood the hall with light.

But in that instant, in the fraction of the second before the switch flicks, I see what I have left outside, in the dark. Trees that cluster at the end of the path. Shrubs like people standing in rows. Objects made out of the dark itself. Moths fly and flatten themselves against them, and disappear.

And everything with a life of its own. Trees, shrubs, every nameless shape. They watched me canter just now, running my own race, all alone, like the fat child who has fallen behind on sports day. The child that anyone with a heart would want to cheer.

Cheer?

I close the door. Not frightened, not anymore. Almost exhilarated. Later, in bed, I leave the curtains open just to see if I can. And I sleep – very, very well. While deep in my skull, at the very edge of a dream I don't remember, I seem to hear cheering.

~

# Chapter Nineteen

Mary Coryn is buying her lottery ticket when I come into the shop. But instead of the smile that I was expecting, she frowns.

'What happened to you, then?' she snaps. 'Get lost on the way to the clinic?'

'Sorry?'

Mary turns to Evie. 'Guess who had an appointment with the midwife and didn't turn up?'

And too late, I remember. The summons to the health clinic, the battery of tests – I'd completely forgotten. But how did Mary Coryn know?

'Mary...?'

'My niece is midwife at the clinic. She's who you were meant to be seeing yesterday. Expecting you, she was.' Mary looks grim. 'What's the matter with you? Everything laid on, and you let it fly out of your head. You girls – you don't know you're born. Tests for this, tests for that; if there'd been a bit more of that in my day, then maybe I would have...'

She stops, pretends to study the numbers on her lottery ticket.

'She looks all right to me, though, Mary,' offers Evie. 'She looks ever so well, I'd say.'

Mary glances at me, nods briefly. 'You've got colour in your cheeks, I'll grant you that. I'll tell John Marsh when I see him next. He'll be glad enough to hear it. Too thin by half, though.'

I touch my cheeks. They are forever pink these days – from being outside, from digging. From the Other Thing making me hot one moment and chilled to the bone the next.

'I forgot to look at the calendar, Mary.'

And this is nothing but the truth. It's three weeks since I came home from London, since the race through the dark. But the days have run seamlessly into each other, left no impression of time passing. Tom has come and gone and yet I have barely seen him. He finds ways to keep himself busy – sits at the computer, spends hours in front of the new widescreen television he bought to replace the old one. Never goes outside. Even the machines don't interest him now.

Sometimes I wonder how we can go on like this, how two people can live together in such a fashion. Then Tom goes away again, and I remember: we are not living together. More and more, we are no longer *we*.

And what have I done? I have dug. I have slept, eaten. Feeding the thing that feeds off me. But I should have noticed Time. Yesterday I walked into the shop to find tinsel twisted along the shelves, dusty fairy lights in the window. And on top of the counter, a large cardboard Santa pointing to a promotion for novelty biscuits. Christmas is coming, and I didn't even notice.

But then Mary forgets to scold me. 'Well!' she exclaims. 'Will you take a look at that.'

She points towards the door. Outside the shop, past the

fairy lights, snowflakes are falling, large and feathery, drifting and rocking on the still air.

'I don't believe it,' says Evie. 'We never get snow this time of year. Not ever. Do you think it'll settle, Mary?'

'No.' Mary is unhesitating. 'Not before Christmas. You get all sorts of weather round here, but you don't get the snow.'

Yet as I drive down the lane, the tyres already sound different, as if we were rolling over icing sugar. And when I press the brake suddenly to allow a vole to cross my path, the car slides forward a few feet on its own, takes out the vole anyway. By the time I reach the bottom, the entire Valley is covered, contracting and tightening under a skein of white. The temperature has plummeted just in the few minutes since I left the shop.

The last time I remember snow was in France with Tom. A week spent in the high Alps, surrounded by it. White roads, white roofs, white everything. Something taken for granted there, impossible to imagine the slopes without it. Here in the Valley, though, it seems utterly strange. Almost supernatural.

I can't see the sky anymore. Flakes are falling faster than ever, a soft throwing down of layers. Maybe this *is* the sky, sinking under its own weight.

Mary's right, though. It can't last. People always talk about rain down here; and sun and storms. High winds and lightning strikes. But when have they ever mentioned snow?

Tom says the same thing when he phones later. 'Snow? At this time of year? It'll be gone tomorrow.'

He speaks with the confidence of a man surrounded by white walls, and beyond them a London sky that hasn't yet lost the look of autumn. Still light. Here it's half past three and outside the snow continues to fall in a darkness that is nearly complete.

He says he's working and keeps the phone call short, but an hour later he's back. 'Sara, are you busy?'

There's a note in his voice that takes me by surprise. He sounds...awkward.

'No. Why?'

'It's Joaquin. He's just phoned me. Turns out he's been in Cornwall since yesterday. He flew down to talk to the people at the Eden Project with some deal he wants to set up there. Anyway...' He pauses.

'Anyway?'

'He was meant to be flying back tonight, but it turns out you were right about the snow. His plane can't take off so he's going to have to stay. And...well, the long and short of it is, he wants to come there.'

'Here? But Tom, there must be ten hotels at least good enough for him...'

'I know, I know. It's just...well, I offered. It seemed the thing to do. I mean look at me, staying at his place week after week.'

'But why? Why would he want to come here?' Wondering if Tom has guessed the answer.

He hasn't guessed.

'You know Joaquin.' Tom speaks with a shrug in his voice. 'He's not that fond of hotels. He likes to have people round him he knows. And he knows you. Though I'm guessing the real reason is he wants to see the place. See what finally got me out of London.'

Except that Tom is not out of London. He is sitting in the

middle of it now. While Joaquin is on his way here, to me. Joaquin here. I feel the blood rush to my face.

'Tom, I don't think that I...'

'I'm sorry, Sara. I told him it would be all right. He's on his way.'

'He won't get down the lane. The snow...'

'He's rented a four-wheel drive.'

'He'll get lost...'

No he won't. I gave him directions.'

'Tom!'

'Just do this for me, Sara. I owe him. I was glad I could make the offer. And he'll be company for you. He knows you're all on your own there. I expect he thinks he's doing you a favour.'

And as he speaks another note enters his voice. Complacent. Probably thinking this is all for his sake, that this is Joaquin, doing *him* a favour.

'Oh and Sara, listen. When you show him round, explain we're not to blame for the decor, all the tat left after the Marshes. Make sure he knows it's a work in progress.'

I feel a reply rising to my lips, something that will make Tom stay away for the next month – but outside the house a light appears, and with it the soft crunch of wheels on snow. Joaquin has arrived.

I move into the hall, wondering if I should go out to meet him, or wait for the knock on the door. I decide to wait here, where the hall mirror has snagged me with my own reflection. There are two bright spots burning in my cheeks, yet my eyes give nothing away. In the dim light of the hall, they are as dark as it is possible to be, as if the pupils have swallowed the irises whole. There's nothing there for Joaquin to see. He'll be like Tom. He'll see nothing.

That's what I believe – until the moment Joaquin walks through the door. With a flurry of snowflakes around him he stops and looks deep into my face, into my eyes. And laughs out loud. 'Ah, my poor Sara. You are furious with me, furious with everyone. Hahaha. Completely enraged.'

And he kisses me on both cheeks. Still laughing.

Now the house seems smaller. And warmer. Heat pouring out of the walls. I touch my cheeks and they are still burning.

Not the same house, not now Joaquin is here.

We are in the kitchen, where Joaquin is taking item after item out of a hamper the size of Marietta's tea chests. Wine, cheese, olives, bread. Sausages glistening red inside their skins and filling the air with scents of garlic and blood. Fragments of straw from the hamper lie scattered round him on the floor, pale strands catching the light.

He should be out of place with his cashmere sweater and Italian shoes, a stranger in the house. But it doesn't work like that. Joaquin reaches for things without looking for them, as if he has lived here all his life. Effortlessly finds knives to slice through string, chopping boards to take the sausage. Chops and slices and crushes, runs his fingers through his hair, leaving the thick, dark curls oily and gleaming.

I don't help him. I don't even ask myself what he is doing or why.

I have come to stand against the wall, as far away as I can be. I have my arms folded tight, and my lips pressed together, trying to make myself unreadable, trying not to draw attention. I don't want him looking at me again, laughing at what he sees.

Although the truth is, Joaquin hasn't looked at me, not since that first moment of arrival. If anything, he is avoiding catching my eye, preferring to apply himself to his hamper, to chopping and tasting. Why doesn't he catch my eye? Is he disappointed by what he saw when I opened the door?

Or is it that Joaquin – of all people – is uncertain? I followed him from the front door and saw his eyes darting right and left. He was looking for the fig tree. Wondering if I had chosen to care for it.

Maybe he doesn't catch my eye now because he looked – and didn't see it.

There's nothing uncertain in the way he talks, though – which is at great length. Explains everything he's brought with him, the provenance of every drop of wine or oil, or morsel of bread. Not out of nervousness or to make conversation, but in all seriousness, as if I am someone who cannot be expected to touch what she does not know, who needs to be convinced of the goodness of everything.

I am beginning to understand Tom, after years of working for Joaquin, wanting all to be just so. Tom who is always fussing and comparing, always anxious that he will be judged by his choices.

But with Tom, that's just imitation. It's different with Joaquin. He is easy as he goes about explaining the food, sounds like a father discussing his children, dwelling on their good points, explaining why they deserve to be treasured. Grieving that not all children can be so prized.

'But I should be making you supper,' I say finally.

'Ah no. I have imposed on you. Would you expect me to come empty-handed? Besides, Sara...' His hand hovers for a moment. 'This is something I have wanted to do for a long time. I have wanted to feed you.'

He looks at me then. And there it is in his gaze: uncertainty. He is unsure of me, and it holds him at bay. Hard as he tries, he cannot read me, not the way he wants to.

He turns back to what he is sure of, the food. Pulls a cork out of the bottle of oil and makes a glistening puddle in a saucer, tears a strip off a large round loaf, sending flecks of flour to float in the air like a second snowfall. I am fascinated by his hands. His fingers are long, with nails wide and flattened, the skin roughened as if by work or weather. How did his hands become rough? So much I don't know about this man.

'You must eat this, ' he says, holding up the bread. He has dabbed it in the oil, making it shimmer as though dipped in light.

I shake my head. The offer of bread is charged with meaning, carries a caseload of significance. If I swallow a morsel of anything from his hand – a pomegranate seed, a sliver of apple, I am lost. Like Eve was lost.

And Joaquin knows it. 'No, you must taste it,' he says and comes to me. The bread glows in his hand. A drop of oil falls to the floor.

'Good bread, Sara. Good oil, you cannot say no.'

I can. I must. Yet he has come to stand so close I have nowhere to put my eyes. I concentrate instead on his mouth, and on his lips which are red, as if forever stained by a dark, full-blooded wine.

I'll find a way to refuse his bread, his oil…

But even as I think this, my mouth comes alive. Tastes of salt and sun are crackling on my tongue, and in my nostrils are the scents of baked earth under sky. While I debated how to refuse Joaquin's bread, my lips had simply opened of their own accord.

Joaquin steps back. He is smiling. 'Are you still hungry, Sara?' he says softly.

And slowly I nod. The truth is, I am hungry. Hungry for the first time in weeks. Ready to faint with hunger.

He pours wine into a glass, offers it to me. I sway towards it, but I don't take it.

'Ah,' he says. 'You're thinking of your child.'

'No.' My voice is sharp. 'Nothing to do with that.'

Which is true. I haven't thought about the Other Thing since Joaquin arrived.

'Good!' He sounds triumphant. He sets the wine in front of me. 'My mother could not have had me without her glass of Rioja every day. And look at the result!' With that he sits and lifts his hands, invites me to look at him. And so I do. I look at Joaquin.

He's turned an ordinary kitchen chair into a pedestal for a living sculpture. Himself. Massive in this small space, he is magnificent. A while ago he removed his sweater. Now, beneath the linen of his shirt, I can see the clumps of hair running riot, black and grey, like a wolf. Suddenly reminding me of the year Tom took up cycling, treating it with the brief seriousness he treats everything before the interest wears off. He shaved away every hair on his body to make himself aerodynamic, because apparently that's what you did.

In contrast, Joaquin would catch every breath of wind that touched him. He could change the weather itself.

As if hypnotised, I move towards the table. It seems to me this man is filling every sense I possess. Not only can I see him, hear him – beneath the scents of garlic and wine, I can smell him. A mixture of leather and soap and Acqua di Parma, which are themselves only the top notes of wilder, deeper odours, reminiscent of what you would detect in the woods. Badger. Fox. Scents to make you wrinkle your nose even as, eager, you breathe them in a second time and a third.

I decide to take the wine he has poured for me, ruby red and glowing in the glass. I'll drink it because I know where it comes from. Joaquin has told me, he has explained the goodness in it.

For the first time, though, Joaquin has fallen silent. He is staring at the wine in his own glass.

'What are you thinking?' Curiosity makes me ask. I can't help myself. But it causes him to laugh for joy, because now it means he can tell me.

'I am thinking that I like a woman who is silent.'

And that disappoints me. But immediately he holds up his hand.

'Oh, not for the reason you suspect. I am not one of those men who like their women to be seen and not heard, like children. No, no, no.' With each no, he knocks the table in front of him.

Then he looks at me, catches my gaze and traps it in his. Threads of connection, invisible, are flying through the air. This is what happens after taking his bread, his oil. Letting him feed me. Allowing the flavours he chose for me to pass my lips. Joaquin says:

'I like a woman whose thoughts are so deep and so concealed it would take a lifetime to read them. More than like. Do you know what such a woman would do to me, Sara? She would haunt me, turn me into a man obsessed. I would do anything, everything – use every trick my father taught me, to find the truth of her. I would make it my vocation, my challenge. I would die in the attempt just to know her.'

He watches as I consider this, holding the glass away from me, the better to see the light caught in the liquid. Wine that has still to touch my lips.

'And what would you do,' I ask, 'once you'd found out everything there was to know?'

'I would put myself at her disposal. If she had a secret, I would keep it for her. If she asked me to stand over her, I would stand with all my might. I would put my – substantial – body between her and the world. I would defend her, protect her if she would let me. Or if it is a different need she has – a way to journey, to advance – I would provide it. I would beg her to use me as a bridge to wherever she wanted to be. And then, if she let me, I would go with her, beside her, watching her. Taking pride in her speed and her grace.'

'You would do that?'

'I would do that.'

'But what if you discover everything about her – and then find you don't like what you know?'

'I do not think that would happen. No, Sara. Never.'

He sits back in the chair. He's said what he came here to say. Now he waits, not knowing if his words have had good effect. Or any effect. His eyes leave mine to search the room.

'What are you looking for, Joaquin?'

'The fig tree. I am wondering what you did with it, Sara.'

A pause. And then I tell him. 'It's upstairs, in my bedroom. The conservatory was too cold in the night. But my bedroom is warm and catches the sun. It's there when I go to bed and it's there when I wake up. It's the first thing I see.'

Once again our eyes meet. Then Joaquin leans forward and slowly takes the glass from my hand. He holds it to my lips and finally, finally I drink.

Wine that is exactly as I knew it would be; the one taste that brings every other taste together – the sun, the salt, the earth – tastes of Joaquin himself. Everything leading to this, to the taste of the wine in my mouth.

'I'm pregnant,' I murmur. 'You know that.'

He puts a hand on my stomach. Holds it so the warmth of it seeps through layers of flesh, sending ripples through that underwater place. But almost immediately I have to move away from it. I am not ready for this, for Joaquin – or anyone – treating what's inside me as something real and alive, when I am not ready myself.

'Tom…' I begin.

'Ah yes. Let us talk about Tom.'

'Did you ask Tom back to London to get him away from here? From me?'

'You mean like David, sending Uriah into the thick of the battle so as to have his Bathsheba? No, of course not. But did I tempt him from somewhere he should have stayed, and never left? Yes. Absolutely.'

So there it is. I should hate this man. This is why I am

without Tom tonight and so many nights. Tom would be here if not for him.

But look who is here instead, where Tom should be. A man sitting with the heavy grace of something cast in bronze, but whose flesh would be warm if you touched it. Who has filled my mouth and nostrils with tastes that are no more than the taste of himself, and having offered, waits for my answer.

My answer. What will my answer be?

The wine glows on my tongue. Its warmth closes my eyes. What would it be like to take from Joaquin? To sleep with Joaquin, carry the scent of him on my skin? In my mind, he isn't even human, not the way Tom is human. He's the beast from the rose garden, the bull from the sea. Offerer of pomegranate seeds. A man who would breathe life into stone and make veins of marble pulse with blood.

The truth is I know what it would be like. There was the dream I had long ago. Dreamt once and never forgot. I know how it would feel to lie against him naked: fine hairs, grey as wolf hair, tickling the length of my body, every line, every curve of me finding its place in him. Wishing I could lie for ever.

The rest – the rest I can imagine. How he would taste, how he would use his hands, his mouth. How his body would be a weight that could defy gravity, and make mine do the same. I know everything and it makes me shiver.

I don't have to sleep with Joaquin to know how anything would feel. And I could weep, because I would have loved to sleep with Joaquin. Loved to.

I stand up. A single glass of wine after so long without wine – now I am unsteady. But firm in my intent.

'In the morning, Joaquin, you will have to go.'

He sighs. But then he smiles. He stirs and the smell of the woods reaches me again. The fig tree is in my bedroom, and we still have to eat.

Although, when in the morning I wake and go to the window, I wonder if it will be possible for him to go anywhere.

Snow. Above us and below. It hangs in the trees, flattens the contours of the lawn. It's in the sky, waiting to fall again. White and bright and burdensome.

It shouldn't be here, all this white, all this snow. Just a cold snap – it was never meant to last. This is weather for people who don't believe in ghosts, proving they were wrong. I go along the landing, tiptoeing past the door where Joaquin lies asleep, trying not to wake him.

But a minute later he is with me. Taking over the making of coffee, beating eggs into which he will dip bread to fry in butter and dredge in cinnamon and sugar. I would be fat if I lived with Joaquin, as fat as he is.

Or maybe not. Maybe it would be enough just to take a taste of everything that comes my way. For the first time, this morning the Other Thing has not made me sick.

We walk to his car, a huge thing, almost as wide as the lane. But the lane is blocked with snowdrifts curved into the shapes of the currents that blew the weather here. Even Joaquin looks doubtful – and then pleased. Sees it as a gift, a reason to stay.

But I look at the sky with its promise of more snow, and say, 'If you go now, you'll make it.'

'If I go now, Sara, you will be all alone.'

'I won't.'

'No?' He looks at me, the way I'm used to now, trying to fathom what lies behind the words. It prompts me to say, 'Do you believe in ghosts, Joaquin?'

'But of course.'

And I believe him. But of course. Joaquin absolutely believes in ghosts.

It's the reason I kiss him, my mouth on his mouth. Happens before I know that I'm doing it. Immediately he kisses me back in a way that makes me forget that we are standing in the cold, with snow about to fall. He kisses me and I am hungry all over again – for cinnamon, for honey, for everything Joaquin would give to me. And yet almost at once I pull away.

Pregnant.

'Mio Dio, Sara,' he murmurs. 'If a tree bears apples, would you expect me cut it down?'

He laughs at the wonder in my face.

But I make him climb into his car. I make him drive away. Telling myself that if I have made a wrong choice, the Valley will put it right. The snow will turn him round, send him back to me. We will go upstairs and lie down together and every imagined touch will become a true touch. Afterwards, I will sleep, un-dreaming, rolled up in all the faint scents of the woods and wild things around me.

I listen for the sound of Joaquin returning, for the snow to send him back. But he doesn't come. I have let the Valley decide and the Valley has let him go, as if this is the way it must be.

And when I turn, a whoosh of snowflakes blows to meet

me. A chill wind which, finding my still lips parted from a kiss, rushes into my throat. Makes me gasp – and then gasp again, this time in shock. It's not the wind. It's *her*, inside me now, filling my mouth, my lungs.

My hands fly up to my lips. But it's too late. I breathe and my lungs are cold and sweet – and filled with her.

Now she's everywhere, rushing through my body. Racing like a child through an empty house. Leaves a trail of ice everywhere she goes. Thoughts of Joaquin are sent flying, to scatter round her like moths. But she moves on, and spellbound, I am ready to follow her…

It's only for a second, though. Shock has delayed understanding. But now I do understand. This is possession, my body suddenly home to two people.

Three. There's me and there's Mandy. And the Other Thing. All inside me now.

No.

By forgetting to be frightened, I let her come in. No living child, now she's inside me. She will fill me as she fills the leaves, the very air of the Valley. I will look in the mirror and it will be her eyes staring back at me. My body no longer my own.

In terror, I turn on her, this creature leaping through my veins, turning them to ice.

Go.

She stops. The race inside me halts.

Go.

And unbelievably, she does just that. This child is biddable. She slips away, leaves me standing the way she found me. Blood, nerves, every dark space grown warm again. And empty.

The terror vanishes with her. And I'm amazed. So used to thinking of her as a ghost, I keep forgetting. She's a little girl, that's all. One who does what she's told. I told her to go, and she went.

Inside, the kitchen still bears traces of Joaquin. Plates smeared with butter and cinnamon. In the cups, the dregs of cold coffee.

Why did I make him go? I could be drinking him now. Tasting him. I have been strong. But to what end? Because I am still with Tom? Because I've broken enough promises? Why did I make him go?

The radio is talking about isolated pockets of freak weather in the South West. People are stranded on hillsides, trapped in their vehicles, waiting until the police can dig them out, having to keep warm any way they can. Some will have to wait for hours.

Maybe Joaquin will come by in that huge car, bringing safety to a lucky few. Pointing them to the flask of brandy in the glove compartment, the blankets he just happens to have piled on the back seat.

Because this is what Joaquin does. He provides rescue. A man equipped to meet every need. Is that why I sent him away? People helped by Joaquin have to be careful not to be helped too much, otherwise they might want to be helped for ever. Make themselves weak just when they need to be strong.

Mid morning the phone rings.

'Sara.' Tom's voice is clipped, the way it is when he wants you to know he's fitting you in between the important stuff.

'You're not expecting me to travel down tomorrow, are you? If the weather's like this, I'm just going to end up stranded at Bristol or somewhere. You know what the trains are like, one small bit of snow.'

'No,' I say. 'I'm not expecting you to come.'

Immediately he relaxes. 'I mean, I would if you needed me to. You know I would.'

'I don't need you, Tom.'

A reply so instant it takes him aback. It's a moment before he speaks again.

'Right – well that's OK then, but if you say the word...' Then he says, 'What about Joaquin? Did he get away all right?'

'Yes.'

'So what did he say?'

'About what?'

'Everything. Me. The move. What I'm trying to do there.'

I don't even have to think about the answer. 'He says he's glad he tempted you back to London.'

'Ah.' For a moment, he is almost too pleased to talk. 'So – you've got everything you need to see you through?'

'Everything.'

'It'll mean I won't get down till next weekend now.'

'It's all right. It doesn't matter.'

And I mean it. It doesn't matter when he comes. Outside the world is white and temporary, and I have everything I need.

After a while the snow stops and I go outside again. Wary at first, wondering if the same thing will happen, if she will try to jump down my throat. But she's a child who does as she's told. Even though the air is filled with her, every snow crystal charged with her, she stays where she belongs, outside.

I go and look at the river. In this still, white world, it is the only thing moving. Dark and sinewy, murmuring over stones, it is busy, in conversation with itself.

Makes me restless, somehow. Joaquin has fed me, filled me with an energy that makes me want to be moving too. I look around – and know exactly what I will do.

It starts with a ball of ice, the first hard centre that will be the core, the heart of what I have in mind. I roll it along the ground to collect more snow so that it gets bigger and bigger. I toil and it grows, puts on weight. And *she* is there, wondering, watching. She wants to know what I am doing.

Making a man, I tell her. A fat man, with a body as tall as it is wide.

Too fat, too wide. I begin to worry that he'll be ridiculous, a figure of fun. So we roll him into the middle of the lawn and start to pile snow on top, where he gets to be taller, and in comparison slimmer. Now this is better, much more like it. He just needs a head.

Which is what we give him. A huge head, cheeks generously packed with snow. Everything about him generous.

We're adding the final touches as the sun comes out – a small pale spot like a drawing pin in the sky, keeping it in place. Our man is over six feet high with coals for eyes and branches for arms. He wears a black fedora hat belonging to Tom, which makes him appear at once distinguished and raffish. His belly is large, and dazzlingly white. I know exactly who he reminds me of.

Warm, worn out, I sit down under a tree where the snow is hard and dry, and close my eyes. Despite the sun, flakes of snow are falling again, brushing my cheek and melting on contact. There's sweat trickling down the back of my neck.

Content. Happy. I could stay like this for ever. Warm when all the surrounding world is cold, the air freckled with snow, and trees standing like wedding guests under a confetti sky. There is nowhere I would rather be. Nowhere I could even imagine.

And it makes me think...

Makes me think there are more ways to be possessed. One way is to have a ghost leap down your throat and fill your veins with ice. But another way is altogether gentler: to become sleepily content, happily submitting to the ties that bind and keep you in one place for ever. You'd never even know it's happening.

A different kind of possession, it has to do with the place itself. It's the Valley, quietly taking control.

~

# Chapter Twenty

And now the snow is gone. Two days later the Valley is bedraggled, filled with the sound of water dripping.

Only the snowman is still there. A shadow of himself – a slow drizzle of rain is finishing him off. I'm about to go outside and say goodbye, when I glance at the calendar. This is the morning I'm meant to be at the clinic.

Shall I go? I'm tempted not to. Stay at home, pretend my body is my own. Then I remember. If I don't go Mary Coryn will know and I'll never hear the end of it.

So I arrive just in time, to be rushed through to a room where a nurse weighs me and takes my blood and tells me about the tests I am having today. She is young with curly brown hair, calling to mind another set of curls.

'Is your aunt Mary Coryn?'

She smiles. 'Spot the likeness, did you? People say I'm the spitting image of her when she was young.'

I find this hard to believe. She is altogether soft with downy cheeks. I'm missing that clear blue stare.

She lays aside the final syringe of blood. 'We'll get on with your scan now.'

In another room she makes me lie down while she slathers

jelly on my stomach and waits for the doctor – a young man – who arrives grinning, picks up the hand piece as if he's about to give me a treat. A moment later there comes the sound I heard the first time. The watery thump, fast and rhythmic. This time I know exactly what to expect. In a moment he'll point me to the screen and I will have to smile, pretend I'm just like all the mothers who lie here. This time I'll be prepared.

But I'm wrong. I look at the monitor, and nothing could have prepared me.

We're back to that underwater place. There's the same wash of black and white, objects swaying amongst unseen currents. But the Other Thing that's there, hooked into the riverbed, has changed. Before it was a mollusc, a blob of uncertainty. Not anymore. This has bones, jointed and hard, glows with a calcium sheen. It has fingers, toes. Flesh that has been laid down in transparent layers. Flesh of my flesh. There is nothing uncertain here. The Other Thing is secure, takes what it needs and grows.

This is what my body has said yes to. Allowed to increase, cell by cell, segment by segment. Jen said the body couldn't lie, but I don't believe her. I can't believe there's any part of me that wants this.

'Oh look!' says Mary's niece, pointing. 'It's kicking! It wants you to know it's there.'

The noise I make – it fools her. She thinks it's a cry of joy. Wonder.

Tom arrives home – and actually hugs me as he gets off the train. Smiles as he picks up his bags and heads for the car.

I know what's happened. Christmas has begun to infect

him, as it does every year. A boy who never got what he dreamt of in his stocking, he's ready to devote long hours to making the present make up for the past. He is laden with carrier bags, bulky but light; willing to make a truce, to create a space, a bubble in which we can both be happy, if only for a few days.

'What have you got there?' I point to the carrier bags.

'Christmas decorations.'

'We've still got all of last year's.' I'm remembering an art house Christmas in black and white, achingly good taste.

'No good. This year it's got to be tinsel. You wouldn't believe it, the stuff is like gold dust. Everywhere is sold out.'

But Tom has managed to find enough tinsel to satisfy even him. Now the house shimmers under a web of silver and gold. He said the look is meant to be ironic, but he arranged it frowning and pondering like a man setting up an exhibition of old masters. Made me stand beneath a piece of mistletoe (also ironic) for him to kiss my cheek. Afterwards he took slow sips of champagne and watched me wistfully, no doubt remembering other times, other years when it seemed he had put the disappointment of Christmases Past behind him for ever.

As we get ready for bed, though, the wistfulness disappears.

I see him in the mirror, his eyes following me about the room, although when I turn around, he is pretending to read. But not before I've caught the horrified fascination in his gaze.

'What?' I ask, although I don't have to.

'You've put on weight, Sara. Suddenly. What is it – ten

days since I saw you? It's like you've...exploded.' He giggles with a mixture of horror and embarrassment.

'It's nearly five months along.' Blood sweeps through my face. 'What do you expect?'

Yet he has a right to be shocked. I don't look like me, not anymore. The Other Thing is growing, has to call up flesh from somewhere; and swift to obey, my body has been busy. Almost overnight, I have grown breasts, a belly. Reservoirs of flesh.

Now I climb into bed beside Tom and lie where I have always lain, aware of this same belly, these breasts. Heavy, they ache from the changes in them. A touch, any touch, would soothe them. A touch would soothe me.

But Tom keeps to his side of the bed, careful about the distance between us. He clutches his book and pretends to read. But then...

'Oh!' A cry has escaped me.

'What?'

'Something's moving.' Startled, I've turned to him.

'Moving? Where – downstairs? You reckon someone's in the house?'

Already he's pushing back the covers, reaching for the phone. Tom has never lost his London head for a crisis, primed to think every sound is an intruder.

'Inside me. It was the...the Other Thing. I felt it move.'

There's silence as Tom stares at my belly. He's wearing the blank astonishment of a man who has discovered a third person in the room. Suddenly the Other Thing has become real.

But now it's my turn to be fascinated. What would happen

if the blank look disappeared? Changing the lines of his face, as shock gives way to something else – a rush of tenderness, a change of heart. What if Tom reached out to touch me now? Where would we be?

Seconds pass. Tom's face is unreadable.

'Tom...?'

He gives a start. With a convulsive movement, he throws himself away from me, further even than before. As far as he can possibly be. And nothing has changed. In my belly the Other Thing moves again.

Now I lie with Tom beside me, and the Other Thing inside me – and I have never been more alone. Even Joaquin's fig tree stands apart, makes me think of nothing.

As soon as it's light, I get out of bed, pull on my clothes and go outside. Immediately, from out of the trees, out of the river, *she* flies to meet me. Not alone anymore, grateful, I go with her, out onto the soil.

'What the...? Sara, what the hell are you doing?'

I jump and turn around. I've been lost in the patch of soil, digging, turning over earth. One moment flowing into the next.

Now here's Tom, dressed in the chunky peasant sweater he bought last winter from an expensive boutique in Barcelona, and with a mug of coffee in his hand.

'Tom...?'

'Don't Tom me,' he snarls. 'Just tell me what this is all about?'

And still I don't understand. He has flung out his arms, causing his mug to fountain coffee in mid-air.

'I've been digging.'

'What for?'

I am bewildered by the question. 'To get at the roots – and the stones and the bits of metal, all the stuff left over from the mine workings…' I break off, warned by his face. 'What is it, Tom? What's the matter with you?'

'What's the matter with me? Take a look around you, Sara. Ask yourself the same question.'

But I don't have to look around. I am standing where I have been for days, weeks. Months. This is where I have been at work, fossicking, hacking, digging. Finding flow. It's only Tom for whom all this is new. He hasn't been outside since I can't remember when. Now he's staring at the lawn where it begins under the trees, making its broad sweep between the house and the river.

Except, of course, it isn't lawn. It's earth. Clean sifted earth where there used to be grass, and under grass, the network of roots, connecting trees to every part of the land. Not anymore. It's all gone. Now there is only one vast empty bed ready to be filled. Brown and folded and ready, it spreads out in all directions, only stops where it runs into the trees. Anything could grow here. No more roots. No more underground paths to the house.

Yet Tom's face is stony. 'So what was the idea, Sara?'

Once again I state the obvious. 'To clear the ground. The same as you were doing. Now you can start planting.'

He gives a violent shake of the head. 'I wanted to make a few plots – not carry out some policy of blasted earth. You've gone and dug up every inch. There's nothing left, Sara. Not so much as a blade of fucking grass.'

'I thought it's what you wanted. I thought you wanted to make things grow.'

'Of course I did. Do. But I had plans, Sara. I had it all worked out. You knew that.'

'No.'

'No? What do you mean, No?'

'No.' I say again. There's a buzzing in my head, like bees swarming. I have to raise my voice over the sound of them. 'You've never wanted to grow anything. Ever. It's all talk. You'd be dead before anything grew here because of you.'

As I speak it comes to me – an image of what I have just said. Tom dead. Under the earth, this earth; and out of him growing a world of trailing things, tendrils and roots reaching up and out of the soil. Feeding off him, thriving off compost that used to be flesh.

I stare at him, spellbound, as if already it had begun, seeds bursting under his skin. Already guilty, just for having let the thought into my head.

'Tom, I'm sorry…'

But he has turned away. There is still the smallest amount of coffee in his mug, and this he pours into the ground between us. It's a gesture of disgust. Brown spilling into brown. I watch him walk away, his shoulders angry and wounded under all that expensive wool.

I should go after him, make it right somehow.

But then, from out of the trees, out of the river, *she* comes. She ran away when he appeared, but now he's gone, and it's just the two of us again.

* * *

Later – much later – I go inside. Tom is in the kitchen. He has the heating on so high it's difficult to breathe. For a few minutes he pores over his laptop, pretends to be busy.

Finally he says heavily, 'I suppose I could just reseed it all with grass. Roll it out flat. We could make a go at having a really good lawn. At least there'd be something to show for it.'

The moment he mentions grass, I know what grass is for. He'll use it to cover up the soil, like throwing a blanket over something he doesn't want to see. Grass made to act like a shroud, to conceal what should be alive.

Not getting any reply, Tom bangs down the lid of his laptop and pushes past me to the back door, slams it so hard that all through the house, tendrils of tinsel twinkle and shiver.

From the window of our bedroom, I watch him.

After weeks of not working the soil, he is out there now. Plods back and forth, busy with wheelbarrows, with bits of machinery that – try as he might – he can't find a use for. He moves jerkily, keeps on dropping things. He looks like a little boy who is in the middle of losing something, a child who's been told he has to give up his room for a stranger.

Now he's gone down to the river. He is standing on the bank, staring out over the water, unaware that I am watching him more closely than ever. And that I am holding my breath.

Because it was there, right there, that I became aware of her. Standing by the river, as he is now, while it ran beneath my feet and turned water into words. Shouting at me, telling me about her.

Is it going to happen to him? Is he going to turn, suddenly sensing – like me – that someone is there, standing behind him? Dazzled by light and informed by water, is it his turn now?

If it happens to Tom, we may still have a chance. The river will change him as it has changed me.

I watch and wait. Wait for him to feel the tingle in the air, breath on his neck.

And it doesn't happen. Tom stands by the river, but he doesn't see, or hear, anything. His mind is elsewhere, playing out the many reasons he has to be unhappy. He is thinking about me, what he would say if I was standing next to him. How I have ruined everything we had, broken a promise that never needed to be put into words. How I have betrayed him. How I have changed.

Under the weight of so many woes, his shoulders slump. Nothing has turned out as he planned – and, suddenly, I feel so sorry for him.

More than sorry. Soft. I feel soft towards him, with his shoulders so defeated under his sweater and his hands hanging useless by his sides. Soft the way I used to be when I would watch him sleep, years ago, when all we had was each other. I feel I could run to him now, take him in my arms. Try to turn this round, every bad thing between us, every broken promise...

But then he does something – and all that softness, it just disappears.

Because Tom is stirring again, preparing to move on and carry the heavy burden of his woes elsewhere. But then he halts. He has noticed something, there, down by his feet. First he frowns; then he touches it, gingerly, with the toe of his boot. Then he bends, and even before he stands up straight again, I know what he has found.

It's the doll. Tom has found her, and is picking her up. Now he's holding her by her draggled hair, up and away from his body, a look of distaste on his face, as though she were an object he needs to dispose of. Something drowned and decaying. He walks away from the river, and I leave the window to stumble downstairs.

Outside he is still holding her, moving with a set, almost stupid look of purpose on his face. As if finally he has found something he wants to do.

I stop in front of him, blocking his path. Stretch out my hand.

'Let me have it.'

'Let you have what?'

'The doll. Let me have her.'

'Why?'

'I've got to put her back. Where you found her.'

'Put her back, what the fuck for?'

'Because...because that's where she belongs. By the river.'

'Don't be stupid. She's just an old doll. Probably been there for months, all covered in mud and crap. She doesn't belong anywhere but the rubbish bin.'

He steps sideways to walk past me. But instantly I move to block his way.

'You're not to put her in the bin.'

'I told you, don't be so fucking stupid. It's just an old doll.'

'She belongs to someone. She was meant to stay where she was.'

About to argue, he opens his mouth. Then snaps it shut.

'Oh I get it. It's that thing again. Ghosts and ghouls and garbage like that. I thought you were over all that.'

I say nothing. Simply hold out my hand for the doll.

Seeing it, his own hand twitches, despite itself; as if his first instinct is to give in, give way. Then his mouth hardens. 'I told you, Sara. Don't be stupid.' He starts to move past me.

'Tom, please. Please let me have her.'

Please – it's a word I should have used in the first place, when I saw the set, stupid expression in his face.

But he shakes his head. 'No, I've had enough. All this crap about ghosts and dead children – you're just doing it to get a rise, Sara. Well forget it. I'm not giving you the satisfaction. She's going in the bin and if you want to climb in and get her, be my guest.'

He is swinging past me. Long legs suddenly giving him the speed, like when we used to go running round Highgate and all at once he would take off without me.

'Tom...' I make a snatch for the doll, but he tosses her into his other hand, holds her high up and out from my reach.

Before I know it, I'm jumping after her, springing like a heavy terrier, and he's laughing. He has her by the hair still and has started to swing her in circles about his head.

'Go on. Jump. Jump for the stupid dolly.'

And I do. I jump and he jeers. We have regressed – two children, one tormenting the other. A doll between them, the reason for it all.

I see what we look like and I stop jumping.

'Tom,' I say again. 'Just give me the doll. Please.'

But something has happened. He stops jogging and turns

to look at me. Too late, I notice his eyes – too bright, feverish. Knowing this is how he'd have looked, twenty, no thirty years ago – the orphan, the one nobody truly wanted. Disappointed every Christmas, unable to win, desperate to get his own back.

'No. I've got a better idea.' He smiles slowly.

He turns and begins to stride purposefully towards the outhouse.

'Tom...'

But ignoring me is part of the performance, making sure all I can do is follow. I force myself to hang back, and keep my mouth shut. But he knows I am right there, behind him, and there's a satisfied swing to his step. Inside the shed he makes for the rack of tools on the wall – and fetches down the hatchet.

'Oh no, Tom.'

'Oh yes, Sara.'

I don't hang back now. He has me glued to his heels, running to keep up, peppering the air with pleas and injunctions. But all it does is add zest to what he's about. He takes the doll to the edge of the trees, to the block where he chops wood for the fire. Lays her down with a certain ceremony that somehow keeps me at bay. She stays where he puts her – a small stiff figure, hair streaming like weed over the block.

Then our eyes meet and we stare at each other. It gives me hope. 'Tom,' my voice is soft, 'I don't want you to do this.'

His voice is even softer. 'I know.'

For a moment there is only silence.

Then I hear it. A warning from the river. Movement in the

trees. A breeze runs across my neck like the touch of a small hand, raises a line of goosebumps where it goes. Tells me someone else is here...

Tom raises the axe, and the same breeze ruffles the hair falling across his brow. A soft touch. Treacherous. Now, about his head, the surrounding air ripples as if he were a picture printed on a page, riffled by that same treacherous breeze. And in the corner of my eye, I see. The flick of a tail by his feet. A cat, reminding me of a cat once seen, long ago.

And suddenly I know what he doesn't – couldn't – know. He thinks we are alone. And he's wrong. He thinks no one cares about this doll but me. And he is still more wrong. Tom raises the axe higher, and truly believes that here, in this place, he is the one with the anger, the power. The will to do harm.

But it's her doll and the anger is all hers. And *she* is what fills every particle in the Valley. Every leaf, every nudging current of air. Remembering that, everything becomes quiet inside me. I have stood back, inside myself. There is nothing I need to do now. It's not me that is going to stop him. For the first time, Tom is going to realise that it's true, every word I've said about her. She is here. She is everywhere. Oddly relaxed now, I watch the trees circle their branches behind him, watch the surge of air gathering to strike.

She is everywhere...

And again it comes to me, the image of before. Of Tom lying under soil, and all the Valley springing to life because of it. Flowers where his eyes once were, cowslips growing from the soft mulch of his tongue. Never again the sound of machines.

This is how a garden grows. Quietly the Valley takes

control of its own. My eyes become heavy as I watch a fate unfold. I feel as if I'm about to fall asleep and dream.

Tom lets the axe hover above his head, fixes me with the empty, brilliant grin of a furious child. And doesn't know about the other child...

No living child. Something snaps awake inside me.

'No!'

I scream the word. But not at him. At her. And Tom only smiles. Brings down the axe, thinking he knows where it will land.

And it's then our two screams mingle. But long after mine dies away, Tom's carries on, splits the air and echoes through the trees. A male scream that seems to have no end.

~

# Chapter Twenty-One

The ambulance arrived and took him away.

But first I had to leave him.

He had lain, staring up at me from the ground, his eyes slowly glazing. I have seen animals in this state. A rabbit left twitching by the side of the road after we had winged it coming down the lane; once, a duck panting beside the river, its breast peppered with pellets.

Now Tom had the same blanked gaze, the same quick, shallow breaths.

'What are you waiting for? Get to the phone.' He whispered the words.

But I didn't move. There was blood. Blood everywhere. Yet I couldn't leave him. If I went inside he would be alone, here – with the trees and the river and a child who could still do him harm.

'For Christ's sake, Sara. I'm going to bleed to death. Get me help.'

But still I didn't move. I had to wait, gauge the content of the air, holding my breath until I was sure. And there – she was gone. Fled, back to the trees, to the river. A child who knew what she had done.

Only then did I leave him, running towards the house, to the telephone. And help.

In the ambulance, he drifted in and out of consciousness. The paramedics had given him morphine for the pain and it took him away for minutes at a time. But every so often he came back and his eyes fell open to stare at me; they asked why I hadn't run for help straight away. Why first he'd had to lie, bleeding while I'd stood, going nowhere, doing nothing.

And how could I explain? I hadn't moved because I was afraid. If I'd left him, what might she not have done? He was at the mercy of a child.

An angry child. I couldn't have left him alone. I wouldn't have dared. She might have used them against him – the trees, the river, the air itself – as she had already used them.

Now he's safe, in the hospital. Lying in a bed with bandages and wires strapped about his leg. The axe cut right through the ligament, and split the bone. Even so he is lucky to be alive. It's what they all say – the surgeon, the orthopaedic doctors, the nurses who change the dressings on the wound – even the old ladies who come round the wards with books and sweets and copies of The People's Friend.

They all know the story: how he was chopping with an axe, how it slipped in his hand; how it came and scythed a valley in his leg, only missing the artery by a miraculous fraction of a millimetre. If he had cut through that, there wouldn't have been an ambulance in the world that could have got to him in time. He so nearly died, and by his own hand. Leaving me, the wife, pregnant with his child.

A tragic accident, that's what it so nearly was. So nearly tragic that even the nurses see him as a special case. With his silk pyjamas and the hair flopping boyishly over his face, they are looking forward to having him around. He'll be there for a long time yet. It's going to be a month at least before he comes home.

It's only me that knows the truth. The first evening, I sat beside his bed and held his hand. The same all through the next day. Gradually it became clear that shock and morphine together had confused him, wiped out the things he should try to remember. After the first drugged sleep of the night, he forgot what he would have asked me in the ambulance: why had I simply stood, not moving while he lay and bled?

Now he lies in bed, aware of his own glamour, of the nurses making a fuss of him. They can't forget the romance of the child nearly born without a father. And he's forgotten how it really was. He thinks it was an accident. He thinks it could have happened to anyone.

He doesn't remember anything he should. It was no accident.

Once again, I am coming home alone. The taxi drops me off outside the house in a limp, grey drizzle of rain. The taxi driver says:

'You going to be all right down here, all by yourself?'

'Of course.'

I pay him, then stand, listening to the sound of the taxi's engine swallowed up by the lane. And wait. Any moment and it will come, the feeling of not being alone. She will come.

But a minute passes, and another. Meanwhile the river runs and sounds just like any river. Wind whispers in the trees and sounds like any wind. Around me the cleared brown earth is no more than a blank, a smudge in the landscape.

And it doesn't fool me. None of it fools me. Over there, beneath the trees, is the chopping block. If I went there now, I'd find the traces of blood where it would have run and collected and cooled between the wood shavings and the grass – unless, of course, animals have come in the night and taken it away, every matted drop, fed it to themselves or their young, wasting nothing.

That's where he lay, writhing from the wound. My Tom. He nearly died. He could have died. And I hadn't even been able to leave him to phone for help because of what she might still have done to him.

I stand in the empty patch. She's hiding. Keeping her distance, keeping away from me. Well, let her. She can stay away for ever. He could have died.

It's only inside the house it occurs to me. Why am I not afraid? I should be. I know what she can do now, this child with the power to hurt. Look what happened to Tom. What if she turned on me? What could she not do to me?

But somehow, the thought has no resonance. He took her doll, and like the little girl she is, she hit out. Boys who bully deserve to be hurt.

Yet she did more than hit out, this child, no living child. Tom lies in a hospital bed with the hushed step of nurses round him. She made it happen, she nearly killed him.

How could she do such a thing? How dare she?

It's still there this morning. Anger. Rage.

Waking up without Tom. Not in London now, but in hospital, with pins and screws keeping his leg together. He nearly died.

Rage. Fury. It drives me out of the door to find her.

But it's the same as when I came home. The Valley is empty. Here there are only woods and grass – and me. She is hiding. She knows what she has done.

I turn on my heel and stride back into the house. I will find something to do there. Something that will make Tom smile when I tell him. Paint a room, or sand a fireplace. Do something to make him happy.

But it's no use. I'm wringing a cloth above a solution of sugar soap when in my belly it comes – the movement inside me. It's the Other Thing, writhing, twitching as it grows. Wanting me to know it's there. I let the cloth fall with a soft flump back into the bucket, afraid, not of her, but of this. I need to be outside, where she is.

Except, of course, she's not there. She's hiding – in the woods, in the river. A child who has done wrong. Anger springs up inside me again. But not so strong this time, not like it should be. I have to remember Tom, how close he came, how very close.

Upstairs, Mandy's door is open when I would have sworn it was closed.

Is this her doing, trying to draw attention to herself, trying to wheedle her way back in? No. Inside is where she cannot come. This is not her place. She didn't open this door.

Meanwhile Marietta's boxes continue to stand, side by side. Silent now, reminding me it's been days since I heard the scrabble of feet across the floor.

Sure enough, the nest of baby mice has disappeared. Nothing to show they were ever here. Did they grow up, then, and scatter? More likely they died. More likely still, their parents ate them, keeping themselves alive, conserving what they had. Wise parents. I'm about to replace the lid of the second box, when I see what I missed the first time I looked in here.

Marietta's cat.

The china cat that sat on her desk all through the years, watching her work, its face curved into a sleek impassive smile.

'Where did that come from?'

I would have been about five, still small. I expected her to mention somewhere that was far away. A place that was just a name, where all the cats smiled like this.

'Oh I don't know,' she said. She had put down her pen. 'Scotland, I suppose.'

I'd have been impressed at that. Even I had been to Scotland.

'It was my grandfather's. They say it was all he took with him to America – apart from the clothes he stood up in. He must have treasured it, Sara. He was holding it when he died, the last thing he touched.'

I had stared, imagining this cat caught in the grip of a dead man. Despite that, my hand reached out towards it.

'No, Sara. Leave it please.'

But already I had it, clutching it hard, like John Ravenscroft on his deathbed, mesmerised by the porcelain smile.

'Sara,' Marietta's voice chided me – and for answer my own fingers had loosened. The cat fell. Fell and smashed. Every bit of it broken, even the smile.

I stared aghast at what I had done. But all Marietta did was sigh.

Later we glued the cat together. So carefully you could hardly see the joins, so even the smile stayed the same. It smiles at me now from the bottom of the box. Reminds me that once, when Tom broke a vase, his aunt took his roller skates – a birthday present – back to the shop.

I was the lucky one. I've always known I was lucky. But what if Marietta had been different, never loved me in her own dry fashion? I know the answer: I'd have been like Tom, always searching, always wanting something others had.

Marietta forgave me because I was a child and she loved me. Makes me realise I can forgive another child.

Outside, the doll is where Tom left her, lying on the chopping block. I pick her up to give her back to the child who lost her. Take her to the water's edge, to her doll's bed of mud and weeds.

Immediately the Valley stirs. Breeze lights upon my skin. But the touch is uncertain, cautious. She still needs to know for sure. Waits for me to tell her. So I do.

*I am not angry. Not any more.*

The Valley sighs and skips. Breathes again. Inside me, the Other Thing flips, asks that I notice it too. But it's no use. I wouldn't even know it was there. Not while I am here, outside, and she is here too. Above, beneath, around me.

She is back. She is everywhere.

~

# Chapter Twenty-Two

Evie tots up my bill, takes my money. Then reaches behind her to pull down a box of Terry's All Gold from the shelf. Pushes it across the counter.

'And these are for you.'

'Evie...?'

'They're from Mary. She told me to give them to you when you come in. She said better make them plain chocolate because plain's more sophisticated.'

'Oh,' I whisper. 'Oh Mary...'

'She'd have given them to you herself, only she's had to go and look after Reenie, her sister, the one who's poorly. But she was that shocked when she heard about your husband. Worried about you, she was, what it might do with the little one, an upset like that.'

'But I'm all right.'

Evie shakes her head. 'She'll want to see for herself. Won't believe it otherwise.'

I pick up the box of chocolates, which I'm afraid will only make Tom sneer. He prefers his chocolate to come from Belgium, seventy-two per cent cocoa.

'I'll make sure to get them to Tom.'

'They're not for him!' says Evie instantly. 'Mary meant them for you. Let you know she's thinking about you. Case you needed cheering up. Thinks about you a lot, does Mary. We all do.'

She laughs when I blush, hardly knowing what to say.

Tom lies, his leg resting above the cover, bandaged and circled by gleaming metal screws. When I lean across the pillow to kiss him, there's the smell of antiseptic mingling with an expensive floral scent – lilies and tuberose.

'You've got more flowers.'

The table at the end of his bed acts like a dividing wall between him and the rest of the ward, screening him off with a huge, jostling arrangement of blooms.

'Joaquin,' he says. 'You know what he's like. Everything's got to be bigger and better.' But he eyes the flowers complacently, as being something else that marks him out. A male patient deluged with blossoms, like a film star.

'So...how are you?'

'Bored.'

A week since it happened. The third day after he arrived was Christmas, to be endured with swarms of carol singers and hospital mince pies. The doctors made their rounds with pairs of foam antlers on their heads, and Tom unwrapped the watch I bought him. He didn't put it on. Dreamy from the painkillers, he had no use for time. Besides, he has the one Joaquin gave him. I should have remembered.

It's a far cry from the Christmas he had planned. But now we are settling into a routine. Today we will sit for an hour or more, not unlike the elderly couple in the next bed – he with the broken femur he got from falling off the ladder when he was decorating their Christmas tree, and she sitting beside him, unwrapping Murray Mints and clearing her throat. Neither of them talking much. They seem comfortable with the silence.

'Sara.'

Surprisingly, it's Tom who breaks it now. Usually he leaves me to think of things to say.

I look at him. I have been forever looking at him over these past days. First I was watching for the ebb and flow of pain, and the morphine washing in and taking it all away. Then the grey drowsed look that came when they stopped the morphine and let his own brain lull him into peacefulness. And now, what he calls boredom, but which is actually the languor of the well-looked after.

But today there's a new look in his face. Alert. He says, 'What did you do with the doll after?'

I pause then say, 'I put her back. Down by the river.'

He sighs and looks away. A nurse passes by with some tinsel that has fallen down, and smiles at him over the flowers.

Minutes pass. In the next bed the old woman unwraps yet another mint and pops it in her mouth. It's so quiet you can hear it click against the backs of her false teeth.

'Sara,' he says again. I feel myself go tense. But his voice is soft. 'I've been thinking. I'd be grateful – I'd be positively joyful – if you would talk to someone for me.'

'Of course.' Wondering how this connects with the doll.

'Someone who could help. A doctor maybe.'

'A doctor? Are you in pain?' I have jumped to my feet. 'I'll get a nurse to come and—'

'Not for me, Sara. For you.'

Slowly, I sit down again.

'It could be what you need. This way you've been behaving – I was thinking maybe you're just...depressed. Maybe it's no more than that. I'm hoping it's no more than that.'

I open my mouth, but nothing comes out.

'I'm not even saying it's your fault. It was a mistake. I can see it now – moving, taking on the whole house, land, country thing. It's made you, well...'

He stops. Starts again.

'I thought at first it was the Other Thing changing you. Then I realised. There wouldn't have been any Other Thing if you'd been yourself. You'd have dealt with it and that would have been that. Now it's there and there's nothing we can do to stop it.'

Again he pauses.

'I suppose I'm trying to say none of this would have happened if we'd stayed in London. I wouldn't be lying in this bed. There wouldn't be a kid about to crap up our lives. And you...and you wouldn't be talking about ghosts and things that go bump in the night. That is, when you're not too busy digging and digging as if there was some kind of engine in your brain.' He frowns. 'You're shaking your head. What's that supposed to mean?'

'Nothing.'

He throws up his hands. 'See?' he cries. 'I'm trying to connect here, but there's no fucking talking to you.'

At the next bed, the old couple have turned to stare at us. The nurse, on her way back past the bed, is more tactful. Looks the other way. He flinches and lowers his voice.

'Look. What I'm trying to say is, it doesn't have to be like this. We came here. We can go back. We can retrace our steps. It'll be just a case of putting everything into reverse.'

'Everything?'

'Well not everything, obviously. It's too late for the Other Thing. But if we could just get back to where we were, if we could just get your head straight, maybe we can turn this round.' He looks at me. 'I could even find a way to live with having a kid. If only you could just...just...'

'Go back to the way I was?'

He nods. Because I have understood him, every word. He means the Sara who thinks of him, only him. Attentive as a mother with her firstborn, her only-born. He says:

'But it can't happen here, I know that now. We need to be back in a place we belong. Where you belong. Jen says the same thing...'

'Jen?'

And he has the grace to blush. 'I've been on to her. I...I told her about the ghost business.'

'What did she say?' I have to force myself to ask, already knowing the answer.

He shrugs. 'She agrees with me.'

'You mean she thinks I'm mad.'

He pretends to wince at the throb in my voice. 'Well what do you expect? She couldn't believe it at first. It's not a sane thing to think, Sara. She knows there's got to be a reason.'

He means a reason not to believe me. The reason that mad people have no friends. I have lost Jen.

'She says you'll be fine if we just get you back to town.'

'We sold the house,' I say. But I am numb from loss. Numb from betrayal. I have lost Jen.

'It doesn't matter. We'll find something else. A flat maybe. We'll do the other thing – the house, the land – but later, when the time is right, when we've planned it better.'

'I thought you'd planned everything this time.'

He laughs shortly. 'You've got to be joking. You clapped eyes on the pink house and that was it. I shouldn't have listened to you. I could have told you it would never work out, not there. Next time, we'll know better. We'll leave the choosing to me.'

He pauses. 'Hey, what's the matter? Where are you going? I haven't finished. There's stuff I need to say to you.'

But I have stood up, sliding back my chair so violently it scrapes across the hospital floor. Makes the old couple look round again.

'I'm going home.'

'But that's what I'm saying to you. We can go home. Properly home. Back to where we belong.'

'This is where I belong.'

He stares a moment then gives a crow of disbelief. 'For God's sake, Sara! For months you've been whining that nobody wants us, that we're the outsiders and all anybody wants is to see the back of us. Tell me how you can possibly say you belong.'

I open my mouth to answer. I'm thinking of the box of chocolates. Mary and Evie so anxious to see me bloom with this child. Reg with his old man's smile. People who care for me.

Tom says, 'Look – you know as well as me, it would take

twenty years. Longer. God, Sara – you'd have to fucking die there. That's the only way you'll belong.'

And hearing that, something inside me stirs. Remembers how nearly he died. How nearly he did belong. But it's nothing he would want to hear.

His voice has become soft again.

'The fact is, you don't belong there, Sara. You could never belong. You can see that, surely. You know what you're like? Truly? You're like those animals we used to see on the Underground, those mice that used to run between the tracks in the dark. We'd watch them moving, remember? Trains never bothered them, or the noise. You'd think that if they could live there, they could live anywhere. Yet you know if you took them out, put them in the country, they wouldn't last two minutes. Owls would get them. Or they'd go mad.'

He watches me a moment. Gently places his hand over mine.

'You're just the same, Sara. The place has driven you halfway to mad already. You're seeing ghosts, fuck it! Digging holes in the ground as if you were planning to bury an army. Your best friend thinks you're losing it. Come with me before it's too late and there's no way back. We'll start again. As for the kid – what we can't change, we can fix. We'll pay people to look after it. Nannies, schools, the works. We don't have to be like Charlie and Jen. We'll fix it so we hardly know it's there.'

He looks into my eyes.

'Just trust me in this. You keep saying you don't want this child. Well I believe you. It's your hormones stitching you up, I understand that now. Hormones taking you over, stopping you from having the termination. Probably the same fucking hormones that've been making you see ghosts. But we can deal with it, Sara. You can talk to someone, take a few pills. We can make everything right. We just need to go back. We can be happy again. Just you see.'

I stare at him, feel the lines of my face become slack. Tom smiles, reaches out and draws me close. His mouth finds my mouth; lovingly, lingering in a way it hasn't for months. The nurse comes by a third time, sees a handsome, boyish man kissing his wife, and looks envious.

I'm driving. Too fast for the country roads, steering like someone who knows every bend, who has lived here all her life. Someone who truly belongs.

But Tom's right. People like us – we say we belong, but it's wishful thinking. We escape from town to village and, five minutes after we've arrived, say it's as if we've lived there for ever. We bring friends to stay, laugh at the locals. We say a place is made for us.

But who else says so? Not the same locals who aren't local anymore because they can't afford the houses they grew up in. Not the farmers who annoy with their smells and their noise, or the teachers whose schools still get closed because rich folk don't send their children there. New people say they belong somewhere, when all it means is that they like it there.

So how can I say I belong? I can't.

Unless there is a way. A way to prove I was meant to be here. I stop the car. I've arrived at the church, where we stopped the very first morning we came. That day I saw something – and put it out of my mind. I didn't want to belong then. Now – now I do want to belong.

The grave stands as I remember it, distant from the other graves – older, greener, keeping its secrets close. I've never come back, not since that first time. Today I fall onto the wet grass, kneel beside it. Eager now, I set my fingers scrabbling at the moss, tearing it away in clumps, searching until I find what I'm after.

And there it is again: Ravenscroft. My name. This is what I didn't let Tom see that day. He would have pointed to it in triumph. *Look, Sara! It's a sign. It shows you'd be coming home!*

But I would have told him then: a name can't be a sign of anything except itself. There has to be something more; something that connects. John Ravenscroft was a miner. He went to America to become John Ravenscroft, owner of railroads, steamships and an ocean of stocks. And a china cat.

But he didn't come from here. He took the boat from Glasgow and left in 1879. Marietta told me. There has to be more to connect that Ravenscroft with the Ravenscroft who lies here.

So I keep searching. But moss clings harder than you'd imagine. It's like trying to flay an animal without the proper tools. I scrabble and search until my fingers bleed, but all I find is a flat green sheen that has become part of the stone itself. Everything else is worn away.

Except this: a name – Elsa.

No date. No mother, no father, no husband, no children. Just Elsa Ravenscroft, the letters shallow, almost gone; and that's all. There is no Elsa in any story I've heard. Nothing to connect.

It means Tom is right. I'm no different from the rest of them – the incomers, the outsiders. Elsa Ravenscroft belongs here, under the turf; but Sara Ravenscroft comes from far away, and could never belong.

Now when I drive, I go slowly, careful with every twist and turn.

~

# Chapter Twenty-Three

Down in the Valley, the woods seem lifeless, sunk into the earth. But if you look closely, they aren't lifeless at all. There are small, hard swellings at the tips of each and every tree. Each swelling a life, a new tree coiled like a spring, pressing against the shell that contains it and which soon will have to split and break and fall empty to the ground.

Things are dying so new things can be born – all in this one place, where everything belongs except me. Mandy died here. *She* belongs.

As I think of her, she comes. Blows cold against my cheek, brings the blood rushing. Why does she come to me? What am I to her?

On impulse I put out my arms – and gasp as she flies into them. I can smell her. A new thing, this – a little girl scent, sweet sour like apples long before they ripen. The warm, waxy scent of hair. It's like holding Pig.

Shocked, I let her go. Immediately my arms feel empty.

Tom phones me.

'Why didn't you pick up? I've been calling for hours.'

I know. All evening I've listened to it ring.

'I knew you were there, Sara.' Tom's voice is accusing. 'But look, I haven't phoned to quarrel. Far from it. I've got good news. Joaquin's been saying he needs me back at work. Well now he's put his money where his mouth is. He's fixed for a room in a private place up in London. Everything can come to me there.' He pauses. 'You listening, Sara?'

'Yes.'

'You see what it does, don't you? It'll make moving back a doddle. We'll put the house on the market, but only in London. Keep it away from the local agents. We want city types with proper wads. Meantime we can start deciding about what we want instead. I was thinking Notting Hill or Holland Park. Or how about Primrose Hill?'

'Tom.' I interrupt. 'I need to ask you something.'

'What?' Impatient, Tom is brimming with plans. His voice tells me what I've already guessed. The Shine is on its way back.

'Have you ever felt you belonged? Here, I mean?'

He sighs. 'That again. I thought we talked it all out, Sara.'

'Please, Tom.'

There's a silence at the other end. At last he says, 'OK, maybe. At the beginning, when it was all new. It felt – great. Like the place was made for us. But then...'

'But then...?'

'Then you had to get pregnant, didn't you?' He snaps these words – but then he softens. 'Even before, though, it had started to go...sour. You saw what it was like, it didn't matter what I did. It began to feel as if the whole fucking place was laughing at me, even the machines. Then came the accident...' He stops. 'If I tell you about the accident, you'll think I'm as mad as you are.'

'I won't.'

He laughs mirthlessly. 'That's the whole trouble. I know you won't. And the thing is, it is mad.'

'Just tell me.'

He hesitates. 'All right – the accident. I've started remembering it wrong. Not like an accident at all. I look back and it's like the place – the whole fucking place again – had turned against me. Made it happen.'

'What do you mean?'

'When I picked up that axe, I was angry, but I knew what I was doing. I wouldn't have let it slip. I was in control. Yet the fucking thing came down, and it was like I had nothing to do with it. Like it wasn't even me holding it. There – I told you it was mad.'

'I don't think it's mad.'

'Yeah, well. But here's the thing, Sara. I don't want to come back there. Can you understand that? I hate the place now. Just like it hates me.'

For a moment neither of us speaks. Perhaps because everything has been said. Tom knows about her. He'll never admit he does, not even to himself, but he knows. There's something here – a child with a child's anger; and it will pay him back for every bad act, the way any child would.

He doesn't believe she exists, yet still he knows. The place is dangerous for him. If he comes home, if he angers her again, she'll hurt him again. She'll put him under the earth, and make it so he stays for ever. Always belong.

Tom says, 'Do you understand why I've got to get out of there? Got to, Sara? I can find a way to live with the Other Thing – but not there, never there.'

He waits.

'Well? Do you?'

'Yes,' I say. 'I understand.'

And I do. I understand more than he will ever know. I know why we can't stay here. Suddenly, just like that, we become *we* again.

She knows what I've done.

I go outside, and straight away she rushes towards me.

*I'm sorry,* I say to her. I'm so sorry.

Flurries of leaves fly from nowhere, the air around me spins.

But all I do is shake my head.

And that's when she grows angry. The breeze flies faster, sends dust skitting upwards, sharp particles to drive into my eyes.

*I'm sorry,* I say again.

Angrier by the moment, she's not going to listen to me. She's just a child, she knows nothing about the promises adults make and feel bound to keep. Helpless, I turn to make my way back towards the house, but a root snakes from underground, catches me and trips me up, sends me sprawling.

Blood fills my mouth. Salt on my tongue. Yet it could be worse. Here, in this Valley, she has power that no child could ever dream of. No living child.

*I have to go.* I try, I try to tell her how it is. There's no way I can stay.

But there's no talking to her. With a roar the wind drives in from the trees. A moment later I'm running; back towards the house, to safety.

*I'll make you stay.* She pursues me with the unbounded

rage of a child. *I'll make you never leave.*

And it's true. Of course she can make me stay. Things are born and they die. She died here; she belongs. She can make others do the same. She has the power. Even Tom knows that now.

Run faster.

Inside the house, safe inside the house, I close the door, drive home the bolts. I'm shaking. I had forgotten how this felt: to be afraid of a child. A child with the power to harm.

How am I to live now?

As so often, the answer comes in the shape of another question. *What would Marietta do?* Even as I ask myself, I know.

Marietta's things; they are my answer. Upstairs, I take them out of the boxes. Masks, statues, painted skulls. Shrunken heads, puppets and claws. Drums with their skin stretched tight, fetishes of blood and bone. What did Marietta say they were for?

Protection. A way for the Dead to ward off the Dead.

I need to be protected now. Until *she* stops being angry, understands that adults can't always do what children want. Until I close the door to this house and leave the Valley for ever. Otherwise she'll find a way to make me stay.

So now they are everywhere, Marietta's things. Next to the windows, the doors – anywhere there is a crack, a way to slip inside. They will be the guards, the eyes to warn and ward off.

I am trusting in the Dead to keep me safe.

But just when I think it's all I need to do, I go back one

last time to Marietta's boxes. And find the photograph of my mother and the china cat, still there, as if waiting to be noticed. Neither of them magic, the way the masks are magic; all the same I take them and put them on my bedside table.

But as I turn to go, something makes me stop.

It's my mother. She smiles at me from the garden where she stands. Young – much younger than I am now, she holds a baby in her arms. Me. Holds me up and laughs, happy. You can see it in her eyes.

Her eyes. Slowly I pick up the photograph. Now we both stand, divided by time. All the years of growing up, I barely thought about her. I was an orphan and she simply never lived long enough.

And now look! I always thought I had Marietta's eyes. But that's not true. Sometimes, when I've been outside, and the breeze has been skimming my neck, when one moment has been flowing into the next and the sun a slow clock above my head – this is when I've glanced in the mirror to find my own eyes looking back at me, wide open and alive. Just as my mother's eyes are looking at me now.

This is what she would have seen – Mandy. These eyes.

Finally, I understand. Eyes that are an invitation, an open door. I have let my own eyes become an invitation, a promise. They made Mandy come to me.

I snatch up the photograph and thrust it in a drawer, face down. Now my mother lies hidden, her eyes unable to smile at anyone. But it's too late. It's been too late for months.

I have her eyes. They made Mandy come, making promises I could never keep. Making her think I was here to stay.

* * *

Now I have to be safe. From her, from Mandy.

A week goes by and Tom is in London, in his private room a world away.

'I'll be all by myself,' he said before he went, almost convincing himself it was true. But he's wrong, of course. It's me that's alone.

Unless you count the Dead.

Every day now the wind tears through the Valley, trees throw their branches at my feet and threaten to do worse. Up in the shop, they call it weather, but I know what it is. It's *her*, still furious, determined to make me stay. Each night I close the doors against her, leaving her outside to rage against me in the dark.

But am I safe? I need to believe that I am. Child of the river, she cannot come inside. But what if that's not true? What if she finds a way to make it not true? Why shouldn't there be a way for her to slip inside, defying the doors and the watching masks, slipping past them the way noise passes through cracks?

Or water that trickles through the smallest space. Why not? She's the child of the river.

I've begun to dream her inside the house. I dream that the river washes against the walls, searches for cracks. Leaches under doors, falls through the spaces in the window frames, spreads a shining carpet across the floor. And it brings her with it.

But only in dreams. When I wake, there is no river. The doors are shut and sturdy. Marietta's masks stare out into the dark and the house is dry and watertight. Safe for now, but for how long?

# Chapter Twenty-Four

Mary Coryn frowns at the circles under my eyes.

'You're looking tired, my girl.'

Evie says, 'My Mum told me she never slept a wink, not in all the time she was expecting me.'

Mary shakes her head. 'You shouldn't be down there by yourself. You need someone to keep an eye. What if anything happens?'

'What sort of thing?'

And there it is – the old look passed between Evie and herself. A reminder that there is something they believe they know, and I don't. Still keeping secrets from me, even now.

But now I have a secret from them. The pink house is for sale again, glued to the window of a London estate agent's. Fortunately Mary and Evie don't know; otherwise they'd think we're fly-by-nights, folk who can afford to taste a place and move on. Never stay long enough to leave a mark.

Better they don't know.

But then Mary points to my basket. 'We'll not be seeing hide nor hair of you soon, will we? You won't be needing us anymore.'

'What?' I feel the blood run to my face.

'Well that's what you came here for, wasn't it? To grow your own carrots and all. What will you want shops for?'

Her words have an effect. They send me flying home to find the packages of seeds Tom ordered months ago. Take them outside, and salt the earth with them; only remembering to read the instructions on the packets afterwards, when it's too late and I realise I've gone and sown carrots and peas a whole two months earlier than I should, before the frosts have finished for the winter.

But you never know – they might survive, those embryo carrots under the earth. They might still grow and prove the packets wrong. A little stunted perhaps, a little bitter from being exposed too early in their lives, but grow nonetheless. Other things do. Although none of it will be for us now.

Yesterday I looked out of the window to find that all the stretch of brown soil had turned silver. In the night, snails had come and thrown a net of slimy threads which caught the sun and shimmered. It's as if they knew that underneath, things were growing that they could eat. So here they were, ready.

And I am growing too, my belly smoothing out and tightening. The Other Thing moves, makes small contours rise and fall in undulations under the skin. Fascinated, half in fear, I watch the accommodations my body makes. I feel like a passenger, a stowaway aboard a vessel not my own.

But Mary approves. 'Beginning to fill out nicely,' she pronounces. 'Only a shame your Tom isn't here to see it.'

She stops smiling, as she always does when she mentions Tom. She hates the fact that he isn't here. Hates it that I am alone, down by the river. I've told her he's had to go to a specialist hospital in London, and now she just worries about me more. She has bullied Evie into stocking fresh orange juice instead of the sweet-acidy long-life kind that used to be a shop staple, and frowns at the contents of my shopping basket. She knows everything that goes into my mouth.

One morning, she catches me by surprise. 'John Marsh is reckoning on stopping by with you today.'

'Oh? Why?'

'Because I told him to,' Mary snaps as if it were obvious.

So down in the Valley, I wait for him, relieved that Mary had warned me. But I should have thought more about him coming. He steps through the front door, and stops dead.

'What are these then? Got a witch doctor staying with you?'

The masks. I'd forgotten the masks. I should have put them away. He's having to see objects designed to keep out a child – his child. The little girl he lost and would give the world to have back.

I hurry him to the kitchen, where he pretends not to notice that we have stripped it all away – the Artex and the country pine, the patterned tiles they were so proud of. Keeps his eyes trained on the mug of tea I have handed to him.

'Mary told me to find out if you needed a hand, what with Tom not being here. Bit of hammering, leaky pipes – if you tell me, I'll sort it.'

'There's nothing,' I tell him. 'Thanks.'

'What about outside? Grass is coming through early this year. I could see if it needs cutting.'

Before I can say anything he moves to the window

to inspect the lawn – and of course there is no lawn, not anymore. He gives a low whistle of surprise.

'Mind if I go out and have a look?'

In the middle of the vast brown bed, he looks around, impressed by what he sees.

'Get someone in, did you? Clear it all for you?'

'I did it.'

'No?' He grins in disbelief. 'Well – it's something, I'll say that. There were tree roots right the way underneath.'

'Tom was furious with me.'

He looks surprised. 'Why's that then? It's a good job you've done here.'

'He never meant to touch much of the lawn. Just the trees. He was going to chop them down, then clear it for vegetables. Kohlrabi, asparagus.'

And for some reason this amuses him. 'I see. Some of those beeches are over two hundred years old. What was he reckoning on using for that little job? A bulldozer?'

I think a moment, remembering Tom's failures with the rotovator. Then I smile. 'Yes. I suppose that's what he would have done in the end.'

'And how exactly did he think he was going to get a bulldozer down the lane?'

As I flounder, he gives a shout of laughter at what city folk think they can get away with. But my own smile has faded. Because that laughter – it shows how, deep down, he has a contempt for us, Tom and me, believing we had the answers to everything. He's laughing because he thinks we are hopeless. Incomers who haven't got a clue. Tom's right – we don't belong. We could never belong.

But the anger dies. *She* is here. Perhaps she heard his voice from the river, heard him laugh and now here she is. I feel her as I always feel her – by the pricking on my skin, the sudden extra beat of my heart.

What about Marsh, though? He's still laughing at the thought of Tom. Can't he feel her? He's her father. If he would only be still a moment, stop the laughing, surely he'd realise straight away. We are not alone. He should listen, the river would tell him.

'Stop!'

And immediately he stops. But the grin is still there.

'Listen,' I tell him. 'Just listen.'

He looks at me. 'Listen to what?'

'To the river.'

The smile dies on his lips. He blinks once, twice. Now, because of me, he does hear it – the river. He hears, and I watch it all come back to him – exactly what happened in this place. There will be no more smiling today.

'Oh,' I whisper. 'Oh I'm sorry. I should never have mentioned the river. Not to you.'

His eyes fly to mine. My own look has said it all.

'You know?' he says in disbelief. 'You know what happened here?'

I nod.

'Who told you?'

'Nobody. Nobody told me anything.'

But he doesn't believe me. And I can't tell him how I know. Convinced he's been betrayed, he shakes his head, starts to walk away. But then he turns again, his face red with a sudden male flush of anger.

'It wasn't her fault. Don't let anybody tell you it was Carole's fault. I shouldn't have left her when she was like that, do you hear me? She tried to tell me and I wouldn't listen.'

'Tell you what?'

But he hasn't heard me; or he doesn't care to answer. He has begun to shake, this hard, compact man, and as he speaks, he raises his hand as if to hit the air – or me. A moment later, though, he lets his hand drop. He is pulling himself together, little by little. His breathing slows and becomes heavy.

'I'm sorry,' I say again.

'I'm telling you. She didn't know what she was doing. Even the police said so.'

Then he turns and walks fast as he can, away from me. His car door slams and there comes the roar of his engine in the lane. Over-revving, sounding like one of Tom's machines.

The car disappears, but not the words. They hang in the air, will hang for ever now. Not Carole's fault. She didn't know what she was doing.

And I am shaking. What did she do, this woman who was cold even on a warm May day? I thought I knew what happened here. The river was to blame. The river took Mandy, but it would have been an accident. As accidental as all the other stuff it carries away. Old boots, watering cans. Pots.

I never wanted to think there might be another way.

What did she do?

I turn to Mandy. But she's gone. The air is empty. Her father told me something I don't understand, but Mandy heard him, and now she's fled. Is this what happens? Are there things that even ghosts try to forget?

A new thought arrives. Crawls into my head, threatens to grow and harden like a grub turning into a fly.

Not her fault, even the police said so.

Inside the phone is ringing. It's Jen.

'Sara...'

I cling to the sound of her voice, pressing the phone hard against my ear. Yearning for the softness of Jen, the largeness of her.

'Sara...are you all right?'

'No.' My own voice breaks, refuses to hold together.

She sighs in distress. 'Oh sweet girl, Tom's told me everything. Everything. Listen to me, though – it's going to be all right. You're coming back. Just hold on to that. Just a little while more and all this will be behind you.'

'All what, Jen?' I ask her wearily, knowing what the answer will be.

'The ghost, Sara. Whatever it is that's frightening you. Whatever you've told yourself is there.'

'She's real, Jen.'

Jen makes a soft noise in her throat; her way of telling me that she doesn't believe me.

'She killed her, Jen. The mother. I think her own mother killed her. Now she's remembered and she's gone. I don't know where she is.'

'Sara...stop.'

'Everybody hurts her, you see. They make promises and then they break them. I'm the same. I'm leaving with Tom and she's going to be alone again. She's angry with me, and she's right to be. I've hurt her. Everyone hurts her...'

'Sara, please. Don't do this.'

'But I'm telling you, Jen. I should have told you weeks ago.'

'Sara,' her voice breaks through mine. 'Just listen. Come to me. Just grab a bag and leave. Tom must be mad leaving you down there. You've got to come away.'

'But you don't believe me.' My voice is wild. 'You don't believe she exists.'

'It doesn't matter what I believe. We can talk about it when you come. We'll talk about everything. But for now, just do as I say, please. Come to me. Come now, Sara.'

She waits and suddenly I am calm again. 'I'll come if you say you believe me, Jen. Say you truly believe me.'

This time it's me that waits. 'All right,' she says at last. And brightly, quickly adds, 'Of course I believe you.'

It's what I expected her to say. I take the phone from my ear, gently put it back in its cradle. Immediately the phone rings again, but I let it ring.

Mad folk don't have friends. They just have people who lie to them.

~

# Chapter Twenty-Five

There's more storm coming. Two weeks of storm, Mary tells me. Batten down the hatches, she says.

I believe her. The air is leaden, heavy with the expectation of rain and worse. Beside the river the trees are steeling themselves. Everything is steeling itself. Tonight and every night will be hard for all those baby things under the earth. Everything may die.

I go to look for *her*, but she is nowhere. She has fled back to the river. Perhaps she goes to forget, currents of water washing away the memories of what her mother did.

But then, as I turn towards the house, she comes. Hurls herself at me, stops me in my tracks. Suddenly it's a struggle to put one foot in front of the other.

She wants me to stay for ever. Wind whips my face. She has the power.

Everybody hurts her. It's unforgivable, the way I force myself past her, back to the house and drive home the bolts to keep her out. Rattle the knuckle bones and drums to shake the Dead awake. Lock the doors and windows all over again, just in case.

And yet I know, if I opened my arms, she would come. Fold herself against me, fill my nostrils with the scent of apples. All she wants is me.

I twist the keys in the locks one more time. Sealing the cracks that would let her in. Tonight I will lie awake, listening to the sound of water, afraid to sleep. Afraid to dream.

And in the morning, I will go in search of her. As if she too were the thing I wanted most.

Meanwhile, the Other Thing twists and turns, pushes against my ribs, as it does all day and every day. Sometimes I notice it. More often I don't. I'm used to it. It's like hearing a lodger moving about your house. It ducks and it dives, does everything it can to get my attention, wants more than its fair share.

Only occasionally can it make me pause. Battering my sides as though desperate to make me remember. I'll even stop to consider it then – briefly. But inevitably I'll forget. What I remember is Mandy, no living child.

Nothing else is real.

I have to be careful as I drive. In the lane, the steering wheel swings under my hands as if other hands were guiding it. Hands that would turn the car into the bank, smear it against the earth, send me careening into foxholes.

Another way to make me stay.

Tom has started phoning me from his room in his private hospital where, it seems, anything is allowed. Always late, always when he is drunk. It's the champagne, he says. Administered on doctor's orders.

'Do you see Joaquin often?' I ask him.

'Not much. He's given me free rein in everything. Finally got the message.'

He is happy. The future is bright again. He talks about where in London we should live. He wants organic supermarkets, good restaurants. He has plans to put a wind turbine on the roof, apply for an allotment – perhaps in Kensington or Chelsea. He says living in the country has taught him what's important in life.

He never mentions the Other Thing.

Tom talks himself to a standstill, until sleep and wine overtake him. But I'm grateful to him because I don't sleep. After he's gone I will be awake. I am listening. Waiting for the sound of water.

Tonight the phone rings – late, as ever. I pick up, ready to hear Tom again at the other end.

'Sara.'

A voice like velvet, caressing the dark. Joaquin. I let myself fall back on the pillow.

'Are you well, Sara? All by yourself there.'

'It's your fault if I'm alone. You took Tom away.'

'I'll send him home to you if you like. If it helps you.'

'Don't do that.'

'Then I won't.' He stops. He's waiting for me to speak again, to tell him what I want.

'I don't sleep, Joaquin.' And feel my eyes scorch, too tired for tears.

'No? My poor Sara.'

And instead of talking, he sings to me. Old songs in Portuguese, which he doesn't bother to translate. Songs his mother had sung to him. Joaquin has a cracked deep voice that wanders in and out of tune, rhythmical as one wave breaking after another. Before I know anything else, he has sung me to sleep.

* * *

When I wake, it's nearly midday. I've slept fourteen, fifteen hours. Dreamless. Now sleep has put colour in my cheeks, rosied my lips as if someone had been kissing them all night. And I'm hungry. I want cinnamon and honey, churned with butter. Joaquin fare.

But I can't go shopping for them. I've lost something, and I don't know where to find it.

An hour later and I've looked everywhere. Emptied every single bag and pocket. Keys, money, shopping lists lie in a jumble on the kitchen table. I've gone round and round the house, pulled open drawers and wardrobes, but it's not there. Now I can't think of where else to look.

But this is what plagues me, keeps me searching: I don't actually know what it is I've lost. I only know it's gone. Something that should be there, that needs to be there. And isn't.

Finally I give up and drive to the village. But I don't have the roses in my cheeks anymore. The strain of looking for something I can't even name has brought the pallor back. It pulls at the skin around my eyes, makes my head ache.

Maybe that's why Mary looks at me, more intently than ever, her eyes so sharp and searching, I thought maybe she could see it. But all she does is frown, as if she too knows there's something, but she can't put her finger on it either.

It's still gone when I come home. An absence. Something that's been lost.

It's not Mandy, that's for sure. She comes swooping from the river, the trees. A child who will not leave me alone, would leap down my throat if I let her.

But then I see something that makes me forget even her. It's my brown bed of soil; there are blades pushing through the earth, everywhere tiny flags signalling growth. Green.

Green! Without thinking I have turned to her, pulling her in close, sharing the delight, forgetting to be afraid. Immediately, in my nostrils is the scent of apples, sweeter than before. Ripening, getting ready to leave the tree.

My head swims. Dizzy, I push her away. For once she doesn't try to stop me. And once inside, I forget to wonder why. Almost physical now, the sense of what is gone, an ache that grows. How is this possible? How can I miss something and yet not know what it is?

But the ache is there now. Always there, like the warning throb of pain to come. Something that's been lost.

~

# Chapter Twenty-Six

But that was earlier and this is now. Now I do know. I know what is missing.

An hour, two hours ago, I came to bed. Lay in the dark, and felt the stillness around me. In the house everything was quiet. Quiet inside me.

The Other Thing has stopped moving. Night – this should be the time, the exact time that it jumps beneath my fingers. Hard bumps of bone I can feel through flesh whether I want to or not. An unwelcome reminder.

But not tonight. An hour, two hours I have lain here, in the dark.

When did I feel it last? Not today. Last night? Last night I lay, falling asleep to the sound of Joaquin and his mother's songs. Yesterday? Yesterday the only movement was around me, in the trees and on the surface of the river. And anyway, when did I ever allow myself to notice?

The day before? I don't remember. The day before that? I lie in the dark and wait.

Three hours now. Four. Nothing. The thing that ducks and dives inside me, does everything it can to draw attention to itself, has stopped. Everything has become quiet, like a lake where the fish have escaped to the sea.

It must be asleep. Everything sleeps. Sooner or later, even I will sleep, and in the morning it will wake me, turning somersaults as if trying to impress. And I will ignore it.

I don't listen for the sounds of the outside anymore. Tonight I lie, waiting for the Other Thing to do what it has always done. Wait for it to come alive.

It happens suddenly. One moment I am waiting; the next I am not. There is nothing to wait for.

It has gone. The Other Thing has gone.

My heart beats once, then stops. Instead of breathing, I feel myself folding over and over. Curling around an emptiness that only seems to grow. I try to grow with it, I try to contain it, but I can't. It's an emptiness bigger than I am.

Yet for a second it doesn't frighten me. There's not anything to be frightened of, not anymore. I imagine myself flying to Tom, hear myself telling him: it's gone, there is nothing to come between us. We can keep our promises after all. For the smallest fraction of time, I feel myself rising, buoyed up on a void...

Only to fall, sucked back into the space where the Other Thing used to be. Not there anymore because it couldn't compete. It swam and it floundered and took what it could. It even managed to grow – a little. Stretched the margins of my body, pushed them into a shape that could contain it and into which I am falling now. But it wasn't enough. It needed something.

Me. And it couldn't have me.

And this is the result. Tired out with trying, it has swum

away, back where it came from. It's gone. There is no Other Thing. There is nothing here but me.

In the dark, someone cries out. A light goes on, fills the room with shadows. Hands rip open the drawer beside the bed, knocking aside a china cat, which leaps and falls and shatters for a second time.

Hands scrabbling, searching till they find it – the photograph lying face down to keep her from calling in a child.

And there she is, the young woman who was my mother. Her eyes find mine. My eyes, laughing and open. Eyes to bring back a child, from wherever it has fled. Call my child back from the sea.

It's all it takes. A single welcoming thought.

*Come back. Come back to me...*

And it works. Her eyes meet mine and there it is – the single look, the welcoming smile. A smile to call a child and bring it back. She has the power. Her eyes are my eyes. She, I can call it back.

Something hears me. Something stirs. I hear it – sound that comes from outside the house. Yet inside me everything is still. The secret lake is empty, laps against nothing. What have I done, then? What is moving? Who is it that I've called?

Downstairs comes the answer. Quietly, quietly, the front door has slipped off its latch. Windows have slid open, cracks are prising apart the walls. Eddies of water are trickling, falling into the house.

This is what I have done. I have called *her* in, the child from outside. The wrong child. A single welcoming thought. Now she is pouring through walls and doors, washing away the masks. Here because she thinks all I want is her.

She comes, while another child – my child – steals away.

Water beats against the sides of the house, bubbles with a kind of laughter. Laps against the stairs, excited, filled with... what? Joy. Of course: I made her think I preferred the Dead over the Living. And it's not true.

But she doesn't know that. Instead, water races, seeking its own level, looking for me. All the house is filling. I can smell the river, dank and alive. I can smell apples.

While quietly, quietly the Other Thing swims away. Leaving only her – Mandy.

'No!'

I shout. Beyond the door, sounds catch and pause.

'It's not you. Not you I want. Go away.'

A voice – my voice – sends ripples through the night. Shocked, a child hears, and understands. Already the laughter has stopped. The house has become still. Everything is still. No more water. No more joy.

But inside me, there is movement. Sudden and powerful as a dolphin leaping. Lifts itself high above the sea in a shining arc. Not gone, still here. My child inside me. It heard me. It came back. Bone moves against bone, flesh against my flesh, alive. No longer other.

Mine. My child. The only sound I hear now is of our hearts, my baby's and my own, rising and beating together. Rhythmic and soft as the sea inside a shell.

But what about her? Mandy. I told her to go and she's gone. Slipped away, obedient as the child she is, back to the cold, to the river, which will take her for the last time. And there she will stay.

Everybody hurts her. Time after time we hurt her. Now it's me. How could I have done that to a child?

Come back!

For a second time tonight, my voice rings out. My baby hears, and rocks toward the sound, but all the life is inside me now. We have found each other, my baby and I. But Mandy, child of the river, she doesn't hear.

I can't let her go. Not like this.

Downstairs, the carpet is dry under my feet. Walls, doors, they are like bone. My hands touch the masks in the dark, and their eyes are blind, empty. It's not just her – I have sent all the Dead away, keeping every bit of life for myself.

Outside it's the same. A night with only a sliver moon and a valley without a child. Even the trees have lost her. But if I close my eyes, I see her. She is standing by the river, one small foot poised over the bank. Waiting. One small step and she will be gone and the river will close over her as if she has never been.

All these years I have dreamt of just this moment. And yet I never dreamt the truth: it was me that put her there. I sent her to the river for the river to take.

No.

Clumsy, I start to run. Thrown off balance by my belly, my breasts, feet slipping on wet clods of soil. Down the slope, down the overgrown path to the river's edge, thorns in my soles.

And she's not there. The bank is empty. I'm too late. Child of the river, to the river she has returned. Nothing but the water now to hold her, hug her close. Yet water was never enough. She wanted her mother. Why else would she ever have wanted me?

In all the years I dreamt, I never saw her take the step. And now she has.

I stand on the bank, where she has stood for years. Below me, the river runs, knows I am here. Waits for no one, unless just the one person…

I step off the bank. Into the river.

Everything. Every thing a preparation for this.

Mud swarms between my toes; river pulls at my knees. Makes my nightdress billow up around me, white and floating, like the small dress I am looking for. Already I am shivering, but water closes around my thighs, squeezes them with the promise it will not always be like this. Cold now, it says, but it won't be later. After a while, I won't be cold at all.

But I will not stay for that. I have a plan, and it's not to stay in the river. One small hand is all I need. I will find her and hold her and bring her home.

She's not here, though. Of course not, why would she be? She'll be further out, where the water flows more freely and memories are more easily washed away. I have stayed too close to the land, unwilling to commit, even now. I need to go to where she is. Deeper.

Up to my waist, then my chest. Water so icy I wonder how she can stand it. It catches at my sides, tries to push me off my feet. River runs and wants to take me with it. If I don't take care, it will have me. And I need to take care. I need to find her, take her home.

But how do I find her, in the dark, with the water hustling me away? Perhaps she will find me. I am all she has wanted.

Perhaps all I need to do is wait and she will come.

Sure enough, as I stand, something touches my hand. I look – and glimpse a trail of bubbles, a small streak already dissolving like moonlight in the water. A moment later and it's gone. So I make myself be still, and once again I see it, a drift of white beneath the surface, close enough to touch. This time I move, so fast my own speed surprises me. Kicking away with my feet, towards the centre of the river's stream, towards it. Towards her.

But the very moment my feet leave the bottom, I know what I have done. I've let the river trick me. Already there is no drift of white, no small hand. My body crashes forward like a whale, sends me plummeting into a world without substance. Triumphant, the river streams over my head, takes me to itself.

I sink. I go down. Deceived by water, I have crossed the line. I have lost my world and entered hers. I didn't even stop to take a breath.

Swim. I have always been a swimmer. Back in London, skimming across the surface of swimming pools, from one tiled wall to another. Swim to the shore, I can do that. But here it is different. There is no shore. I have left all that. I wheel and spiral and there is nothing. Only darkness and a weight of water. Nothing above me, nothing below me. My arms lunge and flail, carve shapes around me – and all they do is propel me further into the black.

So it begins, the transformation of land creature to water. Arms and legs already no longer what they were. Lengthening and thinning out, they are no use for anything. I am nothing like I was. My only talent is my lungs, my centre a barrel of air about to be spent. And my only skill now is for drowning. My arms flail more uselessly than ever, and I begin to spin.

But suddenly the spinning stops. My feet have come into contact with something which, as if waiting just for this, seethes and sucks at my ankles, grips like a soft maw. I am at the bottom, the very bottom of the river, feet thrust deep into the mud. Not spinning now, but swaying, like a plant with roots hooked into the riverbed, nodding in the current.

I have no strength. I have used it all up. It propelled me so firmly to the bottom that I am locked here. And all the air that was ever in the world, I have used up too. In a moment I will have to breathe, and then the barrel that is my chest will split open, and the river will run right through me.

Pain now. Blooming under ribs, where once there was air. In my chest, my head, it grows and blossoms. I try to hold what's left of me inside, try to keep it safe. But I can't. I have to breathe. Have to.

And then I do.

I breathe.

Opening my body to water that rushes in like knives. Not a gentle invasion this. Not a gentle way to die. A pitiless way to be transformed.

But then?

But then...calm. The pain stops more quickly than it came. Cavities are filling, equilibrium is being achieved. Already my body is adjusting. As if made for water, my arms rise up, graceful, swathed in the folds of my nightdress. And the river – the river has kept its promise. I am not cold anymore, and the water is no weight. It holds and settles me. When my knees buckle and I topple forward, it catches me and sets me upright again, gently. Promises it will always treat me gently. As it has always treated her.

Where is she? I can't see her. But she is here, somewhere. Has to be. In a moment I will see her. This is her place. This is where she belongs.

And me. I belong here too. I remember my dreams now, every dream I've ever had. All telling me the same thing: how there has always been another life, another way to be. Diving and swooping and swimming, not even having to breathe.

Everything points to this. Every dream of water. Surely I've come home.

Inside me, my baby kicks and does a small, smart cartwheel of its own. But it's only a reminder that it's never known anything but water. A swimmer, it can swim for ever now. We both can. Already we have taken on the movements of the river. Like weeds, like water.

Because this is where we will stay. This is where we belong. Deep down I believe I always knew it.

Satisfied, the river sighs and loosens its grip. My ankles slide out of the mud and I feel myself rising. The water doesn't have to hold me anymore. It knows I am going nowhere. We are all staying.

My face breaks the surface, and I am on my back. For a moment I stare, vaguely surprised, at the sky, at the sliver moon. A different world. Not ours, nothing to do with us anymore. Then the river tugs and I begin to sink again, feet first, calmly back into that other world. My world now.

And then?

And then, on the bank, I see her. *Her.* Mandy stands, facing me, a small shape silvered by the moon's faint light, no more than a silhouette. But she watches me. And in watching me, tells me the river is not where she is. I will not find her here. I am in the wrong place. Not the river. Never the river.

A hiccup of disbelief – it makes me cough. And cough again. Suddenly, I am a fountain, spewing water. The river feels the emptying and, in alarm, it pulls again, harder, drags at my feet, my legs. But already air is rushing in, where the water was. And she stands on the bank, shows me where she is. Tells me I should be there too.

I try to swim towards her, but it's hard, too hard for me. The river catches my arms, pulls on my waist, is determined to keep me. I can't swim, not like this, weighed down by water and fatigue. Once more I sink. But then I see her again, standing on the bank.

She's doing what she has always done. Waiting. She is waiting for me. For me. Realisation shocks me into swimming, striking out one last time. I swim so hard that, resigned, finally the river shrugs, has to let me go.

Safe on the shore, I pull myself out of the water. I've done what she wants. I have left the river. I have saved myself and I have saved my baby from that other world. Now, too exhausted to raise my head, I am looking for her shoes. Little red shoes standing on the bank. But they aren't there. And when I look up, she's not there. The riverbank is empty.

My teeth have begun to chatter. Skin silvered and freezing in the moonlight. It doesn't matter that I can't see her. I know exactly where she is. In my belly, heat is beginning to spread. It moves into my breasts, my thighs. Sweeps upwards into my throat and down into my hands. Soon there will be no part of me that has not been warmed and made strong again. I'll be able to stand up, go back into the house. But just for these last moments, I stay here, beside the river, curled around the child that is alive, and the other child who is not. They are both here. I can't see them, either of them. But I don't have to. I've found them.

Both of them inside me now, where they belong.

This is what it is to be possessed. This is what I've been afraid of. This is mother love.

~

# Chapter Twenty-Seven

The clinic says she is a girl and she will be born in earliest May. That was weeks ago. Now she's only days away.

I told Tom, waited for his response. It was his last chance to change. And when all he did was sigh, I told him I would not be coming to London. We are no longer we. He would stay there, and I would stay here. Where I belong.

'You don't mean that, Sara.'

'I do.'

Then it began, the storm of protest, the litany of promises broken. But not once did he mention love. Not because Tom has never loved me, but because love is the least important thing compared to other things. He has needs that far outweigh love, leave it floating in the balance.

Finally, though, he exhausted himself. In a voice that had become hoarse, he said:

'Nobody's going to blame me for this, Sara. You drove me away. People will know that. You're on your own now, do you understand? You can't ask me to have anything to do with it when it comes – the Other Thing. Not after what you've done. Don't come to me with it.'

'No. I never will.'

'You say that now.'

'It's a promise, Tom.'

And suddenly he believed me. I thought he had learnt nothing from these last months, but perhaps he knows this much: this is a promise I will keep.

It was then I caught it – the change in his breathing: suddenly lighter as the future is lifted from his shoulders. What was a burden to him, unbearable, intolerable, is gone. He doesn't have to be anything he never wanted to be. He doesn't have to be a father.

Now Jen says he is indeed telling folk I drove him away, but how can I mind? It's only true. She came to stay last week – leaving the children at home with Charlie. The first night she slept solidly for sixteen hours, then mooned around the house, dreamy as a girl. Large and liquid-eyed from enough sleep. Enormous with the baby inside her, blousy with pregnancy and warmth.

'I miss them of course…' she said, meaning Pig and the Duke. Smiled at the unspoken *but*. Then the smile faded.

'What about your ghost, Sara?' Cautious, she asked the question. Watched me carefully.

'Oh she's still here.' And when she looked alarmed, I laughed at her.

It took till the second night before she could bring herself to say what she'd come to tell me. 'Tom's seeing someone, Sara. He's not even trying to hide it. Charlie thinks he's been seeing her for weeks – months. Has he said anything to you?'

I shook my head.

And she shook hers. 'Of course not. Too busy pretending he's the injured party.'

'He is.'

Jen threw up her hands. 'Oh come on, Sara...'

But we've been through all that. The choices are all mine.

Jen said, 'Do you want me to tell you about her, this woman he's...?'

'Yes please.'

She laughed shortly. 'It's not as if you'd even believe it. You'll think I'm making it up. Sara, she's old. Not old, old. What I mean is she's got to be fifteen years older than he is. Sort of magnificent in a way, one of those women who've seen and done it all. But the fact is, she's old enough—'

'To be his mother.' I finished the sentence before she even had time to pause.

Jen stared at me. 'I can't believe you're taking this so calmly, Sara. Don't you mind?'

'Mind?' I played the word over. Tried to imagine Tom in the embrace of another woman. But all I could see was a little boy running joyously into the open arms of his mother. Someone who would never let him down. And never choose another child over him.

'It means you'll be on your own, Sara.'

'Except for you.'

'And Charlie,' she added.

And Mary, and Evie and Reg. And the baby to come. And perhaps someone else whose name we haven't mentioned. Like teenagers, Jen and I were holding out, waiting for the other to be the first to say it: Joaquin. But she didn't say a word. For the first time here is something she dare not mention.

So she doesn't know that he phones every night now. He

calls to ask about me, about the baby, about everything to do with us. Joaquin is attentive and grave as a man enquiring after his own family.

Long before Jen came to stay, I asked him, 'Joaquin, have you ever wanted a child of your own?'

He answered without hesitating. 'Of course, but when I was a boy, I had leukaemia. I nearly died. Many months of nearly dying. Those songs I sang to you, my mother sang them to me all the way through, when there was nothing of me, a thin little twig in a bed. As you see, I lived, but the drugs – those wonderful drugs – they took their toll.'

'I'm sorry, so sorry, Joaquin.'

'On the contrary, my belief is that often a clever woman waits until after a child is born. Only then does she choose the father. I am hopeful, Sara. Many things come to those who wait.'

Jen went back to London. The Valley is turning green in fifty thousand shades, and all the great brown bed has disappeared under a sea of shoots. Every now and then, I wade in to weed – only to wade out again wondering what damage I have done. I don't know a dandelion from a carrot top. It doesn't seem to matter. It all keeps growing. Everything around me grows, inside and out. I am waiting.

And all the time *she* plays at my feet. Twists in and out between them like a cat. Steals into bed with me at night. Too light to leave an imprint in the earth or on the pillow, she waits with me. Always there, part of me.

What will happen when my May girl is born? Will she know about Mandy? Be one of those children who never quite believe they are alone. Certain that somewhere, there is a twin, another version of herself. Constantly dreaming of a child who stands beside her by a river?

Mary Coryn came down yesterday with a bag full of cardigans and bonnets and crocheted boots. This baby will be dressed like a child of the nineteen fifties. Woolly and balloon cheeked, thriving on orange juice and the brand new NHS.

She bustled about the house, pretending not to disapprove of the bare walls and floors. But stopped when she saw the china cat, the result of another day patiently spent mending, glueing the smile back together.

'Well for goodness sakes! I haven't seen one of those in years. It's the Trewith Cat.'

'The...?'

'The Trewith Cat. There was the pottery in Trewith, just down the river from here. It's closed now, of course. But all the old folk used to have them, right from when they were kiddies.'

'This was my great-great-grandfather's. We thought it came from Scotland.'

'Well you were wrong there. That cat is Cornish.'

Outside, as Reg started up the car to leave, she pointed to the sprouting things on the bank with their splotchy stalks. 'And that's giant hogweed, that is. You want to chop all that down before the baby comes. Get any of the sap on you and it's worse than being stung by jellyfish. Get Tom to do it.'

'We're not together anymore, Mary.'

She slipped her arm through mine. 'No, love. I thought probably not.' After a moment she said, 'You know, I haven't been down here since I was a child with my sister, Reenie. We used to play here all the time.'

I look at her, surprised. She's never mentioned this.

'Reenie.' Mary's voice was a mix of sob and exasperation. Reenie died a week ago. 'She was the daft one. Always seeing things, she was.'

'What sort of things?'

Mary's reply was instant. 'Nothing. It was just her own reflection in the water, silly girl.' She changed the subject. 'You done your shopping yet? Proper shopping, I mean. For cots and clothes and bottles and all?'

'Soon. I'll go tomorrow, I promise.'

I wanted to ask what Reenie saw, reflected in the river, but Reg tooted his horn and she had to go.

I keep my promise. I go shopping.

I need a carrycot and sling, blankets and Babygros. A pushchair, nappies. Jen mentioned a shop in St Ives where they have all the stuff I could find up in Primrose Hill – designer everything for the perfect child. But Mary Coryn has told me about the Mothercare in Tavistock over the river, so that's where I'm going. I'll get everything I need and more.

Now, as I walk to the car, the Valley has a more than usual hush, an air of things half asleep. The trees stand, tossing sunlight between their leaves, while beside them the river runs, its surface an innocent glitter. It does this – a game it plays with itself, with me. Pretending it's nothing but any river in any valley. But I'm not fooled. Under the surface, the river will be cool and dark and silent.

Indignant because it could not make me stay.

As for *her*, she'll wait for me under the trees, jumping from patch to patch of sunlight. She never leaves the Valley, not even to come with me.

After months of shopping in Tremaine's, Mothercare is a shock.

For moments I stand, transfixed. It's the habit of a marriage, forcing me to see things briefly through Tom's eyes. The clash of primary colours, the kitsch and the cute. Ducks and teddy bears, clowns and cats. Shiny fabrics, plastic and rubber. And people – lots of people with lots of children. Toddlers running underfoot. I know exactly what Tom would do if he were here. He would stand, gazing at it all, silently mouthing: the horror, the horror.

Then I stop seeing through his eyes, and all I can think is that I have come to the right place. Exactly the right place. The baby thinks so too. Elbows me in my groin, a reminder to get on with things. Not much time now. But it doesn't matter. Everything is here.

And everyone. For there, on the other side of the shop, is John Marsh. He's standing next to the children's clothes, surrounded by boys' things: miniature boxer shorts and Ninja Turtle pyjamas. Thomas the Tank Engine dressing gowns. He hasn't seen me, is too busy with the little boy who's there beside him, about eighteen months old, chunky and solid. A child with his feet planted square on the ground, next to a box of bedroom slippers with spacemen on them.

This must be the baby I saw all those months ago in his mother's arms. Older now. A toddler. Marsh's son, with the stamp of the father on him. Already I can see how at this age John Marsh would have been just as solid, just as stubborn. Yet soft, soft as butter. Now here they stand, father and son, a reminder that time passes. Things move on.

In a different world, Tom would have stood like this, one not-so-distant day, facing up to a child with a mind all its own. But that's not going to happen, it's a day that will never come. At which thought, something aches inside me, a throb for what might have been. Not for my sake – but for Tom's. Tom will miss this. He will live and die without it all.

An ache which passes as I watch John Marsh.

He has given up. Defeated by a small child, he stares across the shop, eyes pleading for help. For half a second I even think it's me he's appealing to. Then I realise it's someone else, behind me. I turn and there she is, Carole Marsh. Standing amongst the girl clothes, laughing at him for being so useless, for allowing a small boy to keep him anchored to a display of spacemen slippers.

And she's different, nothing like she was…

But before I can gauge what that difference is, my eye is caught again. A little girl is standing next to her, half hidden by a rack of Barbie nighties. She wears a pink dress and has long dark hair tamed by brushing. She must be about five – the same age as Pig, but verging on the plump, and without Pig's sharp eyes and quick mouth. Pig you might remember just for the way she glares at you. This child you're more likely to see once and forget.

Except for the hairband that she wears. A black velvet band keeping all that thick, dark hair off her face, it has her name written across it in large shiny letters.

M A N D Y.

Mandy. I watch her lift a hand to wave at Marsh and the solid little boy who must be her brother, and the world jigsaws and fades into black…

I open my eyes. The shop has contracted around me like a telescope that has snapped shut, and now all the faces, small heads and little dresses are closing in – children, their small mouths open like fishes. It feels like in the river again, pressed by the weight of water, not able to breathe.

'Get back, all you. Give her some air.' The voice, a woman's, is familiar.

There's a murmur in the crowd. Children protesting. 'But what's she doing? Why's that lady lying down on the floor?'

'She fainted, that's all. Now stand back when I'm telling you.' It's the same voice. Firm. The faces turn mutinous, but they move away, and I can breathe again. Now the only face I see is her face. Carole Marsh.

A noise comes out of my throat. She puts her head closer to mine, but carefully, mindful not to crowd me. And now I can see what is so different about her. She is not pale, nothing like pale. Carole Marsh has firm, red cheeks and eyes blue and steady that hold mine.

I whisper, 'Mandy. I thought that the river…'

Carole Marsh's eyes flicker, but they keep hold of mine. In fact, it's her eyes that save me, hold me as the world begins to spin once more. Stop me sinking through the floor, beneath the surface of things.

'What's happened?' This is John Marsh's voice. Then it comes again, harsher, made rough by surprise: 'That's Sara Lewis!'

'I know. She fainted.'

He says something about me fainting before, but she ignores him. Her words are all for me.

'Everything's all right, Sara. You'll be all right. Don't you fret about a thing. We'll look after you.'

Her eyes hold mine; and what she seems to say is: *I'll* look after you.

They get me out of the shop and into the nearest cafe. I walk and she is there, holding me, her arm firm around my waist. Inside me the baby responds to her touch. I can feel its head butting towards her hand, wonder if she can feel it too.

Now there's a clatter of different noises around us – babies crying, the hiss of the coffee machine. Parents telling off their children. They sit me down on a bench seat against a table, and slot themselves in around me – John and Carole Marsh, a little boy.

And a little girl. Mandy.

I try, I try not to look at her, but I can't help it. She sits with her legs swinging, knees dimpling, eyeing up the ice cream counter.

'John, get us all a cup of tea, lots of sugar for Mrs Lewis. And something for the kids. Keep them quiet.'

Obedient, he gets to his feet. It seems amazing to me now, but she's the one in charge, telling him what to do. And still her eyes hold mine, keeping me fixed, keeping me steady. After a moment, the little girl slides off her bit of the bench seat and goes after John Marsh who has taken his place in the queue. Stands beside him there.

'I thought she died,' I murmur. But I don't know if Carole

can hear me over the clatter. 'I thought the river took her. I thought that you...'

I tear my eyes away to watch Mandy – a small, plump child in the shadow of her father. Beside me, Carole does the same.

Maybe it's only us. Maybe there's no one else here that can see her. Somehow I brought her with me from the Valley, fleshed her out and gave her substance. Now it's only us who know – her mother and I.

But at that moment the woman behind the ice cream counter bends across and smiles. Mandy points to the chocolate ice cream and the woman picks up her scoop. With that the cafe begins to spin again like a whirlpool, and I am about to be sucked down.

Someone takes my hand. It's Carole Marsh. A woman who keeps me from sinking. She waits as the cafe steadies and resumes its normal clatter, while beside her the little boy plays with the sugar bowl.

'I thought she died.' For the second time I murmur the words. 'I was so sure the river took her. Mandy.'

This time she hears me.

'Whoever told you that?'

'No one. No one told me anything.'

'Did you ask?'

'Oh yes.' Time after time of asking. 'But no one talked about it. It's why I thought that she...'

But I can't say it again. I can't say I thought she died when Mandy stands in front of us, watching her ice cream being scooped into a cone.

Her mother smiles wryly. 'That's what happens, isn't it?

Small places – you try to keep things quiet and folk just end up thinking the worst.'

'But the river,' I am stammering now. 'Are you saying nothing happened there? Nothing at all?'

The wry smile fades and her mouth twists the other way. 'Oh no. Something happened.'

She glances across the cafe, at the two figures at the counter, and down at the little boy paddling his fingers in the sugar bowl. There's a silence, which I break. Staring at the table as I speak, afraid that I will break:

'If you don't tell me what happened, if I never know, I truly believe I will go mad. And nothing will help me. Nothing will bring me back. Do you understand?'

I am pleading with her. Terrified she won't believe me. After all, why should she? She doesn't know about a child, no living child. She doesn't know how the river kept me, and held me. She doesn't know about the Dead, keeping the Dead at bay. She doesn't know that I am speaking the truth.

I will go mad.

And yet when she looks at me, I see. She believes me. Colour flares in her cheeks, tells me this is a woman who knows about madness. Carole Marsh nods, and finally, finally begins to tell me what no one else would.

The cafe goes quiet around us. We are the only people in the world.

'I'll start where you came in, that day you arrived in the valley.'

She glances at me, checking that her tone is right, that her voice is a voice I can listen to. This is a story into which both of us need to be eased; only when she is sure does she carry on. 'We were desperate to sell that house. Desperate. But you knew that, didn't you? You took one look at us and you knew. I could tell.'

I nod. Grateful that we understand each other, she and I.

'Six years we'd lived there in the Valley, right from after we got married. It was John who made us go there. He wanted the space. His dad had just died, so he had the money and could do what he liked. I didn't argue. I thought we were lucky, having a place like that, right from the day we were wed, when most couldn't afford to have anywhere. When people said they couldn't bear to live somewhere so cut off, I thought they were just jealous.'

She smiles, rueful as she recalls a young woman who loved thinking herself lucky, envied.

'Anyway, it's not how it was. I knew everybody up in that village. I grew up right next to the church. My mum and dad had moved away to the coast, but Mary Coryn was still there. Used to babysit me, she did, when I was little. If I wanted company, all I had to do was jump in the car.

'Besides, I never was by myself, not in the beginning. I worked the switchboard at John's station, did all the same shifts as him, even the nights. It's how we got together in the first place. Happy we were, happier than anything. But then…' The smile fades. 'Then I got pregnant, didn't I? I had Mandy, and everything changed.'

Our eyes turn towards the counter, where a small plump child in a lettered hairband is frowning at her ice cream, considering which side to lick first. Carole says:

'Not the sort of thing you want to be hearing about in your state, is it?'

'It doesn't matter. Just so long as I know.'

She nods, and starts again.

'She'd been a lovely birth. Nothing hard about it, not like it can be for some. I was on cloud nine. It was summer, I thought nothing could be better than this. Having her, having John. Coming home. But then...'

She swallows, touches the table in front of her. Suddenly the colour has paled in her cheeks. She's back, the woman I met nearly a year ago, cold on a May day.

'First it was the air. It's the only way I can describe it. Three days after she was born, John went back to work. He drove off and it was as if he'd taken every bit of breathable air with him. No warning. Like a lid had come down on the Valley and he'd escaped just in time. I thought there must be something wrong with the weather. Then Mandy started to cry in her cot, so I went to pick her up...' she stops, chokes on her words, '...and I couldn't. I couldn't touch her. She just lay there – angry, ugly. Like a different baby, nothing to do with me. I took one look at her and walked away.'

She darts another glance at the little girl. Looks away again.

'I'm lying. I didn't even walk. I ran. Even though she was crying. Right away, down to the river. Anywhere else and you could still hear her. But there it was all right. The sound of the river drowned everything out. I couldn't hear her anymore.

'I stayed there I don't know how long. I told myself it was the heat, making me odd. But it wasn't. I went back to her and it was the same. And the next day and the next. She'd cry and I'd run away, down to the river so as not to hear her, stay there till I could go back, make myself touch her. I'd feed her, change her, and wait for John to come home so I could hand her over. Then I'd just go away and sleep. I'd have slept the clock round if I could. Never have woken up.'

Her hands drop into her lap and I imagine a woman laying down her head, wishing that sleep would take her, never give her back.

'I lost track of time after that. Months went by and suddenly Mandy wouldn't be left, not anymore. One day she simply climbed out of the cot. It's like she'd had enough, and decided if I wouldn't come to her, she'd have to come after me. Ten months old, and she was walking. Running, more like.'

'You couldn't go to the river, then?'

'How could I? Moment she started, I had my work cut out just keeping up with her. Soon as she learnt to put one foot in front of the other, she was off. Down into the flowerbeds, up under the trees. But more than anywhere, she'd want to be by the river. Always the river. In the end, she kept me so busy running to keep up I forgot I'd ever wanted to walk away.'

Suddenly, she's smiling again, eyes lit up and remembering. And, catching the look of surprise in my face, laughs at me. 'I was happy, you see. Back to the way I was. Whatever happened after she was born, it stopped. One day I woke up and realised it was all in the past, I didn't feel like that anymore.'

And to my shame, I am almost disappointed. A woman was sad, then she was happy again. Is that all there is to know? Is that all that happened by the river?

Yet, as if able to read my mind, she shakes her head. 'Only then...well, then we went and had another baby. Mikey...'

She turns to the toddler on the bench beside her. He's building stacks out of sugar sachets, oblivious to us, his cheeks bright red in the heat of the cafe. There are streaks of escaped sugar all over the table and under it. Sweetness everywhere. At which point, John Marsh arrives with a tray, Mandy beside him. He frowns at the mess, as if preferring to focus on that instead of on what's passing between his wife and a relative stranger.

Carole says, 'I'm telling Sara what happened. After Mikey was born.'

He blinks swiftly, but says nothing. She turns back to me.

'You can guess, I suppose. It was like with Mandy, but worse, much worse. Again it was three days after the birth. Happy till then, until suddenly I didn't want to go near him. I couldn't even look at him. I wanted to tell people but I didn't dare. Not even John. I was afraid they'd think I was mad, a bad woman. I forced myself to take care of him, told myself if I could just keep him fed and warm, he'd be all right. Then I'd be able to walk away. Go to the river.

'But he wasn't all right. All he ever seemed to do was cry. It was like he was angry all the time, wanting me every minute of the day. Didn't matter what I did. It meant I couldn't leave him. He'd just open his mouth and scream. I was afraid he'd die of screaming.

'And the worst thing was, there was Mandy. She was getting on for four and she needed someone there, watching. Watching her all the time.'

She points to Mandy.

'You won't believe it now, but all skin and bones she was back then. It's my mum and dad who've made her plump. They give her too many sweets. They just want to spoil her, keep her happy after...after what happened. Back then, though, she was like a wire. And never still, always wanting to be by the river. I'd see her sometimes, suddenly going stiff, alert-like. Then off she'd go, running like someone had called her name.

'I tried to keep her close to me, but she was clever. One day she went and made a pile out of all of John's police books, right next to the front door. She climbed up and worked the latch. I looked out of the conservatory, and there she was, right by the river, all by herself. Standing on the bank with her foot out, like she was just waiting to take a step.'

From deep in my throat has come a choking sound.

She hears me and stops, thinking I have something to say. But I swallow, shake my head, and she carries on.

'I threw the baby down and ran outside, picked her up from the bank. Spanked her I did, hard. I bruised her. I knew, I knew I shouldn't have, but I was out of my mind that day. And...'

Carole looks at me. Not only is she pale now, her eyes have grown old. No longer the eyes of a young woman.

'And that's how I stayed from that day on. Out of my mind. You see, once I'd seen Mandy by the river, about to take that step, I knew.'

Her voice has barely changed, but I see John Marsh's hand edge towards hers. I see their fingers touch, and know we are close now.

'What did you know?' Softly I ask the question.

'How it was just a question of time. One day I'd take my eye off her and it would have her. The river would have her, my little girl. It even told me so! I could hear it talking to me. Waking me in the night, running under my window, telling me it was going to have her. It was going to carry her away.

'I told John. I was so sure he'd understand. He lived there too. He had ears. I thought he must be able to hear it – the way the river got into your head, telling you what it wanted, what it was going to do. I thought we could both hear it.'

Marsh looks haggard. Shakes his head and looks away.

'He said I should just keep busy. Get out and about, go and see my mum. He didn't believe me when I said I couldn't drive anymore. I couldn't drive anywhere, not with Mikey screaming. I knew what would happen. He'd cry so I'd drive into the wall or another car. Or the river.'

Carole Marsh stops and takes a breath. Now, now we have arrived.

'It was a Saturday. John offered to take Mandy off shopping with him, give me a rest, he said. And oh, it was a relief! I didn't have to watch for her. I didn't have to go round the house twice, three times, making sure every door and window was locked and bolted. For once, she was safe from the river. Safe with her dad, like she never was with me.

'But then the baby started to cry again and I realised. Nothing had changed. There was always going to be Mikey, wanting me. Just like there would always be Mandy, wanting the river. Soon she would come home and it would all start over again. The three of us here – Mikey, Mandy and me. And the river, waiting.

'And suddenly I felt so sorry for him, for Mikey. For this

baby that cried all day and all night because he knew I didn't want him. I could tell he'd never be right, never be happy, or grow to be the man he could have been. There'd always be something he'd want, and never have. Never. And it was my fault, for not loving him like I should. All my fault.

'That's when I heard it again, the river. Didn't matter that the doors were closed – I could hear it, louder than I ever had. Running right through my head, shouting at me.'

'What did it say?' I hardly dare ask this.

'It said it had the answer!' All of a sudden, she's almost smiling, eyes shining as she remembers. 'It told me I could make everything right for everyone. I just had to take Mikey and go. It said it could make it so Mikey could have me for ever, never have to be alone or unhappy. And Mandy would be safe because now John would look after her, better than I ever could. The river explained it all to me, and for the first time since Mikey had been born, I saw how I could do something right.'

Beside her, a noise comes from Marsh's throat. Wordless.

'It all seemed simple then. Easy. I just picked up a shawl and put it round Mikey and me, wrapped him tight to my chest. Right away he stopped crying! Snuggled up against me, and fell asleep like he'd never done before. Having him happy like that, it just seemed to prove it, showed I was doing the right thing. And I walked out of the house.'

She looks at me.

'I walked down to the river, Sara. Right to the river. You could get to it then. There were no bushes, no brambles. I went straight to the water. Into the water. It was so cold, but Mikey – he didn't even cry. Even now I don't understand it.

Maybe it was because I had him so tight, like he'd always wanted to be and never was. And then, when I was ready, I just lay down. I lay down in the water like we were in bed, and let the river take us.'

There is another noise beside us. John Marsh has begun to shake. This is what he has been remembering, every time he came to the river. This is what he saw, and will never be able to forget.

Tears have gathered about her eyes. But she doesn't seem to notice. And she doesn't stop speaking.

'That's when I heard a scream. It was Mandy. The sound of her cut through the air like a knife. But it didn't stop me. I just held Mikey and ducked my head under. It was the river you see, telling me what to do. But Mandy kept screaming and screaming, and John came running. He'd had to run anyway just to catch her. They'd come back early and she'd jumped out of the car and run down to the river. The very thing we'd always tried to stop her doing.'

Her voice has fallen almost to a whisper. I have to bend in close to hear.

'And that's when he saw us, Mikey and me. He ran and swam, and somehow he got us. Brought us back to the bank, both of us. But by then it was too late. The river had gone right over Mikey's head. John tore the blanket off him, but he just lay there, not breathing. Mikey was already dead.

'But John wouldn't have it. He picked him up and shook him. He kissed him and breathed into him and banged him – and he brought him back. He got him breathing. Somehow he did it. And that's how Mikey died and came alive again. It's how he's here now. That's how we are all here.'

Slowly she reaches across the table, touches her husband's arm. And slowly his shaking stops.

She turns to me again. She's coming to the end of the story. 'I went to this big hospital up in Devon after that. Big, dark place with high walls. Benton. At first I thought I was in prison, where the police put people like me. Women like me. It was only gradually I found out it wasn't a prison at all. I was just there to get better.'

Dark walls swallowing the sun. I know the place. The very place.

'They told me I had post-natal depression. They told me I wasn't mad, I wasn't even bad. They said I was ill, in a way that some women do get ill after children. They promised I would get better, and they were right. I did get better. But it wasn't just because of the drugs and the treatment, and the kindness – endless kindness. The truth is, I'd already started to get better. I started the moment Mikey began to breathe again, and after, when we all sat together on the bank waiting for the ambulance. It started with John holding me, telling me he loved me. Telling me he'd always love me. Most of all, I got better because she'd gone, that woman who couldn't love her children.' She stops. Looks at me. 'The river had taken her, you see. Just like it promised.'

As she speaks, she puts a hand to her face. And when she takes it away, her eyes are clear. Try as I might, I can see no trace of her, the woman who walked into the river, and took her baby with her.

'Of course, I had to come home, back to the Valley. But we already knew by then, we couldn't live there anymore. John, he couldn't abide the river, couldn't even go near it. But that was nothing compared to Mandy. She'd seen too much.'

'That day we came. She wasn't there.'

'No, she'd stayed with my mum. We were only there because you'd asked to see the house. We were living with my parents by then. We had to, because of Mandy, still waking in the night, still screaming. Yet if it hadn't been for her, always wanting the river, she would never have seen us. John would never have come running. And Mikey and me, we wouldn't be here.

'But it was hard. For months, no one would touch the house. No one local. People knew too much. They thought if bad things could happen to ordinary folk like us, they could happen to anyone. They put it down to the place, being so cut off.'

She takes her hand from Marsh's hand. Lays it over mine.

'But you came along, and it saved us, you taking it. We're grateful to you, Sara – to you and your husband. Tell him we're so grateful.'

Then her hand is gone. She has turned to take Mikey in her arms, and instantly he nestles against her, his body a soft extension of hers. Mandy pops the last bit of her wafer cone into John Marsh's mouth and with a small pink tongue explores the ice cream moustache above her own. The sounds in the cafe, which seem to have hushed all this long while, pick up again. People chat and the coffee machine hisses. The Marshes smile at me, but keep their best, their most secret smiles for each other.

And the story is over. I know what happened. No one died. Everyone is safe. There was no ghost. There never has been.

And yet I saw...

I saw nothing. I felt, heard, tasted, smelt. But I saw nothing except what was there: wind, river, trees, moths.

Carole Marsh says, 'Tell Mary I told you all this. Tell her she never had to go keeping secrets, not for my sake. Look what happens when you do. People end up believing all kinds of things.'

Like ghosts. And little girls. And rivers that sing of carrying them away. And none of it true.

~

# CHAPTER TWENTY-EIGHT

Now I drive down the lane as I've driven two hundred times and more. Twigs drag along the side of the car with the dry scratch of things complaining. Ferns nod as I pass, and in the rear-view mirror the lane curves and disappears in to a V: a vanishing point.

At the bottom, I stop the car and get out.

And, as always, it takes a minute. But I wait until, from under the swish of leaves and the rattlings of woodpeckers and the hum of a plane flying its way west, it comes: the sound of water. The noise of the river.

It's the sound of any river.

When I left, there was magic here. The Valley was drowsy with it. Now there's nothing, just a lot of trees and a river running by. A beautiful place, a remarkable place. It has an air, an atmosphere all of its own.

But that's all it has: an air. An atmosphere. Trees move and river runs, but there is nothing out of the ordinary. When I left, I thought Mandy was here, jumping from shadow to shadow. And she's not. She's with the people who love her. No one died. Everyone is safe. Now all that's left is to listen and look – and hold my breath.

For this is the test, the real test. There is no ghost here. There never was.

So what now? If there is no ghost, if the river is just a river, what else is there?

I ask the question, and in my belly the baby flips, as if in fear of the answer.

For if there is no ghost, if there never was a ghost, no invisible twin, what is there left to love...? Does everything go back to the way it was?

The Valley sways. Empty. There is nothing here but me.

But then...then a sudden flap and fluster of wings. A bird has broken out of the trees, to fly straight and true as a rocket into a deep-blue sky. Describes a single arc high above the Valley – and swoops back, into the Green. And something happens: inside me the baby describes the same arc. Swoops and dives and vanishes, back into the Green.

My baby. My May girl.

It's like waking up from a dream, and finding the dream is still happening all around you.

Hardly any time left now.

I need to finish the room, make it ready. Mandy's bedroom isn't pink anymore. I've painted the door white and the walls yellow to catch the sun, but there are still the skirting boards to be glossed and the pink carpet taken up. Makes me wonder if I'll be ready in time.

But I'm tired. It's been a long nine months. The claw hammer I'm using to lever out the nails feels heavy in my hands, too heavy to use. What if I just left it? A pink carpet – a baby could live with that...

*Keep going.*

A voice that can only be my own. Makes me jump almost. But obedient, I do as it says. I reach again for the hammer.

Marietta – she would have attacked this carpet with ten times the determination. Skinny arms braced for the task, she wouldn't have let tiredness stop her. With Marietta in mind, I fit the hammer to another nail and try again.

And look what happens, doing it Marietta's way. The hammer rips up not just a swathe of carpet, but half an entire floorboard. It comes away in a rush, sending me flying backwards, so that for a moment I lie, pinned by the weight of my own stomach, legs in the air, like a beetle flipped onto its back. In my imagination, Marietta's mouth twitches.

Meanwhile the carpet flops back into place with the floorboard underneath it.

I get back onto my knees. I need to see the damage. Somehow I've managed to splinter perfectly good planks by main – if surprising – force. Careful now, I lift up the carpet to inspect the section of floorboard that comes with it.

And when I look again at the plank, it's obvious: it's not broken after all. Both ends of the section are trimmed and smooth. I didn't snap it; it was meant to come out, leaving exactly what there is here – a neat rectangular hole in the floor.

A hole? A hiding place. What else can it be?

I don't even have to stop to think. A moment later I'm struggling to fit an arm through a space that even Marietta would find difficult. Confident that hiding places nearly always have something hidden. Kept safe.

Which is what has happened here; what I find is a

newspaper. Just a newspaper, its pages crisp and creamy as if I had gone out and bought it this very day. But the date in the corner says otherwise: 22nd December 1875. Kept dry, kept dark, it's as well preserved as grave-goods in a sealed tomb.

And it's wonderful. I turn it over, charmed by the advertisements for cough medicines and parasols and different shapes of hats, all inserted between reports of farming prices and crop sales. A local newspaper – a little bit of history, as old as most of the gravestones up in the churchyard.

But why is it here, hidden away? As though waiting to be found one day, long after everyone mentioned – all these farmers and land agents and merchants – is dead.

Then I see: three small paragraphs reporting a crime and its aftermath. I read, first quickly, then a second time, slowly. Then a third, by which time of reading I have every word committed to memory. A story, sown into my mind as if it had always been there.

'On the 12th December, Dr Phineas Grey the County Coroner examined the case of Elsa Ravenscroft, four years of age, daughter of John Ravenscroft, miner, the said child having drowned at the hand of her mother, Margery Ravenscroft, in the Tamar River on the 14th August of this year. Doctor Grey heard that the woman – known to be a loving mother – had but three days before given birth to a stillborn, causing such a madness of grief as to suggest her to be incapable of knowing her own actions. Dr Grey judged the killing to be unlawful, but was content merely to commit the aforementioned to the Benton Asylum, where she will be detained for her own protection.

'The father of the deceased, John Ravenscroft, having lost

both mother and child, has ordered the family home to be placed for public auction, to include all contents thereof with the exception only of certain trinkets etc dear to his daughter. A man known to be much afflicted by his misfortune, he has since left the County, for a northern destination.

'A point of interest to many of our readers is Benton Asylum itself. It is here that all advances in medicine and the mind are put to the greatest benefit of mankind. The men of Benton are determined that by their efforts Science will speedily yield answers to an affliction common to all levels of society, to whit, the strange and tragic mania which troubles so many of our wives, sisters and daughters following the rigours of childbirth…'

I put the newspaper down. I don't need to look at it anymore.

No thoughts now – only images. Images of a little girl, a river. A mother who killed the thing she loved the most. A father who fled, first to Scotland, then to America. John Ravenscroft who came from Cornwall, and after became a different man altogether. He became rich. He became my great-great-grandfather.

But Elsa stayed. Born here, she died here.

Yet something of her escaped: blood. It ran down through the years like a thread, trickled through the generations, from her veins into mine. Shared blood that bound us. It gave me dreams, it made me come here. It brought me home. *She* brought me home.

Elsa. Elsa Ravenscroft.

So what does she want, this little girl, whose blood binds us? What has she always wanted?

The answer reaches through the window – the river. It clatters over stones, turns water into words. The river tells me what she wants, and it's easy. It's what any child would want. She wants her mother.

But how can she find her when she belongs here? She is tied here. I feel her cling. She is tied to me, tied to this place. How do I help her?

I only know one way: *tell her.* Tell her what she needs to know. Whisper words, praying they are the right words. Praying she can hear me. You are Elsa. And you don't belong here, not anymore. Go and find your mother. She loved you. Go and find her now.

She hears me.

I know she hears me; because suddenly she is closer than she has ever been. I can feel her – the press of her body against mine. I can smell her – a child's breath, warm, as her mouth kisses me goodbye. And I can taste her: apples and water, cream on my tongue. Outside, the river runs and hurries on its way.

They must have been the right words, because then she's gone. Elsa is gone. All she ever needed was her name, and someone who loved her.

Then suddenly it's just us, my baby and me. Two where we used to be three.

Already there is space. Room for someone else.

# Chapter Twenty-Nine

I ask, 'Did I do the right thing? Letting her go?'

'Of course. How could you not be right? What child doesn't need her mother?'

*Our* child lies between us in the bed, our May girl. Born three days ago, she is small and folded, with limbs that unfurl like bat wings when she stirs, jointed and graceful. She has dark hair covering her head, soft as mouse hair, hands and feet that wear their nails like tiny beads at the end of each finger and toe, pink and polished and perfect. She arrived wet as a mermaid from that underwater place. Left me tired and aching and weak with longing.

Joaquin held her even before I did. Closed his eyes as he held her, this father I have chosen for my child. Our child.

'She smells of apples, Sara.'

He cradled her a moment more, then handed her to me. Kissed my mouth with the first of many kisses to come.

And he was right. She smelt of apples. And something else – water. Rainwater, river water – water that would have cradled her and lapped softness into her skin all through those months when I didn't know I wanted her. I held her that first time and felt a howl gather in my throat.

That I could ever have called her Other...

Then her fingers curled around mine, and the howl vanished.

Fainter now, that scent of apples. Three days since she was born and it's a scent overlaid by soap and camomile and the same cream that Jen has used on all her babies – three of them: Pig, the Duke and Ivor (already called the Engine).

Yet if I press my face into the crown of her head, where the hair grows in whorls, I can still find it. Apples. Water. The fact is, we all smell of each other. Rubbed into Joaquin's skin are the scents of milk and blood and the damp bosky notes of recent birth. And worked into mine, the scents of woods and badger and musk. While between us lies our child, with the scents of all of us combined.

Three days, though. Three days since she was born. A thought strikes me and, in sudden terror, I turn to Joaquin. 'What if it happens to me? It was three days each time. What if it happens again?'

He looks at me gravely.

'Look at us, Sara. Tell me if you think it will happen.'

So I do. I look at Joaquin, and I look at our baby. I look for a long time. He is terribly large and she is terribly small and together they fill the room, the house, the whole world. Long before I stop looking, the fear has vanished.

One moment flows into the next. Time runs through our veins.

We've called her Elsa May.

a&b

OTHER TITLES AVAILABLE FROM
ALISON & BUSBY
BY PENELOPE EVANS

| | | | |
|---|---|---|---|
| ♦ First Fruits | 9780749005436 | Paperback | £6.99 |
| ♦ A Fatal Reunion | 9780749082789 | Paperback | £6.99 |
| ♦ My Perfect Silence | 9780749081843 | Paperback | £6.99 |
| ♦ Saving Grace | 9780749079963 | Paperback | £7.99 |

All Allison & Busby titles are available to order
through our website
*www.allisonandbusby.com*

You can also order by calling us on
0207 580 1080.
Please have your credit/debit card ready.

Alternatively, send a cheque made out to
Allison and Busby Ltd to
Allison & Busby
13 Charlotte Mews
London
W1T 4EJ

Postage and packaging is free of charge to addresses in the UK. Prices shown above were correct at the time of going to press. Allison & Busby reserves the right to show new retail prices on covers which may differ from those previously advertised in the text or elsewhere.